She's the one I've be[en]

LASS

HARLOE RAE

LASS

Copyright © 2019 by Harloe Rae, LLC

All rights reserved. No part of this publication may be reproduced, distributed, or transmitted in any form or by any means, including photocopying, recording, or other electronic or mechanical methods, without the prior written permission of the copyright owner and the publisher listed above, except in the case of brief quotations embodied in critical reviews and certain other noncommercial uses permitted by copyright law.

This is a work of fiction and any resemblance to persons, names, characters, places, brands, media, and incidents are either the product of the author's imagination or purely coincidental.

Cover design by T-Red Designs
Photography by Reggie Deanching & R plus M Photo | www.rplusmphoto.com
Models: BT Urruela & Jess Birks
Book design by Inkstain Design Studio

LASS

NOVELS BY
HARLOE RAE

RECLUSIVE STANDALONES
Redefining Us
Forget You Not

#BITTERSWEETHEAT STANDALONES
GENT
MISS
LASS

Watch Me Follow

*This book is dedicated to Melissa (MPP),
Tijuana (SDP), and Talia (LMM).
For all you do, always.*

PLAYLIST

Space Cowboy by Kacey Musgraves
Over and Over Again by Nathan Sykes and Ariana Grande
Say Something by A Great Big World
Like I'm Gonna Lose You by Meghan Trainor & John Legend
Little Do You Know by Alex & Sierra
Secret Love Song by Little Mix & Jason Derulo
The Story Never Ends by Lauv
Friends by Marshmello & Anne-Marie
Kiss Me by Ed Sheerin
All I Want by Kodaline
I Can't Fall in Love Without You by Zara Larsson

PROLOGUE

SHANE
Reason

My father told me that a single second can change everything. In this moment, I finally believe him.

She walks toward me, this life-altering girl. An erratic beat echoes in my ears, and I seem to have lost the ability to breathe properly. Am I awake? I've experienced surreal dreams countless times, but this isn't the same. All of my senses are going haywire—misfiring and crossing—but set directly on her.

"Dude, what the fuck is wrong with your face?" Trey says from beside me. I barely hear him, much less care what's coming out of his mouth.

My co-worker doesn't appreciate being ignored and jabs me in the ribs. "I'm talking to you. Why are you staring at her like that?"

I shake my head, clarity creeping in. "Huh? What was that?" I glance at him as heat stings my cheeks.

Trey squints at me. "You're an odd duck, Shane."

I shrug, rolling his words off me. Nothing I haven't heard before. I've been scorned for my differences since I was little. To say I'm socially unaware is a huge understatement, but it's not entirely my fault. I was raised in a tiny, almost non-existent community where church is the only social gathering. Garden Grove is an entirely new dimension. Most days I just stumble around, taking in the hectic activity buzzing along Main Street. Everyone has somewhere to go and the choices seem endless. I didn't have a clue where to begin and had been wandering aimlessly, until now.

A gust of sweet apples suddenly overpowers the bar's ever-present popcorn and beer stench. This new aroma makes my mouth water, and I immediately want more. I turn to find the source, my newfound breath stalling again.

Why is she standing at our table? Is she mad I was looking? I couldn't help myself. This is exactly why my mother was constantly seeking forgiveness for me. But I've never seen anyone like her, and it's liberating. The girl speaks up before I can attempt an apology.

"Hey, cutie. Welcome to Dagos. What can I get for you?"

I stare at her angelic face, getting lost in a fog of red hair, brown freckles, and green eyes. I should resist this pull, fight the urge building inside me. That's what Pastor Raines would command. But the control he once held over me no longer exists. Resolve infuses my spine, and I don't shy away. I keep looking at her, ignoring the years of harsh commands demanding otherwise. This right here—*her*—is the reason I left. All doubt melts away. The remaining regret churning in my gut evaporates. I'm escaping their constricting clutches and narrow-minded beliefs… permanently.

This beautiful temptation waves in front of me, and I blink slowly. "Did you hear me? Are you okay?"

I swallow once, then again.

"Cat got your tongue?" She giggles, and my gut clenches.

What the hell is going on with me? I'm certain my mind is playing a cruel trick. No one can be so… *perfect*. I manage to find my voice. "S-something like that. You, ah, work here?"

She leans on a chair, and her ponytail flips, cascading all that long hair over one shoulder. Her hip pops out to the side, creating a hypnotic curve. I trace her body, unable to look away. Hell, I wouldn't move if this building went up in flames. She points to a name tag pinned on her shirt.

Addison.

"Sure do. I doubt the boss man will ever get rid of me."

"Addy's the best damn server this place has. Grayson would be lost without her. Or at least lose half his customers," Trey says.

Addison gawks at him. "Was that a compliment?"

He rolls his eyes. "Don't read too much into it. I'm just hungry, and you're the one to fix that."

She huffs. "Sounds more like it."

My neck almost snaps while I look between them. Trey knows her? A fiery wave crashes over me and I curl my hand into a fist. I stare down at my shaking arm, steam covering every inch of me.

A soft palm lands on my shoulder, and the fire snuffs out. I fling my startled gaze up and find her looking at me.

"You okay?" Her brow is creased, and my finger itches to smooth those wrinkles away.

I give a slow nod as too many thoughts pile up. This girl is free, relaxed, and calm. I've never witnessed anyone move so effortlessly. She talks to everyone with ease. It's perplexing, but makes complete sense considering her profession. It's probably just her, though. She's everything opposite, and that draws me in. A whisper of my mom's threats wiggles into my mind. She'd scare me off. Tell me this is exactly what she was afraid of. I should come home, repent, but my ass remains firmly planted on this chair.

What can I do to make her like me?

Trey chuckles. "We're still trying to figure this guy out. He showed up out of nowhere, asking for a job at Jacked Up."

I scowl at him, not appreciating his interruption. Even if he's right.

"You two work together?" she asks.

"Uh-huh," I mumble.

"Jack treating you well?"

"Yes." I grin at his name. My boss, Trey's uncle, has been nothing but kind. I'm not used to such genuine hospitality, and he extended it without hesitation.

Addison smiles too. "No surprise. Jack is a great guy. He'll give you the shirt off his back."

He pretty much did, letting me move into his loft until I get settled. I don't tell her that, choosing to remain quiet and appreciate her presence. She seems to realize I'm not planning to speak up and fills the silence between us.

"I haven't seen you around. Just move here?" I nod again, and she laughs. "Man of few words. I like that."

She does? I sit up straighter and expand my chest without being too obvious. Girls need guys to watch out for them, right? Maybe I'll be her protector. I'm strong and built like an ox according to my father. He enjoyed having me around for the heavy lifting. I'd like to show her my worth.

Someone whistles, stealing Addison's attention. She gives them a signal and turns back to me. "Wanna order? Or did you need a few more minutes?"

"I'll take my usual," Trey drawls.

Food is the last thing on my mind, but I need to say something. I'm not ready for her to leave. "You look like an Irish lass," I blurt.

Addison stares at me while Trey laughs. I blush, my face going up in flames.

"Ah, you're a charmer," she says.

"I'm not sure what you mean," I reply softly. And I really don't. Is she making fun of me?

Her emerald eyes sparkle. "Are you from there or something?"

I shake my head. "No, not at all. It's just something I saw in a magazine."

Trey hoots beside me. "Was it the dirty kind? Damn, newbie. Didn't know that was your style."

I glare at him, silently shoving him until he's almost off the chair. "No, it was a travel brochure." But it might as well have been Playboy the way my mother reacted. Her screech still rings in my ears.

"Yo, Addison, this isn't social hour. I'm thirsty," hollers a man sitting at a nearby table.

She huffs and waves him off. "All right, I gotta go. Want some food?"

I cast a quick glance at the menu. "I'll just have whatever Trey ordered."

"Got it." She nods and takes off. I feel her absence immediately, like a kick in the shin. Sharp and painful.

Trey gives me a hard nudge. "Dude, what the hell is wrong with you? Haven't you ever seen a hot chick before?"

It takes serious willpower to peel my eyes off Addison and look at him. "Huh?"

"Pick your jaw up off the floor already. You're drooling all over the place and making a fucking mess," he complains.

I stare at him, unsure what to say. The truth is I haven't been around many girls my age. My sister doesn't count. The handful I saw at worship sure as shit don't look like her. My frame of reference is miniscule, but it doesn't matter.

"Listen, Shane. I told you to speak up more often, but I was clearly wrong. You need to stop talking." He doesn't seem aware of the turmoil swirling within me.

I ignore his barb. "Do all women in this town look like her?" I know the answer even as the question comes out. Addison is a knockout. Whether in a secluded space or crowded around supermodels.

Trey scoffs. "She's just a chick, bro."

My blood pressure rises at his words. "No, she's definitely not."

"I mean, sure, Addy's pretty chill and all. But don't lose your head over her."

I grind my teeth and mutter, "Thanks for the advice."

He smirks. "Yeah, whatever. Where are you from again? You never told me."

"Not important," I say. I can't think about home. The disdain on my mother's face when she discovered my plans will forever haunt me. I can't open that door. Not this soon, maybe not ever.

Trey crosses his arms and squints at me. "You really gonna take classes at Concorite? Twenty-three is a little on the old side to be starting." His mention of the local technical college is a welcome change in subject.

"That's bull. Age is just a number."

He crosses his arms. "Most guys I know are done already."

"We aren't them, clearly. I'm absolutely going. Already have my schedule."

I've never attended an actual school. Any education I received was from my mother, which was lacking in every department aside from spiritual. This small, insignificant thing that most kids take for granted means a great deal to me. When I heard Jack mention that Trey is enrolling, I immediately registered. He seemed surprised by my eagerness, but these opportunities weren't offered at home. Just one more thing I'd been missing out on. But not anymore.

"I'm more than ready," I add.

"Why? It's just school."

"This will give me real training and a degree. I grew up fixing farm equipment, mostly with diesel engines. What I currently know is from family and far from professional."

Trey shakes his head. "But that's good enough. If Jack didn't give me an ultimatum, I'd happily avoid it."

"Quit complaining. This way you're guaranteed to co-own the shop when Jack gives his okay," I say. He doesn't get how lucky he is. Having that chance is beyond the scope of my imagination.

He thrusts his palms out. "Exactly. It's a power play."

"Didn't Jack graduate from there?"

Trey pinches the bridge of his nose. "Sorry I brought it up. Too bad you can't take credits for me."

"Still complaining about college?" Addison pipes up, appearing out of nowhere. She sets our plates down, but I barely notice. My heart thunders almost painfully with her this close again.

Trey groans. "Seriously? How did you hear about it?"

"Myla overheard Jack bragging about you. He's so proud," she tells him.

"My ass. He just wants a more qualified protégé," he grunts.

Addison flicks his ear. "Don't be a dick. Jack only wants the best for you."

His eyes roll skyward. "Give it a rest, Addy. I didn't order a side of sugary shit with my meal."

I finally glance at my lunch, happy to discover Trey's usual is a burger with fries. My stomach grumbles loudly as the smell of grilled meat hits me.

"Glad you approve." Addison quirks a brow at my abdomen and I want to crawl under the table. "Need anything else?"

I shake my head while automatically folding my hands together.

Trey says, "Nah, we'll be outta your hair soon enough."

Addison smiles. "No rush."

When I look up, she winks at me. I expected to be surprised at what exists outside of my family's compound. Nothing could have prepared me for her. Now I have to figure out how to make her mine.

CHAPTER 1

SHANE
Red

"Go talk to her already," Mitch says.

"I dunno," I reply.

He gives me a flat stare, one I'm very familiar with. My friend has been listening to me obsess over Addison for three years. I met him on my first day at Concorite, and we bonded over a mutual appreciation for tools. Only difference is Mitch uses a wrench to fix pipes instead of engines.

"Shane, brother, you do this same song and dance each time we're here. Didn't you just hang out with her recently?"

I nod. "Yeah, at Boomers. It was an ambush of sorts. Trey didn't tell me they were all there celebrating."

"But you got to see Addison."

"I didn't say it was a bad surprise."

Mitch shoots me another stern look. "So, what gives? She's totally into you."

I scrub a palm over my forehead. "Not buying it. We had a conversation surrounded by friends. It was very platonic, like always."

"Dude, she gave you her number weeks ago."

"Because she was having car trouble."

He points at me. "That's another excuse."

"Maybe it is. But what am I supposed to text her?"

"For fuck's sake, you're like a tween with his first crush. I'm honestly not sure how to help you."

I search for Addison across the crowded bar, finding her filling a tray with drinks. I release a pitiful sigh that deflates my chest. "Me either."

There's been a handful of occasions we've seen each other outside of Dagos. But it's always with others in a group setting. Her bubbly personality is fascinating, but intimidating. A few comments led me to believe Addison was flirting, but it never goes further than a couple of laughs. I'm always holding back because believing in more is too tempting. What could a girl like her truly see in a guy like me?

What started as a seed of doubt has grown into a full-sized tree, blocking my path to her. I've settled for these stilted interactions and pleasant exchanges when I visit her at work. I deserve this suffering, I suppose. It's my penance for leaving home in search of a more... exotic life. Back then, I avoided the opposite sex in fear that impure cravings would arise. Turns out that threat is very real. The lust inside of me is a sin my mother would be scandalized to learn about.

The conflict is eating away at me, but Addison's lack of real interest is far worse. Her indifference is a hot stake driving through my heart. The pain hasn't eased over time. Neither has my desire for her. I've tried to play off this intense attraction, pretending I'm interested in meeting other girls. That couldn't be further from the truth. There's only one I want. Too damn bad Addison doesn't seem to share my need.

So, I'm stuck silently pining after her.

Mitch coughs, yanking me from my miserable musings. "You're going to die a virgin at this rate."

I scowl at him. "Will you keep your voice down? No need to tell the entire town."

"Not like it's a secret. You're practically a monk."

"Not on purpose. That's how I was raised," I remind.

Mitch claps me on the shoulder. "I know, man. And I feel for you. I can't imagine growing up so closed off. But stuff is different for you now. You've got to make a move. A real one. If you don't change the status of this situation with her, no one will. Some other guy is going to swoop in and steal her away."

White-hot anger strikes when I picture another man's hands on her. I shake my head to clear that poison away. "If it was that simple, she would've been mine on day one. Talking to people so openly is still an adjustment for me, and Addison is another level entirely."

He juts his chin toward her. "Don't overthink. Just do."

I inhale deeply, the familiar scent of fried food and stale beer providing a sliver of comfort. "Okay, I'm going to ask her to have dinner with me."

"Yeah, buddy," Mitch hoots and punches me in the arm.

"Thanks for making a scene."

He laughs. "Go get your girl."

I stand slowly, taking time to straighten my shirt and ballcap. I make sure my steps are steady and measured even as my thoughts spin on a sloppy loop. Stray popcorn kernels crunch beneath my shoes, making me sound like a herd of buffalo. But no one seems to notice.

What should I say? Dammit, this was a bad idea. I'm not ready.

No, fuck that. This moment has been suspended long enough. I swallow the bundle of nerves lodging in my throat and focus on her.

Red.

That's all I see.

The color is a taunt, luring me in and calling to my depraved desires. I want to bury my fingers in her long hair. Have those sinfully painted lips covering mine. Feel her artfully coated nails digging into my skin. I shiver just thinking about it, my dick twitching in agreement.

Addison is talking to another server as I quietly approach. I don't mean to eavesdrop on their conversation—it happens by proximity.

"She left on Monday," Addison tells the other woman. I think her name is Myla.

"Tania stopped by over the weekend to say goodbye. We'll miss her around here. How's the roommate search going?"

Addison groans. "Not well, as in nonexistent. I don't know where to start."

"Have you asked around? I'm sure Marlene has suggestions,"

Myla laughs.

"No way. If I give that nosey Nellie an inch, she'll run off with a mile. Talk about added stress."

"Gah, can you imagine who she'd come up with? I'm sure Betty would toss her name in the hat."

Addison shakes her head. "Not happening." Her shoulders rise and fall with a big breath, the weight seeming unbearable. "Where do I find someone reliable and responsible and easy to get along with?"

"Right here," I blurt.

Both girls whip around and gape at me. Myla's surprise quickly morphs into a grin. Addison can't seem to pick her jaw up off the floor. She sputters, "How much did you hear?"

I can barely make out her words over my thundering pulse. "Enough."

"You wanna move in with me?"

My heart beat skyrockets, threatening to bust a vein. What the hell did I get myself into?

"Shane?" Addison prods.

"Uh, yeah?"

"Were you being serious?"

"Yes?"

"That doesn't sound very convincing." She raises a brow. "Are you really looking for a place to live? Raven mentioned something along those lines."

I learned early on how fast word gets around in this town, so I'm not surprised people are talking. "I am, yep. My lease is up and I'm hoping to relocate."

Addison crosses her arms, pouting those plump ruby lips. "And where have you been looking?"

I scratch the back of my neck. "Um, I don't have any leads yet."

Myla elbows her and shuffles to the side. "Problem solved. I gotta check on my tables. Fill me in later."

Addison gives her a look I can't begin to decipher. Her green gaze swings back to me. "So, you randomly stumbled into this conversation, and it just so happens I have space available?" Her tone is light, but suspicion rings out. I don't blame her disbelief one bit. Even carefully constructed plans rarely turn out this smoothly.

Coincidence? I doubt that.

"It seems that way," I mumble.

Addison takes two steps closer, and I tower over her small frame. She has to crane her neck to look at me. She appears delicate and fragile, needing someone around to keep her safe. I'll never tell her that, though. What Addison lacks in stature, her attitude covers tenfold. Feisty and sassy as all get out. I love that about her.

Love.

I snort. What could I possibly know about that word? My fingers curl into a fist as I shake those thoughts loose. Now isn't the time.

She clears her throat, peering up through long lashes. "Do you want to stop by and see my place? My shift ends in an hour. It's not far from here."

That would be the rational thing to do. But all reason flew out the window long ago whenever Addison is involved. "That's not necessary. I trust you."

She gawks at me, blinking slowly. "That's not usually how this goes."

I dip my chin. "I've, uh, never done this before. Jack took care of everything last time."

"Ah, okay. That makes sense. So, you'll blindly sign a rental contract? Just like that?" She snaps her fingers.

"Why not? I don't require much. If you have a room, that's all I need."

Addison bites her lip. "Well, for starters, we barely know one another."

"That's not true. I eat here at least twice a week. Usually three or four," I argue.

"But that's just small talk. I'm not sure I can judge your character based off that."

I furrow my brow. "What do you want to know? I'm neat and orderly. There won't be any clutter issues because I barely own anything. My friends call me low maintenance, whatever that means."

Her mouth opens, closes, then opens again. "I still think you should check out the apartment before agreeing to anything."

"Nothing will change my mind. If you're okay with this, I'm good to go." And that's the truth. I'm sold on this wild-ass idea, even if it's spinning out of control.

Addison rests a palm on the top of her head. "Yeah, I guess. Trey seems to tolerate you well enough and he doesn't like anyone, so that's saying something. Suppose that's a good enough reference."

I shrug. "Works for me."

Her face practically glows, a huge smile exposing straight teeth and the tip of her tongue. I have to hold back a disgraceful groan. Her expression will keep me warm on the coldest nights. "When could you move in?"

"Tomorrow?" I suggest quickly. I'm sure my dopey smile gives the eagerness away.

She giggles. "That's a little too soon. Maybe next week? I have to get the papers drawn up."

A twinge of disappointment hits, but I'm no stranger to being patient. "Sure, you're in charge."

"I doubt that very much," she says softly. "Does this seem crazy?"

"Why?" To me, everything is finally falling into place.

Addison wrinkles her nose, those adorable freckles winking at me. "I have no clue. It's very unexpected."

"Do you need time to think things over?" I ask, not wanting to force myself on her.

She looks away. "That isn't the issue."

"Not sure what else I can offer. Figured this was something I could help you with. You're not happy?" My skin prickles, and I try not to fidget.

Her gaze darts to mine, green colliding with brown. "I am, really. This has been weighing me down since Tania announced she's leaving. You're doing me a huge favor stepping up like this."

I offer a weak smile. "It's my pleasure." She has no clue what lengths I'd take to be near her.

"Is it?"

"Yes." I force every ounce of confidence into that word.

"O-okay. I just thought… um, never mind." She curls a stray lock of hair around her finger.

"What?"

Addison smiles again, but the expression seems forced. "It's not important. Maybe this is… good. Yeah, this will be good," she repeats.

"Are you sure?" Because she isn't acting like it.

"Yeah, this will solve the questioning." That doesn't sound so great.

I rock back on my heels. "About?"

Splotches of red stain her cheeks. "Ah, well… if this," she motions between us, "was heading in a romantic direction."

I feel the blood drain from my face. "What do you mean?"

"If we're living together, the potential of us dating is zippo. We'll be roommates and friends, but that's all. Otherwise it will be awkward and tense and blah. No, thanks. Setting this boundary will cut out the possibility."

I choke on the brick lodged in my throat. "Wait, what?"

"Can you imagine the mess we'd be stuck in if things went sour? Better to not chance it, right?"

No.

No, no, no.

I blink slowly, trying to process her words. Is this an unwritten rule I wasn't aware of? And what, now I'm trapped in the friend-zone? I avert my eyes, glaring at a neon sign stuck to the far wall. An outcome that doesn't involve us as a couple seems impossible. Shit. I rapidly search for a counter-argument, begging for a way out of this clusterfuck.

What the actual hell?

Addison keeps talking, unaware of my turmoil threatening to level me. "The back and forth has been heckish. Does Shane like me? Why isn't he calling? Was I imagining things? So, yeah. This is the optimal solution." She gives me a solid nod.

A boulder slams into my gut, and I feel even worse. The floor disappears and I'm suddenly free falling, unable to speak or move or even breathe.

Her warm palm gently landing on my forearm calms the chaos in my brain. "Don't worry, this will be fun." She winks and adds, "Roomie."

Somehow, I highly doubt that.

CHAPTER 2

ADDISON
Bits

I lift the steaming mug to my lips, inhaling the rich aroma. I moan when the heavenly mix of vanilla and hazelnut hits my tongue.

"Girl, you make drinking coffee sound erotic. Let's make a commercial. I'll have a line around the block," Delilah announces and signals down Main Street from the front window. She turns off the open sign, whips off her pink apron, and plops down on the cushy chair next to mine. I take another generous sip, making sure my enjoyment is heard loud and clear.

"Now you're being over the top," she says.

"You brew damn good beans. I'm only showing my appreciation of your mad skills."

My best friend shimmies her shoulders. "That's right, keep stroking my ego."

I laugh, but she deserves all the praise. Everyone in our small town would tell her the same. In less than a year, Delilah has set up a very successful—and profitable—business. Her coffee house, Jitters, is everything Garden Grove had been missing and she delivered big time. "How's business this week?"

She fluffs a decorative pillow before slouching deeper into the seat. "Kinda slow thanks to summer winding down, but you won't hear me complaining. After that hectic season, I'm ready for a break. The profit margin is totally worth it, though." Her eyes flutter shut, and I'm pretty sure she's going to fall asleep.

I nudge her lightly. "You're such a boss."

"Thanks for noticing." Delilah peeks over at me. "How're you hanging in there? Usually you don't stop by for an evening boost unless it's been a rough day."

I glance around the empty café, recalling the very unexpected events during my lunch shift. My belly gets all tingly and warm, along with the rest of me. The smile lifting my lips feels like a reflex, cropping up whenever I think about him.

Delilah springs to attention, suddenly rejuvenated. "Oh, snap. Something actually happened. I figured Marlene was just exaggerating."

I groan and cover my face. "That woman needs a better hobby. She has ears everywhere, I swear."

She scoffs. "She'll be busy with great-grandbaby number twenty soon enough."

I snort. "Pretty sure this is the first one. Peter and Becky stopped by Dagos while they were here visiting. I heard all about Marlene's extravagant plans."

Not that she's ever secretive about anything. The old lady has a reliable reputation of spreading all Garden Grove gossip far and wide. Trying to keep news private around here is a task and a half thanks to her.

Delilah steeples her fingers. "Even better. All her attention will be solely focused."

"True story."

Her eyebrows jump up and down. "So, let's get back to your sordid affair this afternoon. Tell me everything."

I feel my cheeks heat and scratch at the burn. "Uh, well... Shane stopped by to eat. Mitch was with him. They sat in my section."

Delilah pretends to snore. "Oh my gosh, snooze-alert. Get to the good stuff."

"I was doing a slow build-up for the ultimate climatic experience."

"Damn, that sounds sexy. But save it for the bedroom. With Shane," she stage-whispers.

I don't hold back my exaggerated eye roll. "That's all shot to shit. Turns out he's really looking for a new place to live. And it just so happens I have a room available. Somehow, he walked up at the exact moment I was whining to Myla about Tania leaving. Shane couldn't speak up fast enough."

She blinks at me and shakes her head. "Wait a second. He actually wants to move in with you?"

"Hey!" I shove her lightly. "You make it seem like such a hardship."

"Oh, please. It's just surprising considering his wishy-washy behavior. This is a fairly huge commitment. He can't flake out on you."

I bite my lip. "Shane is pretty positive about living together. He didn't want to come by first or anything. Just agreed blindly and ready to go." A pebble of doubt rolls in my stomach recalling his over eagerness that quickly changed to hesitation. I squint at Delilah and say, "That closes the door for a relationship between us. I made sure to let him know our status would be friends-only. No bed-sharing." I sigh and slump my shoulders. "Kinda sucks, right?"

She crosses her arms. "I call bullshit."

"What? Why?"

"You honestly think lines won't be crossed? I give it a few weeks, tops. No way he can resist you. That man has it so effing bad, girlfriend."

"Sure has a funny way of showing it," I reply.

Delilah shoots me a flat stare. "Don't be a downer. Sounds to me like he pounced on this opportunity, assuming it would bring you two closer. I take it you're the one with the silly boundary rules?"

"D, leaving the possibility open is a disaster waiting to happen. It's far easier to shut this down before anything happens. I'm thankful to have a decent roommate option. I won't blow it because he's hot and my lady bits want his beef stick."

She sticks out her tongue. "Thanks for the visual."

"Please," I say through a giggle. "You're far worse than me."

"She's right, D," Raven calls from the hallway. My other bestie strolls toward us, a streak of flour across her forehead like war paint.

"You win the battle?" I ask.

Raven plops onto the couch across from us. "It was touch and go, but I pulled out ahead."

"That's what she said," I joke and we all laugh.

Raven claps. "We should totally binge *The Office* tonight."

I smile at her. She's a much-needed addition around here, and not just for her masterbaking. Raven managed to turn Trey's permanent frown upside down and the entire population of Garden Grove is thankful. That guy is still unruly, but he's far better these days.

"I'm in," I chirp.

Delilah bumps me. "Shouldn't you be preparing for a certain someone to enter your domain?"

"You make it sound so dirty," I reply.

Raven holds up a hand. "I missed something. Please explain." They're both looking at me, and I exhale slowly, mentally preparing for another round of questions.

"Shane is moving in with me," I murmur.

"Since when?" Raven's pitch raises several notches.

I pick at my nails. "Um, today?"

"You sure about this?" she asks.

"I'm suddenly very unsure," I admit.

Delilah chimes in. "Why?"

"Because I'm weak and he's so attractive," I wail with a fist in the air. They burst into a fit of cackles.

Raven wipes under her eyes. "I don't see the issue."

I form a square with my fingers. "Let me paint you a picture.

What starts at flirting turns into heavy petting, which obviously leads to sex. What if it's terrible? Then we're stuck in the same apartment, avoiding each other until his lease runs out. That's really uncomfortable to imagine."

Delilah shrugs. "Would you rather be constantly wondering how fantastic it could be? Take it from me, don't miss an opportunity."

"Not to mention all that wasted chemistry," Raven adds.

I fake-sob. "It's tragic. Shane came out of thin air. Seriously, where is he from? Suddenly he's barging into my personal space with his woodsy cologne and bulging muscles. No man should look so hot wearing a ball cap. Oh, and don't forget dimples." I smack the table. "Those bad boys are lethal. How am I expected to resist?"

My friends are wearing matching grins. I search their expressions. My gaze bounces between them, waiting for all the answers. Their lips only lift higher.

Eventually I crack. "Okay, what're you two thinking?"

Delilah rubs my back. "You're already sunk, sweetheart."

I balk at that. "No way. I hardly know the guy. Sure, Shane has stepped in when I needed help a couple of times, but he rarely speaks to me. Today was our first decent conversation in months."

"You're a special case," Raven says. "Shane talks plenty. Pretty sure he drives Trey a little mad when they're working together. Mostly blabbing about you, I'm sure." I roll my eyes at that, but she keeps going. "Addy, he doesn't hide it well. At all."

Delilah's blonde hair swishes when she nods. "He loves sneaking up on you, swooping in at the perfect moment. Holi-Daze was my favorite. He would have pummeled those guys with your permission."

I glance at the ceiling, prickles trailing up my spine. "You weren't even there."

"Feels like I was with the amount of vivid detail you provided. What's his nickname for you again?" she prods.

I shiver just thinking about him calling me lass in that deep voice of his. The word rolls off his seductive tongue like candy. Why is that so hot? My gaze jumps to the traffic outside, continuing to avoid her all-knowing stare. "Not sure what you mean."

Delilah elbows me. "No way you're playing this game. We both know you remember like it was yesterday."

I huff. "He calls me lass."

Raven's brow crinkles. "Huh?"

"Like an Irish girl," I supply.

"Don't you hate redhead stereotypes?" she asks.

"This is different," I mumble.

"So gone," Delilah whispers to Raven.

I bite my lip. "Do you think living with him is a mistake?"

A knot tugs in my chest when considering backing out of our deal. I've already grown attached to the idea, my wavering be damned. These more than friendly feelings toward Shane can be dealt with later. I'm completely capable of controlling myself.

"It's a fantastic plan. I've already told you. All of Shane's needs will be met under your roof," Raven says with a bounce in her brow.

"Yup." Delilah agrees. "What could possibly go wrong?"

"I feel like you two haven't been listening to any of my concerns,"

I complain. "What would my mother say about living with a guy? I can't even think about my dad."

Delilah scoffs. "Lucky for you, they're living very permanently in Florida."

"Retirement suits them well," I say.

"Seriously your mom is a fox. You've got great genes. Must be nice knowing that's how you'll look at sixty. I bet your dad still has to chase men off her tail," Delilah laughs.

"Ugh, he's used to it. They've been together forever. She's always kept him busy." I shudder. "I don't want to think about that."

"Right, so what's your next excuse?" Delilah asks and motions for me to spit it out.

I cross my legs and pull at the fraying hem of my shorts. "How will this impact my dating life?"

"You mean the nonexistent one?" Raven laughs.

I giggle at her snark. "Shut up over there."

Delilah pokes my arm. "I'd say it's going to be really helpful getting Shane locked down."

I muffle a groan between my fingers. "D, that's not the point of letting him move in. I have to consider other options."

"Addy, you've lived in Garden Grove all your twenty-three years. The male prospects aren't suddenly going to change. I'd say this is your best bet. Plus, he's the one you want and has been for quite a while. Let's not lie," Delilah drawls.

"Are you searching for an escape clause?" Raven arches a brow.

I shrug. "I just want to explore all avenues."

"Because the possibilities are endless." Raven's words are coated in a heavy dose of sarcasm.

Delilah makes a sound of agreement. "Girlfriend, this is a match made is roommate heaven. Green light means go for it. You won't hear me trying to persuade otherwise."

I squint at her. "Being in love sure does change a person."

She flips some blonde hair over her shoulder. "I know, right? Looks good on me."

Raven laughs and points at me. "You're next."

"Why did I bother bringing this up? Both of you are total instigators," I accuse.

"Guilty as charged," they reply in unison.

I smile in spite of the unease coursing through me. "Now I know how it feels when we play two-against-one in the dealing with men department."

Raven winks. "Isn't it lovely to be outnumbered?"

"Yeah, what else are friends for?" Delilah jibes.

"That's the best question I've heard so far this evening," I mutter. Their expressions sober, and my stomach twists at ruining the humor between us.

Raven leans forward. "Are you honestly worried? I figured we were mostly messing around about this. It already seems like your mind's made up."

I blow out a long breath. "It is. I was just looking for a bit of support. Maybe to back up my friends-only rule."

"Is that really what you want out of this?" Delilah asks.

"Yeah?" The word is wimpy, even to my own ears.

"Addy, let's be honest. Shane is transparent about his feelings, but he's not the only one," Raven comments.

"Deny all you want. The constant fidgeting alone gives you away. But we'll just see what happens," Delilah says.

"You know how much I like going with the flow," Raven quips.

I roll my eyes and stand up. "Great plan. Thanks."

Delilah grabs my wrist. "Where are you going? We haven't discussed this topic in nearly enough depth."

I shake her off with a playful shove. "You're just trying to further delay the cleaning chores." She doesn't dispute my assumption. I take a moment to study the quiet café. "Not sure if I tell you often enough, but the setup in here is fantastic. Comfortable furniture by the window. Regular table and chairs closer to the counter. I love the layout. Very welcoming and customer friendly."

Delilah tilts her chin. "And I think you missed a true calling as an interior decorator. Your apartment alone is proof."

I wave her off. "I'd never be able to do that as a job. Especially around here. There aren't enough options."

"Just for fun, in your free time. Those inspiration boards of yours are a-mazing. I'm seriously jelly of your creativity. You should help people redecorate," Raven suggests.

I shrug. "Maybe. I'm happy working at Dagos for now."

Delilah sniffs. "Yeah, yeah. Rub it in."

I smirk at her. "You ready to match my salary?"

"Nope. Still can't afford you," she admits.

"Quit your bitching. You've got the best baker in the state," I say. "Grayson would love to expand our desserts menu, but no one can compete."

"Damn straight," Raven cheers.

I slowly step toward the door, attempting a clean getaway. They snicker at my not-so-stealthy retreat. "Off to prepare your love nest?" Delilah drawls.

A shiver rolls over me as I let my imagination run wild. I don't bother hiding my grin. "Maybe."

CHAPTER 3

SHANE
Advice

I reach for a wrench and get cranking, thankful this work has become second nature. My brain is focusing elsewhere, on a certain girl miles down the road serving the lunch crowd. I glance at the smudged watch on my wrist. Only forty-five minutes until break.

I'm attempting to find a groove when Marcus, another mechanic at Jacked Up, appears around the car's trunk. "We getting grub soon?"

"Just about done with these spark plugs. I'll be ready shortly," I say. "Where to?"

I catch Trey's laugh from across the garage. "As if you need to ask."

"No one's forcing you to join us," I bite out. If it were up to me, I'd eat all my meals at Dagos. Visiting the bar three or four times a week seems excessive to most. To me, it's barely enough.

Trey turns to face us. "Good because I'm not listening to you obsess over Addison's ass on my free time."

Marcus makes a noise of agreement. "But you gotta admit, she's got a fine ass." I glare at him, and he holds up his palms. "Just an observation, man. Don't kill the messenger."

"Well, look elsewhere," I growl.

He raises a brow. "You finally claiming her?"

Trey snorts loudly. "Shane called dibs the second he moved to town."

I don't dispute that, although Addison is hardly mine. That very solid fact leaves a bitter taste on my tongue. What the fuck am I going to do? Obviously, the logical solution is to live together just as friends. I'm such an idiot.

Marcus nods. "Ah, that's why she offered you her place. You're finally gonna seal the deal."

I kick the stained floor, not wanting to admit the truth. "We'll see."

"No doubt about it," he says.

"Yeah?" That one word holds too much hope. I'm a lost cause.

Marcus wipes his dirty hands on a rag. "She'll be all over you in no time. Just give her time to warm up. Set the mood, spoil her rotten, don't make resisting an option."

I look away, squinting at the sunlight pouring in through the open door. "What do you, uh, suggest?"

"You're seeking advice from this guy?" Disbelief rings clear in Trey's voice.

"And you're any better?" I widen my stance.

"Fuck no. But I don't pretend to be." His accusing stare fixes on

Marcus.

"Meh, he's right. I'm a fucking hound dog. I take no offense," Marcus replies.

I look between them. "So, I just wait to see what happens? Let her take the lead?"

"Good Christ," Trey mutters. "Do that and you'll never get laid."

My patience is slowly unraveling and I take a deep breath. "What do you recommend then?"

"You looking for sex or love?" Marcus cuts in.

I open my mouth only to close it again, not sure how to respond. This seems like a private topic of conversation. Trey unknowingly comes to my rescue.

"Dude, he wants forever with this girl. I recognize that look," Trey says. He lifts a brow at me. "I'm not giving you shit, rookie. I know how it is."

"Yeah, pansy-ass. You're locked down," Marcus hoots.

"And you're jealous," Trey shoots back.

"Of your blonde honey? Abso-fucking-lutely. I'd like to hit that—"

"You better stop talking," Trey growls.

"Pussy-whipped," Marcus coughs out.

Trey is visibly tense, about ready to pounce on our douchey pal. Through clenched teeth he spits, "Social hour is over. This is fucking worse than a high school locker room. I can't hear this shit again." Trey slides under the rusty truck he's been working on.

"Hurry up with this shit so we can get outta here. I'm hungry, and I bet you're starving." Marcus winks and humps the air. I grimace at his crude gesture, but cover it up with a half-smile.

"Sounds like a plan," I tell his retreating form. He offers a wave before disappearing into the gravel lot.

I shift closer to the engine, trying to hurry this job along. The faster I finish, the sooner we can go to Dagos. Easier said than done. Each minute feels like an eternity, seconds ticking by like molasses. I'm jittery, muscles twitching with excessive energy flooding my veins. I can't seem to stay still for more than a few moments. It's been this way all week. But what do I expect? In a couple days, I'm moving in with Addison.

We're going to share a space, my belongings blending with hers. But more importantly, she'll be sleeping a few feet away. I squeeze the wrench in my hand, imagining something far softer against my skin. If only dreams were reality. Living together won't include everything I was picturing. Addison was quick to slap stipulations on our situation. Strictly platonic. I can't move past that factor.

More like an enormous roadblock.

A hand clapping my shoulder startles me from these racing thoughts. "Something on your mind? Keep tightening that bolt and it'll strip."

I glance at Jack, catching the concern marring his brow. A ton of bricks lands on my back having him worry over me. I scratch my neck and mutter, "It's nothing."

He moves closer and takes a glimpse at the Ford's engine, joining me under the open hood. "Nice work, not that I'm surprised. Between you and Trey, I'll be retiring early. You'll be running this shop in no time." Jack straightens and crosses his arms, watching me with a knowing stare.

Growing ten feet tall with his praise, I can't keep the grin off my face. I'm still getting accustomed to having compliments sent my way, even though my boss doles them out almost daily.

"Appreciate that," I tell him.

"Now, what's bothering you up here?" He points to his temple.

A heavy exhale deflates my chest. "Uh, just got something coming up."

Jack's head tips to the side as he continues studying me. "You're not usually the distracted type. Must be important."

I hear Trey groan from the adjacent stall, only his feet visible while he works on the vintage Chevy.

"Why'd you have to ask? He was finally piping down about her."

Jack looks toward his nephew's mostly hidden form. "Like you're one to talk, kid. I can't get a word in edgewise when you ramble on about Raven."

"Bullshit," he barks.

Jack ignores him and focuses on me. "So, a girl?"

I shrug while fire blasts my skin. Fucking Trey and his big mouth. "Well, I wasn't gonna say anything."

Trey wheels himself out from under the truck. His chuckle is dark as he stands up. "Dude, give it a rest. Her name is running on repeat in your one-tracked mind. She's gonna take back her offer."

I blanch, but quickly add a glare. "I wasn't talking to you."

His finger circles around the garage. "Kinda hard to miss in here."

"Don't listen to him," Jack says. "Who's the lady?"

Metal clangs on the concrete floor. Trey points at me, and I can practically hear his molars grinding. "Don't start. I'll knock you out with that wrench. Then you can meet her in dreamland."

"Hey!" Jack turns fiery eyes on him. "Knock it off. You need to get laid or something? Feel free to take off early."

Trey mutters under his breath but listens to his uncle. He disappears out the side door with a slam. The tension instantly eases, and I relax against the car's fender.

We remain silent for a couple beats, staring in the direction he stormed off. I should probably apologize to Trey for talking about Addison nonstop lately. But the dam is broken and all these feelings are rushing out. I can't seem to close them off again.

"I don't know what the fuck is eating him," Jack complains. "I think he has a lot of good days but damn, this isn't one of them."

I shuffle my feet. "I, uh, probably have everything to do with that. I've been bothering him this week. Marcus doesn't help either."

"Don't take responsibility for his shit. Trust me, it's a waste of time."

I shake my head. "No, really. He wasn't lying about me being a broken record. I've been talking about Addison more than usual."

Jack raises his brow. "Addison Walker?"

"Yup. She's the one." I dip my chin at that, not wanting him to catch my double meaning.

"What about her?"

"I'm moving into her apartment." No point in hiding the truth.

His eyes bulge. "How'd you slip this by me? I didn't even know you two were dating."

I cough to cover the grip suddenly squeezing my throat. "Because we're not. This is strictly roommates only."

Jack rubs his jaw. "I see. And this came about how?"

"Well, I need a place to live. She has a room available. Kinda just clicked into place." I lift a shoulder.

"You're all right with this arrangement?"

"I'll take whatever she's willing to give," I tell him honestly.

"Shit," he spits. "You're already screwed."

"I wish."

He laughs. "Hold tight to that humor. But really, you've gotta go into this prepared. Living with a chick isn't easy. Especially when there's feelings involved. Get your guard up."

I furrow my brow. "What do you mean?"

"Your limits are about to be tested."

"Not sure I have any." My face gets hot thinking about Addison pushing my nonexistent boundaries. I'm more than willing to give her free reign.

"Damn, you're worse off than I thought." Jack scrubs a palm over his mouth. "When is this happening?"

"Day after tomorrow."

"So soon? What's the hurry?"

"Why wait?" My pulse pumps faster thinking about invading her space. I'd already be living there if she let me.

Jack tips his head back and exhales loudly. When he's facing me again, his eyes bore into me. "Let me give you some advice, rookie.

You all think I'm some old fool—"

"Aren't you like thirty-five?" I interrupt.

"Damn straight, but that's beside the point."

"I don't think you're old or a fool. You're a successful business owner before the age of forty. That's impressive."

He grunts. "Part of this chat isn't about stroking my ego, but I appreciate that. You need to pull your head out of your ass."

I rock back on my heels, his words an unexpected blow. "What?"

"You're a good man, and I'd hate to see that change. The last thing I want is for you to get hurt."

Smoke coils in my gut at his insinuation. "Addison won't—"

"I'm not saying she will," he argues. "Can I offer some advice?"

"Please do." Did he hear us talking earlier? Maybe he's taking pity on me.

Jack blows out a silent laugh. "You said there's no romance involved. I'm not trying to be a dick, but it's damn clear how you'd like things to be. Not sure how I missed it before now. Don't come on too strong, but show her how you feel. Treat her right and go slow. If she doesn't want to cross lines, there's a reason. Don't push too hard, but show her what she's missing. Give her reason to want more."

I crack my knuckles. "You live with a woman before?"

Something stormy passes through his gaze, but it's gone in a blink. "Yeah, once. Probably won't happen again." He laughs, but the sound is flat. "Learn from my mistakes, yeah? If you want Addison, don't let her slip away. Protect that big heart of yours and just be… careful."

I flare my nostrils, breathing deep. Since leaving home, Jack has been my greatest source of guidance and support. I know he means well, but I'll plow over any warnings when it comes to Addison. I'm all in.

"Thanks, boss," is my gruff response.

He knocks on the car's frame, an echo ringing out across the shop. "And another thing, this deal is gonna raise some eyebrows. In this town, everyone will demand all the details. I'm sure you've figured that out by now. Watch your back and get ready for the gossip hounds to descend. There's gonna be questions you'll have to answer."

I smirk, more than willing to spread the news myself. "I'm counting on it."

CHAPTER 4

ADDISON
Cloud

I rearrange the row of jars for the umpteenth time. He probably won't notice the candles adorning the mantel, but I want everything to look perfect. Just in case. My hands tremble slightly and I shake them out. Why am I nervous?

A knock on the front door answers my silent question. Shane is here, to move in with me. He's standing right outside, waiting for me to let him in. Oh, shoot. I'm going to vomit. My heart is a jackhammer, crushing bone into dust. Breathing is a chore, and I gasp for air. The last-minute decorating is long forgotten while I get my head in the game.

There's no reason to freak out. Be cool, confident, and collected. He's just my new roommate, not an extremely attractive man I want to climb like a tree. This is going to be like living with Tania. I groan and smack my forehead. There's no comparison—Shane couldn't be more different. There's no use pretending.

I've been preparing for this moment. What am I scared of? I know Shane... kind of. I'm not intimidated by him. This just feels really... personal. He's going to be so close all the time. My control is about to be constantly put to the test. But we'll set boundaries and stick to them. That should help, right?

Another knock startles me out of my mental pep-talk.

"Coming," I announce. Dirty thoughts immediately come to mind, images of a very different scene playing out between us.

Dammit, I scold myself. Not going there.

I whip open the door in a flurry and almost swallow my tongue. The sight of Shane, in all his masculine glory, makes my knees tremble. Are those angels singing? I should have stalled a few more moments.

Abort, abort, my brain screams. *Mayday, mayday. Lady-bits are a lost cause. Need immediate back-up.*

Looking away isn't an option—moth, meet flame. All I can do is stare. I slowly scan his muscular body, starting at his broad shoulders cloaked in a plain white tee. His biceps strain the fabric and seem to bulge under my perusal. The cotton can't hide the obvious sculpt of his pecs and washboard abs. Whoa, I'm in trouble.

"Hey, Addison," Shane murmurs.

I snap my focus off those sinfully low-slung jeans. A ball cap covers his head, but I see the amusement lifting his lips. Embarrassment stings my cheeks, and I offer a finger wave. "Hi, you."

I shiver from the intensity in his stare. Combined with a shy grin and those seductive dimples, his expression melts me into a puddle. My resolve pipes up from somewhere in the faraway distance.

No, be strong. Remember the boundaries.

I shake myself out of the horny-haze and slap on a smile. With newfound control thrumming through my veins, I open the door wider. "You're right on time. Welcome to my—our—humble abode."

Shane bows his head and steps inside. "Thanks."

I glance down at his lone bag. "Need help bringing in the rest of your stuff?"

"This is it," he says and hefts the large duffle onto his back.

"Are you a purge and pack type of mover?"

I see his brow furrow under the hat's curved brim. "A what?"

"You know, toss more than you take," I explain.

"Nah, I just don't own a lot. My last place was furnished so I mostly have clothes. I'm pretty easy that way."

I trap my inappropriate response desperate to escape. Roommates only, I remind myself for the zillionth time. "Cool, I can work with that," I tell him with a nod.

Shane takes off his hat, exposing thick dark hair. The strands are just long enough to run my fingers through and tug. His wide chest expands with a deep inhale. He takes in the space, looking this way and that, his eyes scanning every corner. I watch Shane digest it all and wonder what he sees. How did this sex-on-a-stick slip past me for so long? Oh, yeah. He ignored me. A bitter pill hits my tongue and I look away. That's the reminder I need. He isn't really interested, and

I shouldn't be either.

He jerks his chin at the bay window. "You've got a really nice setup." His compliment lifts my spirits and I can't help smiling.

"Really?"

Shane's gaze makes another slow sweep around the room and I follow his path. "Everything has a spot. It's clear you put a lot of thought into decorating. I feel like this should be a magazine cover." He points at the layout.

I beam at him. "Oh, stop. It's not that fancy."

"Just being honest," he murmurs.

We're caught up in one another for far too many beats. His honey eyes eat me up, and I return the favor. My ears are hot, and I fight the urge to look away. What's happening? When Shane blinks, the trance breaks, and our focus bounces in opposite directions. A stuttering breath puffs off my lips at the loss.

"So, uh, where's my room?" he asks.

"Oh, shit. Sorry. That's kinda important, huh?" I laugh nervously. "It's right down the hall, waiting for you."

"Great, thanks." He doesn't move, seemingly waiting for something. I haven't the foggiest idea as to what that might be. I peer around, searching for a distraction from the awkward. Our silence is interrupted by a knock on the door.

I lift my brow at him. "Expecting someone?"

"That's probably my mattress."

"Ah, good thinking."

"Figured that's a necessity," Shane says and walks into the foyer.

He lets in two burly men carrying a massive monstrosity. I gawk at the large box spring, trying to wrap my mind around the size. I didn't know beds could be so big. The guys leave and return a moment later with a king size deluxe on steroids. I bite back a laugh as they struggle to haul the thing into Shane's room. Hopefully that's all they've got because I'm not sure anything else will fit. Strings of expletives accompany the sound of things banging into unsuspecting surfaces. I hang back, not wanting to overstep or intrude. Other than the cursing, the seamless execution is fairly impressive to watch. Their entire process takes maybe five minutes, in and out.

I'm deciding between making coffee and watching Netflix when Shane reappears. He wipes his sweaty brow and moves toward me.

"Wanna check it out?" Excitement shines from his megawatt smile and sparkling eyes. He reminds me of a kid on their birthday, and the feeling is infectious. I soak it in, my own mouth stretching wide. I've never seen this side of him, and that gives this moment some sort of special meaning. Delving further into the why seems like a bad idea so I nod and follow behind him.

A gasp escapes me when I turn the corner. The enormous fluffy cloud practically extends from wall to wall and takes my breath away. The pristine white glows, popping out against the boring beige carpet and paint. I immediately imagine diving onto the middle of that cushy memory-foam padding, letting it swallow me up. Talk about a dream. But really, this is a bit excessive.

I let out a low whistle. "You planning a slumber party? This sucker is big enough for five." I gesture at the newest item on my wish list.

Shane laughs. "That an invitation?"

"Nope." That's all I say. I'm done fueling the crazy-train.

His smile dims, and I feel like a brat for stealing the sunshine surrounding us. But I reinforce my decision by remembering his radio silence a few months ago. Shane's fists stab into the back pockets of his jeans, gaze darting around his new digs. "I've never splurged on anything. This seemed like a good treat," he explains.

"I'd say. Very nicely done."

He smirks at me. "Jealous?"

"Insanely. But I buy crap for myself all the time. I've never considered the largest bed ever made." I mirror his pose, adding a little sway to my hips.

A flush races up Shane's neck. "I might have gone overboard."

"You'll be comfortable, that's for sure."

He quickly glances at me. "Already feels that way."

Tiny bubbles fizz in my belly, and I twist to hide my grin. We're so not going there. I fiddle with the hem of my shirt, which gets me thinking. "Where's your comforter and stuff?" Shane's sheepish cringe keeps me talking. "I can loan you a pillow and blanket, free of charge."

He peeks over at me. "I'd appreciate that. Guess I forgot some essentials."

I shrug. "What are roommates for, right?"

He visibly freezes at my words, eyes locking on mine. It's only a few seconds, but I catch his reaction. Weird. Shane exhales heavily. "That's right. I'll have to get used to this."

"Me too. I have a feeling your habits are the opposite of mine."

"What makes you say that?"

I give a meaningful glance to the bare mattress in front of us, then swing my gaze to his single piece of luggage. "Just a hunch."

"I'll gladly learn a thing or two from you."

My cheeks burn, and I press a palm against the blaze. "We'll see about that," I manage to choke out.

His warm honey eyes reel me in. "I look forward to it."

"Uh, right." I purposely glance away, concentrating on the blank walls. "Feel free to decorate however you'd like. I left it plain so you can add whatever. It'll be fun to see your style."

"I didn't think about any of this."

"Don't worry. It unfolds pretty easily. One step at a time. You've got a bed. Check. What's next on the list?"

"I better start one," he chuckles.

"Maybe groceries? Or something for storage? The closets are pretty small," I say.

Shane nods. "Yeah, sure. I suppose that makes sense."

I shake my head. "You're such a guy."

"Are you calling me forgetful?"

"Not necessarily," I defend.

He laughs. "Because you'd be right. All those extra options don't cross my mind. I'm very basic. Find something to sleep on, go to work, eat at Dagos. Wash, rinse, repeat."

"Now your constant presence at the bar makes more sense."

He starts to say something but stops himself. "Yeah, I guess so."

"You'll be busy for a while. Moving is an undertaking, but it can be fun."

"For you, maybe." Shane's tongue drags along his lower lip, and I'm locked on the movement. "I have a feeling you'll be helping me a lot."

I take a step back, and the pressure in my chest eases. Time to get this show on the road. "So, maybe start with ordering custom sheets. No way you'll find this size at Sew Lovely. Bet you'd even strike out at Target."

Shane scratches the scruff on his jaw. "That's a really good point."

I edge further away, almost to the hall. "I have a laptop if you want to use it. Although I'm sure your phone works just as well." Unless he's using it to call someone--that seems to be an issue. I hook a thumb over my shoulder and say, "I'll just be in the kitchen doing, uh, something. Holler if you need me."

"I'm terrible at this shit," he complains. "I should have planned things better." Shane's somber tone halts my retreat.

I swallow roughly and offer an easy smile. "Impulse buys are the best. It'll all come together. Only thing that matters is you're happy and have no regrets."

His stare is suddenly searing into me, and I feel his heat racing along my skin. Is his effect on me obvious? I sure hope not.

"I'm very satisfied so far," he rumbles. My thighs clench at his sexy timbre. Pretty sure we aren't talking about the mattress. He licks his bottom lip and asks, "Are you?"

And now I'm certain.

I blink quickly, attempting to get my raging hormones under

control. "It's a bit early to tell."

His eyes flare, and the temperature in this tiny square has suddenly skyrocketed. I practically leap out of the room with the need for fresh air clawing at me.

"Would you like some iced tea? I'm parched." My voice is all squeak, but my main concern at this point is to keep my clothes on. I dart away before waiting for his answer.

The tension between us is suffocating, and it's been less than an hour. How am I going to manage living with him, being surrounded by nonstop temptation? I whip open the fridge and stick my flaming face inside. Just as I'm getting my control corralled, his sultry voice comes from right behind me.

"So, what happens next?"

CHAPTER 5

SHANE
Keys

Addison spins around so fast that I almost reach out to help maintain her balance. A rosy blush covers her skin from head to toe, at least from what I can see. Her parted lips are glossy, the red stain matching the paint on her nails and all that shiny hair. The long waves cascade down and around her shoulders. That's Addison's trademark shade, and the color never fails to draw me in. She's sweetly seductive, and I'm a goner.

I should be flooded with guilt for having these primal urges, but the opposite is true. Addison makes me alive, shooting energy directly into my veins. She's the greatest gift, and I'll never take that for granted. How can something so good ever be considered bad? Simple—it can't.

I'm choosing to ignore the lessons I received under my family's roof. Those beliefs belong back there with them, not in this new place I call home. Lord only knows my mother wouldn't survive the news of me living with a woman, unless she's my wife. I take another greedy glimpse of Addison and imagine her in white.

Not a bad picture. She's so beautiful.

Digging a finger into my temple, I chase those crazy thoughts away. What the fuck is wrong with me? My brain is so full of Addison that I'm blind to everything else, like buying bedding. She must think I'm an idiot.

I close my eyes and focus on the sugary scent wafting over me. My mouth hasn't stopped watering since I walked through the door. The lit candles scattered about could have something to do with it, but I suspect my craving is solely for her. Apple cinnamon fills my lungs, and a warm slice of homemade pie comes to mind. My overzealous taste buds are begging, and that could be an alternative—hopefully a temporary one.

Maybe Addison has a recipe.

When I dare to look at her again, she's still looking at me. I need to fill this awkward silence, and my grumbling stomach does the trick.

She lifts a brow. "Hungry?"

I smooth my expression, hoping the mental deprivation isn't reflecting there. "Something like that. An iced tea would be great for now."

"Okay." She stretches the word out, hinting at her disbelief.

Addison reaches for two glasses from the cupboard, the back of her shirt hiking up in the process. A tempting sliver of skin taunts me, and I shuffle forward without hesitation. I clamp my mouth shut to trap the moan from rushing out. Desire stirs in my blood, collecting below the belt. Addison always calls to me, but this is another level entirely. I've never felt such strong need.

What the fuck am I going to do?

Jack's advice comes back to me. I should take this chance to learn more about her. "What do you usually do on a Saturday afternoon?"

She hands over the cold drink, and I take a generous gulp. Addison laughs before taking a sip of her own.

"I actually have to work soon. This is Dagos' busiest night of the week, as you might know." She winks at me.

My nod is quick and jerky. "Oh, yeah. That's right."

"Were you hoping for something more exciting?"

"Do you bake pies?" I blurt and immediately want to take back the question.

Addison visibly stiffens, the ever-present smile wiping off her face. "No, why?"

I inhale, savoring another serving of spiced apples. "Had a sudden hankering."

"I think we need to get a few things straight." Her flat tone twists my gut.

"Uh, okay."

She squints at me. "Just because I work as a server doesn't mean I'll wait on you at home."

I hold up my palms. "Wait, what?"

"You can't come in looking like that," Addison gestures wildly at me, "and start demanding things. It's not my job to cook and clean and tend to all your needs. Who doesn't remember sheets? Or a pillow? What about a plan for food that doesn't involve eating out? You're a grown-ass man, Shane." Her chest rises and falls with heavy breaths.

Shit, this is a train wreck. I desperately search for an explanation so she doesn't assume I'm a chauvinist asshole. "My mom used to make crumble cake on the weekend. Mostly for church. Just got me thinking," I mumble.

"Are you homesick?"

The furthest thing from it, but I don't say that. "Um, no."

She tosses up her hands. "Then what the heck?"

"You smell really good, okay?" I explain in a rush. "And for some stupid reason I was curious if it was from more than just you. Like, if your hobbies include baking."

That snaps her mouth shut. Addison stares at me, those green depths swirling. She gulps, the movement vibrating her slender neck. "That's actually kinda endearing." She sucks on her juicy bottom lip. "I'm sorry for jumping to conclusions. Guess I'm just on… edge."

"Don't apologize to me. It was a stupid thing to ask. I'm ready to forget that part of our conversation."

"Doesn't happen that way," she says.

I smirk. "Figures. Well, consider my foot firmly shoved into my mouth."

Addison giggles. "There's a sight to see."

"I really would like to know more about you," I tell her honestly.

"And asking about pies is the best way to start?"

"Never said I was any good at this."

"Idle chit-chat?"

I rock back on my heels. Clearly my attempts at flirting aren't coming across. I search for a safer topic, and my eyes land on matching plush chairs. The tan couch in the middle has bright red accent pillows. An orange blanket hangs over one armrest, waiting to be used. The large patterned rug in the main area stands out against the dark wood floor. There's a shelf over the fireplace and bookcases along the far corner. Rows of random items line the available surfaces, shedding a bit of light onto Addison. Romance novels, a vase with dried flowers, jars with sand and seashells, and the assorted candles. Framed black and white pictures catch my eye, the images appear to be popular Garden Grove landmarks. With another glance around, I realize how relaxed my body is. This is where I'm supposed to be. I want to make sure Addison feels the same way. She seemed happy when I mentioned decorating before. "Are you into interior design?"

That earns me another huge smile. "It's something I enjoy. I take a lot of pride in finding perfect pieces."

"It really shows. I like your style."

"I love finding new ideas. I'm a bit of a Pinterest junkie."

"Is that a show or something?"

Addison gapes at me. "You don't know what Pinterest is?"

"Should I?" I scratch my scalp, feeling out of my depth. I didn't have access to the internet until a few years ago so I'm always playing catch-up.

She grabs her phone and unlocks it. After tapping the screen a few times, she shows me the screen. "It's a website for inspiration mostly. People upload pictures, recipes, crafts, decorating layouts, chic designs, anything really. I could spend hours on this app. You can pin favorites to boards. It takes up much of my free time."

I glance at the array of colorful images as she scrolls. "Wow, okay. I'm not sure that makes any sense to me."

Addison giggles and puts her cell away. "It's not for everyone, but I love it. Same with Etsy." I blink at her, and she laughs again. "Never mind. What's something you like to do?"

"Anything really. Where I grew up, options were limited so finding new things to try is easy."

"Where are you from again?"

Frost seeps into my veins. I force away the shiver from my limbs. "Oaklain."

She purses her lips. "Where's that?"

"In the middle of nowhere. You won't find it on a map."

"How'd you end up in Garden Grove?"

"Sheer luck."

You left alone?" she asks and I nod. "Doesn't your family miss you?"

Another wave of unease crashes into me. It's far too early to expose my sins, but I can give her a little. "It's difficult to explain without boring you, but I didn't belong there anymore. We don't keep in touch so I wouldn't know either way."

I frown thinking about my younger sister, the only one I'd like to hear from. I'm haunted with images of her being punished in my absence. She's strong-willed like me. I have to believe she's all right.

"Huh," is all Addison gives in response. I'm grateful she doesn't question me further. I don't know how to explain this shit.

My skin is crawling and I veer away from toxic territory. "Have you always lived here?"

Her face lights up. "Yup, born and raised. I'm a lifer, like Delilah and Trey. We'll never leave, at least not permanently."

The certainty in her words chases off the whispers from my past. That sense of belonging, given and received, is what I desire most. Being part of something supportive and positive. I've never had that, until now.

"I'm glad. You fit in this town. It would crumble without you, especially Dagos."

"Make sure to tell Grayson that. Maybe I'll get a raise," she jokes. "So, did you always want to be a mechanic?"

"It's the only training I have. I fixed engines on my family farm, and it's good work. Comes natural to me. But I might take more classes at Concorite, see what else is available."

Her eyebrows bunch. "You're not happy at Jacked Up?"

"I am, but it never hurts to have more skills. Knowledge is wealth and all that," I say.

"That's true. I probably won't work at Dagos forever. Who knows what else I'd do, though. I make decent money as a server thanks to my tips." She gives me a knowing look, and I grin. It's no secret I'm always satisfied with her service.

"You could make more Pinterest boards," I suggest.

"I don't get paid for that."

I cross my arms. "Good thing you're not seeking advice from me."

Addison glances at the clock. "Okay, I have to leave soon. Let's see," she says and taps her chin. "Use anything you'd like. I'm not picky about my stuff. If you're going to have a bunch of people over, just let me know so I can steer clear." I bark out a laugh, and she lifts a brow. "What's funny?"

"Me having a party where you wouldn't be invited."

Her freckled cheeks blush. "Well, the option is open."

I nod. "Noted."

"I think we work opposite schedules so you won't have to worry about bumping into me much. You'll have the place to yourself that way."

My heart sinks. That wasn't the point of this arrangement. I rub at my chest and stare aimlessly over her shoulder. More cold and lonely nights are in my future. Maybe I'll get a job at Dagos. Or would that be too obvious?

"What's wrong?"

Her question breaks into my disappointment. "I don't mind having you around," I admit.

Addison's green eyes widen. "Oh, that's sweet. I'm sure you'll get sick of me--"

"I very much doubt that," I interrupt.

She ducks her face, but I don't miss her grin. "Okay."

"Anything else you wanna tell me right away?"

Addison glances around. "Oh, you'll be needing this." She snatches a key off the counter and drops it in my palm. The significance weighs a ton. Her finger tickles my palm, leaving a streak of heat behind.

"Thanks for trusting me with this. And in general," I say.

She looks up through thick lashes. "Doubt I could find anyone better. You're a good guy."

I know she's talking about our living arrangement, but secret meaning hangs between us. I'm making a huge deal out of this situation, but it's everything I've been waiting for. Addison will finally be in my proximity, all the time. Even if she's not physically here, I'll be surrounded by her. I immediately want to kick my own ass for thinking like a creep.

But I'm not lying about my intentions. This plan will pan out one way or another. If we do end up being just friends, I'll be okay with that. Being around her is good enough. It has to be.

Plus, I don't think the attraction is one-sided. I might be as inexperienced as they come, but Addison is giving off some vibes that make my dick twitch. As if reading my dirty mind, she tosses her head back and finger-combs through all that long hair. She twists the red strands into a bun, the movement lifting her shirt. I'm treated to a view of her flat stomach and have to adjust my semi. Shit, just a quick flash of skin turns me on faster than any porn site I've stumbled across.

"What's that look for?" Her question yanks me from my filthy musings.

I cough to cover the arousal clogging my throat. "Just thinking about later."

"Big plans?"

Hanging around Dagos is my usual, but I try to avoid freaking her out. "Apparently shopping for new stuff."

Her eyes sparkle. "Lucky. I'll try not to be jealous."

"Want me to wait until we can go together? Maybe tomorrow?" I want to erase her earlier comment about never seeing each other. She looks unsure so I try again. "I'm not sure what to get. You'd be doing me a huge favor. I'm a grown-ass man," I say, copying her, "who needs guidance."

Her head bobbles back and forth. "I dunno."

"Please?" I stick out my bottom lip. Her focus is locked on my mouth, and I don't mind it one bit.

"All right. That'll be fun," she mumbles.

I want to pump my fist in victory, but refrain. "It's a date."

Her jaw drops with a garbled exhale. "What?"

"Kidding," I tease and force a smirk. Her reaction is a harsh jab to my gut and I glance away.

Addison squints. "Really? I'm not so sure."

"It can be whatever you'd like," I tell her honestly. The lines she's setting are titanium and wrapped in barbed wire. *Do not cross.*

"Friends," she reminds me.

"You're the boss."

"Hardly," she huffs.

I motion around the room. "In here you are."

She smiles. "I like the sound of that."

"Me too."

Addison pops her lips. "On that note, I've gotta go. Will I see you at the bar tonight?"

I'm nodding before she's done talking. "Where else would I be?"

"According to you, at work or sleeping."

I laugh. "Wash, rinse, repeat."

CHAPTER 6

ADDISON
Rules

Ready for a truth bomb? My roommate is seriously sexy. Real shocking, I know. I've been drooling over him since he stepped foot in my apartment. That was seven days ago. This wouldn't be bad if I hadn't eliminated the potential of becoming more with him.

We're just friends, thanks to me.

But there's no harm in just looking. My experience in this department is zero. I've never been attracted to someone off-limits before. At least the cloying need to jump his bones has loosened its grip on my nether region. I'm managing to keep my outright ogling to a minimum. It doesn't hurt that I'm getting treated to a daily scoop of eye-candy no matter what, though. I'll eventually share how much I appreciate the teasing glimpses of his ripped abdomen. That succulent arrow of muscle leading down to his promised land makes me light-headed.

Damn, I'm in trouble.

The only consolation is I'm not alone.

It's fairly obvious Shane's interest hovers over the boundaries I slapped down too. Avoiding his lingering stares has proven to be very... hard. Yeah, there's no hiding my effect on him. I get giddy goosebumps whenever he adjusts himself. His actions have always screamed louder than words, and I couldn't be more thankful. Knowing he shares in these somewhat forbidden feelings makes me feel like less of a leering weirdo.

Good news? The initial tension brimming between us seems to be easing with each passing day. Although, it's a bit soon to tell. Shane has only been living with me for a week. Keeping these lines from blurring is going to be a challenge. So, I'm choosing to ignore the signs and let the sparks fizzle out. Eventually things will cool completely, right?

Fingers crossed.

I'm trying to focus on being unfazed, at least on the outside. Shane manages to appear calm and collected, but that's his norm. I fill in the silence with silly blabbering while he sits back and listens. I'm quickly learning just how opposite we are. Maybe I'll drive him bonkers, or perhaps we'll balance each other out? For now, I'm following Raven's advice—going with the flow.

So, here we are, strolling the aisles of my favorite store along Main

Street. Poppy Petals is the type of one-stop-shop I'm obsessed with. It's a combination of crafts and home goods, also known as my safe-haven. Shane walks slowly beside me as I *ooh* and *ahh* over random treasures. I pause by a display of assorted mugs.

"Which of these do you like best?" I ask him.

Shane peers over my shoulder. "That one."

His choice has a bold ruby glaze and Piping Hot scrawled across the front. I lift my brow, not surprised in the least. The few kernels of information I've learned about Shane include a talent for working on cars, being extremely tidy, a preference for pasta, and always choosing the color red.

I circle the rim. "Do you want it?"

"I'll buy it for you," he replies.

"We're supposed to be shopping for you," I remind him.

He grabs the cup and stashes it in our cart. "We can share it."

My belly dips imagining passing it back and forth, his lip touching the same spot as mine. I tug at the collar of my shirt, the short-sleeve tee suddenly stifling. "Ah, o-okay."

"Glad you agree." His brilliant smile makes my legs weak.

That's another thing I'm noticing. Shane's demeanor suddenly exudes confidence while I'm bumbling to string a sentence together. Talk about role reversal. I dip my face and trudge toward a basket of fuzzy socks.

"Not sure I can get away with wearing any of these," Shane says.

I pick up a neon pink pair. "No? I think they'd do wonders for your wardrobe."

He grunts. "Not sure I'm that desperate."

"Your loss. More for me."

"And here I thought we were picking out stuff for me."

"I can only resist for so long. You should be proud of me."

"Oh, I'm very impressed with your patience. Or maybe it's your ability to freely indulge without feeling guilty."

I shrug. "Mostly just the small things. An extra coffee mug never hurt anyone."

He quirks a brow. "And the overflowing sock drawer?"

"Another collection," I say. "The funkier the better."

Shane watches me thumb through the bin. "I'll remember that."

I offer a lazy smile. Our banter is getting easier and more entertaining. I'll have to find more silly topics to discuss. This place is a goldmine for that. Who knew Petals could get any better?

From the corner of my eye, I catch sight of Marlene and Betty. I've managed to avoid a confrontation with the gossip-queens since Shane moved in. I'm sure their old-fashioned feathers are beyond ruffled about my new roomie.

My posture goes ram-rod as I consider my options. Can I make it to the bathroom without them noticing me? After a quick glimpse in their direction, I discover it's far too late for an escape.

"Oh, here we go," I mutter.

Shane shoots me a questioning glance as they stop in front of us.

"Hello, Addison," Marlene coos. A waft of stinky perfume accompanies her close proximity.

I give them a finger-wave. "Well, hey there. What a lovely surprise."

Betty peers down her powdered nose at me. "Likewise, dear." Her narrowed gaze swings up and up some more, latching onto Shane. My shoulders instinctively hike up as I prepare for the onslaught. "And you are?" she asks him.

My jaw drops at that. He doesn't appear fazed and holds out a hand in greeting. "I'm Shane, pleasure to finally meet you ladies." They take turns slipping their dainty palms into his massive one.

Marlene elbows her friend. "Don't be silly, Betty. You've seen this fine gentleman around town. He works at Jacked Up."

The other woman nods. "Oh, that's right. Of course. You were the one who fixed up Ronald's Cadillac."

"Sure was, Ma'am," Shane says with a wink. Both biddies titter at that, wearing matching grins.

My shock ping-pongs between them, settling on him. "How have you not met them before?"

He shrugs. "I keep a low profile."

"Like, avoid all social gatherings? These two know everyone in Garden Grove," I sputter.

Marlene huffs. "You make us sound so nosey, Addison."

I give her a flat stare. "Really?"

Betty fluffs her bluish-grey curls. "I suppose, on rare occasion, a few slip by our notice. Yet, you," she points at Shane, "are hard to miss. Not sure how that happened."

Marlene snickers. "I've heard he spends a lot of time at Dagos."

I groan, ready to sling one of their lessons in manners. "Isn't that kinda rude? We're standing right here."

"Yes, dear. I'm aware. Just catching everyone up to speed," Marlene says.

"Your specialty," I say under my breath.

Her lips purse, and I wince. Here comes the third-degree. "Is this the man sharing your apartment? Your *very* male… housemate?"

My what?

"Um, well," I stammer. My throat is suddenly bone-dry, and I can't spit out the words. I need to tread lightly. They'll use anything I tell them against me and spread it around Garden Grove in a hot second.

Marlene takes advantage. "Quite scandalous, Addison. People are starting to whisper about this."

Shane slings an arm around me, and I swallow a gasp. "We're just friends, Ma'am. No funny business under our roof. I'd appreciate it if you kept that in mind."

Inhaling deeply is a mistake. His woodsy pine scent assaults me and sends a shiver from head to toe. I manage to stop my eyes from crossing, but sway into him.

Marlene's voice snaps me out of it. "Well, she works in that drunk den. I can only assume what happens after hours."

I cough loudly. "Excuse me? Hasn't assuming gotten you into enough trouble before?"

She blinks quickly. "That's none of your concern, young lady."

"Neither is my living situation," I retort.

Marlene shares a look with Betty. "Very well, dear. Sorry to be a bother. I wouldn't want to be considered rude." She tosses my earlier phrase back at me.

I roll my eyes. "Right."

A rumble rises in Shane's chest. "So long as there's no misunderstandings. Addison is a respectable lady."

Betty's mouth opens, but nothing comes out. Marlene sighs dramatically. Apparently they're having a hard time agreeing with his statement. I give them a few more moments to reply, feeling a smile grow on my face.

Times up.

"This sure has been fun, but we better get going," I tell them.

Shane chuckles beside me. "I'm sure we'll be seeing you two soon."

The women perk up at that, charmed by his smooth timbre. These birds seem mighty taken with him considering they'd never met ten minutes ago. Oh, who am I kidding? My own lips are lifting high into my cheeks being this close to him. He's intoxicating.

"Looking forward to it," Betty says.

Marlene pats his cheek. "Such a sweet boy." She glances at me. "Be nice to him, Addison. Funny business or not."

I laugh because there's no reasoning with these two. "Will do, thanks."

While they're sashaying away, Shane drops his hold on me. "Sorry for taking liberties."

"Never apologize for defending me."

A dimple dents his cheek. "I shouldn't have told them anything about us."

I wave off his concern. "People are talking either way."

"Good," he says.

"You don't care? Mister Keeps-a-low-profile," I giggle.

"Nah, why would I? You're boosting my popularity by a billion. Plus, spending time with you isn't a burden."

I hide my grin behind spread fingers. "They'll probably assume we're dating."

Shane shrugs. "Let them think that. Doesn't bother me."

His comment is a silky caress, and I shiver. "Me either."

He lowers his lids, giving him a bedroom effect. "No one would believe them."

"Why not?"

"Because I'm the quiet outsider. You're gorgeous and outgoing."

"What you really mean is loud and obnoxious," I correct.

He shakes his head. "Even Marlene and Betty won't peg us together."

I flatten my lips. "Because I couldn't land a guy like you."

He grunts. "Just the opposite."

"I don't see the issue. That's how rumors work. But let's not worry about it. We know the score," I tell him.

"Right." Shane coughs into his fist. "So, are those two always like that?"

"Brutally honest and digging for dirt? Oh, yes."

"I was expecting them to be more polite, as dignified older women and all."

I snort. "Keep waiting."

"You handled it well."

"I'm used to it. We all are. Just grit your teeth and wait for them to leave."

Shane frowns. "That sounds... painful."

I stroll forward and start perusing again. "Meh, not really. They're fairly harmless. Didn't you have drama in your hometown?"

His voice is hollow when he says, "Not that kind." And that's all he gives me.

Whenever I bring up Shane's past, he brushes it off. I haven't pushed too hard because it's not my story to tell. He might be reluctant to share for a reason. Not everyone grew up in adorable Garden Grove with parents who shed nothing but love. Their marriage is something to envy and represents everything I want.

Good luck future husband—high standards for sure. But expecting that level of commitment and adoration is second nature. My father worships the ground my mother walks on and vice versa. I grew up absorbing their affection.

I peek over at Shane. Does he know what that type of love looks like? I'm too chicken shit to ask. Plus, we're not nearly close enough friends for me to poke around in potentially private memories.

I bounce on my toes, ready to turn this conversation around. "So, more shopping? Or something else?"

That earns me a small smirk. "What'd you have in mind?"

"Jitters?"

His honey eyes sparkle. "Yes."

Another thing I've learned—Shane has a sweet tooth. Big time. His initial baking comment makes far more sense with this nugget of knowledge. The way to a man's heart is his stomach, right? No wonder Trey is so enamored with Raven. Shane has to settle for me buying the cupcakes.

We step outside and the late August heat clings to my skin. Maybe I'll suggest a trip to Grove Park so we can cool off in the lake. The thought of Shane shirtless, all those muscles on display, makes my body burn up for an entirely different reason.

"You okay?" he asks and slides on a pair of aviators. Good grief, he's lethal to my control wearing those. As if he wasn't sexy enough. Shane lightly touches my upper back, his strength soaking in. "Addison? Still with me?"

I nod and fan my face. "Just hot."

"Sure are." He swallows roughly and clears his throat. "I mean, yeah, you look a little flushed. Better get your coffee over ice."

I kick at the cobblestone sidewalk, trying to focus on the uneven footing rather than the man beside me. As if hearing the havoc inside of me, Shane's hand grazes mine. I jolt as if electrocuted.

My lashes flutter as I peek up at him. He's already staring down at me. Screw it, spontaneous combustion be damned.

"Wanna go swimming?"

CHAPTER 1

SHANE
Reminder

I recline further into the high-top stool, the padded back supporting my slouch. Being at Boomers, surrounded by two engaged couples, is becoming more common for me. Addison invited me to tag along to the bar, but her intentions are clear as always. Or lack of intentions—we're just friends. The safe distance separating us is a megaphone announcing our platonic relationship. I might be sitting beside her, but we're very much apart.

I hate the empty space.

Yet I don't want to be anywhere else. Why would I? A gap between us or not, this beats hanging at home alone. Being here, I can smell the apple lotion lingering on Addison's skin. Watch those red nails drum on the menu. Get lost in the tumbling waves flowing down her back. Catch her green eyes glitter in the overhead lights.

When Addison bites her glossy lower lip, I choke on a moan. We've shared a wall for two weeks now. Fourteen days of being close to her, but not near enough. She's torturing me without realizing it. My dick is always hard, and the ache never goes away. The constant throbbing is beginning to feel like my new normal, which is warped as fuck. I skipped over the wet dreams phase of youth, and it's coming back to haunt me. This is a lesson in control I don't wish on my worst enemy. But I've found a new level of strength and patience. Plus, my fantasies keep me company at night.

Addison provided more than enough visual stimulation on our visit to the beach. Her bathing suit was mostly strings held together by triangles of fabric. The tent in my shorts was shameful, but she couldn't blame me. I might be inexperienced, but my imagination isn't innocent. I wanted to rip that red bikini off and touch her. Kiss every inch of freckled skin. Suck along sensitive spots that would make her moan.

The lines between right and wrong are getting fuzzy. My need to be near Addison has taken control, driving me straight into the gutter. Pastor Raine's sermons are faint whispers, echoing reprimands that no longer hold power. I should turn away and banish these desires. But what I continue to do is swim deeper into the depths of lust. Potent desire swirls in my blood, the mixture a heady cocktail. When will it consume me completely?

"What's on your mind?" Addison asks.

I look at her, diving into those green waters staring back at me.

I'll gladly drown. "Thinking about the lake." My voice is gruff, giving away the tension simmering inside of me.

She hums. "That was a great afternoon."

"We should go back," I suggest.

Even in this dim lighting, I see her cheeks get rosy. "I'd love that."

"Tomorrow?"

Addison frowns. "I work a double. Maybe Monday?"

I clench my teeth. "I've got the closing shift at Jacked Up."

She sighs. "Mismatched schedules screwing with our fun."

No shit.

She wasn't lying about our opposite schedules. I'm realizing having the same afternoon off is a rarity. Addison's focus goes to her drink, and she takes a long pull through the thin straw. I count the beats of my pounding heart, willing it to slow down. There's nothing to be excited about. The silence stretches between us and I look across the table.

The band hasn't started playing so we can still hear each other. The others in our little group don't seem interested in conversing with us, though. They're distracted with one another, lost in a different element. Zeke is whispering in Delilah's ear. Trey is nipping Raven's fingertips. It's like watching romantic reality television, but I can't change the channel. Something sour burns in my gut, and I peek over at Addison. She's looking at them, her shoulders slumping in a pitiful droop. Shit, I'm being a bad date. I mean, friend.

"Another round?" I ask and point to her glass.

Addison nods. "I'll take a—"

"Vodka soda with a splash of cranberry and lime," I finish.

She arches a brow. "Impressive."

"Hardly. Want some onion rings, too?"

She twists toward me. "How did you know?"

"I pay attention."

"Well, all right then. I can get used to this treatment."

I wink at her. "Good."

After ordering from the server, I turn back to Addison. She's smiling at me, and my pulse kicks up all over again. Things I've recently learned about her include food and beverage preferences, but there's so much more. Addison is crazy smart, wickedly so. She picks up on shit so quick it makes my head spin. And her memory is a steel trap. If I ever slip up and say something stupid, she'll never let it go. She collects a lot of random stuff, like mugs and socks. Her parents live in Arizona and rarely find their way back to Garden Grove. Addison loves dogs, and I often find her scrolling through pet adoption sites.

"Tell me something about you." Her question drags me away from my mental checklist.

I rub my forehead. "Like what?"

"How about your full name."

I press back in my seat. "Shane Rookston."

Her lips quirk up. "Yeah, no duh. I wanna know your middle one."

"It's embarrassing," I complain.

"I'll tell you mine. Addison Jaymes Walker," she says, and I grin.

"I already knew that," I murmur.

She tucks a few red strands behind her ear. "You're so observant.

It's sweet."

"And you're trying to butter me up."

Addison pouts. "Please tell me?"

I scrub over my face, already regretting this decision. But there's no denying her. "Edwin," I mumble.

A snort of air puffs from her mouth. "Really?" The humor in her voice echoes across the crowded bar.

I glare at the industrial ceiling, tracing the black rafter beams. "Yes."

"That's so… um, rugged?"

I roll my neck and turn toward her. "Don't lie on my account."

She slaps a palm over her enormous smile. "I'm not," comes out as a muffle.

"You so are, Adds."

She sobers and leans forward. "Adds?"

I feel the heat rising on my skin and look away. "Uh, yeah. Everyone calls you Addy. Figured I'd be different. But I don't have to."

She grabs my arm. "I love it."

"Yeah?"

Addison nods quickly. "Big time. I figured you were still calling me lass."

I glance at her hair. "That's just between us. And Trey, I guess. He was there that first day."

Her eyes get real big, and she cringes. "Ah, right. A secret..." Addison trails off, and I smirk.

"You already told them?"

"It might have slipped out a time or two," she says softly. "I'm sorry."

I rub her shoulder, and she shivers. "Don't be."

Addison licks her lips. "So, uh, what's your nickname?"

I shrug. "Don't really have one."

"Why not?"

"I dunno."

"Well, we can't have that."

I rest an elbow on the table. "No?"

She taps her chin. "How about sugar or cupcake? You're a big dessert fan." I wince, and she laughs. "Yeah, those are bad." Her eyes flick to mine. "What about honey?"

"Because I'm so sweet?"

Addison's lashes flutter. "Uh, maybe. Um, never mind. Maybe something related to work?"

"Like bolt or wrench?"

She huffs. "Ugh, no."

I gesture toward Trey. "The guys at Jacked Up call me rookie. Makes sense since I am one in many ways."

Addison blinks slowly. "And your last name."

I want to smack my forehead. "That too."

Her green eyes light up. "Rooks? That's got a nice ring to it. And it's the little tower piece in chess. You're the corner of our castle, holding it up."

My body gets warm when she whispers that. Whenever she ties us together in any capacity, my ego swells tenfold. I stretch to sit taller, my shoulders and chest expanding. "I like Rooks."

"Good, it's settled."

"What is?" Raven asks.

"Oh, you want to be social now?" Addison teases.

Raven purses her lips. "Really?"

Delilah breaks away from Zeke. "What's happening?"

Addison rolls her eyes. "Shane and I were discussing nicknames."

Her friends share a knowing grin, and I shake my head.

"Not mine," Addison scolds. "Shane needed one."

He's already covered," Trey says.

"Yeah, from you all at the garage. This is for me," Addison announces.

Delilah just about falls off her chair. "Bathroom break?"

Raven squints at her. "Didn't you just go?"

Delilah swats the air. "Don't be dense, Rave. Girl talk."

Raven winks. "Right, great idea."

The two blondes lift their brows at Addison.

"Uh, sure?" she mutters.

All three are gone in a flash, their high-pitched giggles carrying over the bar noise.

"Women," Trey mutters.

"They always travel in packs," Zeke adds.

"Guess so," I say.

"Don't worry, rookie. You'll get used to it. Those three tell each other everything," Trey explains with a smirk.

I scratch the stubble lining my jaw. "Everything?"

"Oh, yeah. No secret is safe," Zeke replies.

I think about Addison sharing lass with them, skirting around admitting the truth. Guess her reaction makes sense. "Huh," is all I reply.

"Pretty much expect us to know anything that happens, like one big dysfunctional family," Trey says.

Zeke chuckles. "Yeah, you got the screwed-up part taken care of."

"Oh, fuck off. Don't burn a freshly mended bridge, Krue." Trey's gaze swings to me. "Why does it look like someone punched you in the balls?"

"Not sure what you mean," I reply.

He squints at me. "You've got that same expression as Zeke when Delilah was shutting his ass down."

Zeke shoves him. "Didn't you just call me out for talking shit?"

Trey jabs right back. "You deserve it for being a pussy."

"Takes one to know one," Zeke grits out.

Trey holds up a palm at him. "Truce." Then he points at me. "You make things official yet? Or still playing polite houseguest?"

Zeke snorts. "Such a way with words."

I scowl. "It's been two weeks. I'm good with what's happening."

"It's obvious you wanna fuck her," Trey drawls.

I curl my fingers into a fist. "Shut up, man." But he's not wrong. Getting Addison beneath me would fulfill every wild fantasy.

"You gotta marry her first or what?" he taunts.

I open my mouth, but nothing comes out. I can't deny the truth. Picturing Addison in white is no challenge. I settle on, "It's not your business."

"Lame as fuck. You don't know what you're missing," Trey says.

"Not everything is about sex. We're friends, and I'm good with that." Conviction clangs in my voice.

He scoffs and tilts back in his chair. "Fucking pansy. Someone else is gonna steal her from under your nose. Better claim her for real or you'll be sorry."

"Your advice sucks," I reply. I rarely lose my cool, it's one of the qualities my mother actually complimented. But Trey pushes me too far when talking about Addison like this.

"I got the girl, right? What do you have? Empty hands," Trey jeers.

Zeke's focus is ping-ponging between us. "All right, let's move on."

Trey flicks him off, then glances at me. "Just looking out for you, rookie."

I've never hated that name before now. "Don't bother."

"Who needs another?" Zeke interrupts and holds up his bottle.

I take a deep breath, letting Trey's words roll off me. "I could use one."

Trey signals to his near-empty glass. "Fill up the cup."

Zeke gets up to order us a round while Trey and I exchange glares. After several tense moments, he says, "I'm just fucking with you, man."

"Could've fooled me," I grumble.

He knocks on the table. "But what the fuck, dude? Stop blowing her off."

I jab a finger at my own chest. "I'm her friend. That's what she wants." A slithering sensation snakes up my spine and I hold back a shudder. I hate admitting Addison's feelings toward me, or lack thereof. Especially to Trey.

He chugs what's left of his beer. "Put on your big-boy boxers and grow a pair."

"Let's drop it, okay?"

Trey's jaw tics. "Don't be a moron. Chicks almost break their necks checking you out, Addison most definitely included."

I snort, tilting sideways from his abrupt mood swing. "Why are you being so... encouraging all of a sudden?"

His eyes roll toward the dartboards and arcade area nearby. "Fuck if I know. This is all Raven's fault." He blinks and looks back at me. "Is Addison buzzing about Fall Haze?"

I cross my arms. "No? It's over a month away."

Zeke returns with our drinks and passes them out. He laughs, overhearing my response to Trey. "Doesn't matter. Girls are planners. They're thinking about shit years in advance."

Trey grunts. "For fucking real. At least your woman isn't going crazy thinking up new recipes. I swear, it's one festival after the other around here. Raven bakes her butt off nonstop." He pats his stomach. "I reap all the benefits of that shit."

"Quit bragging. I'm building Jitters a new stand so they're a step above in all ways," Zeke says.

"Show off," Trey groans. "Raven won't let me live it down."

I scrub over my face. "I'm lost. What should I be doing to prepare for this?"

They silently stare at me for a full minute until I'm practically squirming in place. Trey cracks up, and Zeke grins.

"Shit, man. You've got so much to learn," Trey says.

I'm beginning to realize he might be right.

CHAPTER 8

ADDISON
Haze

October wind is a harsh breeze, the bite of autumn nipping my skin. I shiver and tug on the collar of my coat. Regardless of the temperature drop, this season is my favorite. I love getting bundled up and cozy in sweaters. Not to mention Garden Grove's most popular festival—Fall Haze.

The town rents a huge field from Sumpter Farms for the event. An array of striped tents, food stands, carnival rides, and game booths dot the flat landscape. I hop on the balls of my feet as we approach the gate. Shane laughs, the sound deep and gruff. I feel my lashes flutter, which causes me to stumble.

He grasps my elbow. "You okay?"

I nod too quickly. "Uh-huh, yep. Just a rock or something. I'm a little chilly, though."

"Want my hoodie?" Shane asks and slings an arm around me. He's been finding subtle ways to touch me—innocently, of course—and I can't seem to get enough. I hunch my shoulders to get his warmth closer. The combination of woodsy cologne and motor oil greets me. I attempt to keep my indulgent inhale under wraps. When I tremble again, it's not from the cold.

"Maybe we should come back tomorrow if you're already freezing," he suggests.

"No way. I'm fine." I suck in a deep breath and add, "You're keeping the cold away."

Shane peeks down at me, those dimples on full display. "Happy to oblige."

Heat washes over me and I can barely feel the brisk air anymore. We stroll through the main entrance and pass over our tickets. I squint against the early afternoon sun, digesting my options. Powdered sugar and fried dough waft over. My stomach gurgles, and I give it a loving pat. Shane's hold on me tightens when I start walking toward the funnel cakes.

"Where're you running off to?" he murmurs.

I lick my dry lips. "Food first, explain later."

He chuckles at my nonsense and lets me lead the way.

That's one thing I lo—nope, like about him. Shane has settled in nicely, along with our friendship. I never knew spending time with a guy could be so fun. He makes me cackle obnoxiously loud and swoon like a damsel. But more than that, I'm at ease with him around.

My guard is nonexistent, and that's a treat I've never tasted before. I can be myself without concern. Shane accepts my goofy behavior with an easy grin, always proving he gets me. I'm floating on a relaxed cloud, without a care in the world. I know he'll be there… as a friend, of course.

He's game for anything, like accompanying me to the Haze. I'm not sure if he's actually interested in attending or just appeasing me. Either way, my smile hasn't dimmed since he agreed to go. Boys I've dated in the past wouldn't go within a mile of this place, unless it involved sneaking into the beer garden, of course. Shane is different.

Man, is he ever.

My body is buzzing but not with nerves. There's always a jolt of voltage zapping between us. The chemistry is undeniable, our signals mixing more by the minute. I'm a live-wire with a warning label—don't touch or I'll go up in flames. My skin is static-cling and wants to rub against a certain someone.

I'm careful not to overstep our lines, but it's getting more difficult. With a quick glimpse up, I get another hit of why. His honey eyes are focused on me—my slightly parted mouth—and he leans closer. The standard five-o'clock shadow shades his jaw, the dark stubble contrasting with his tan complexion.

"Like what you see?" Shane whispers.

My blink is sluggish. "Yes."

A rumble rises in his chest. "Fuck, Adds. What're you doing to me?"

"I dunno," I murmur into the barely there space between us.

Shane hugs me, tucking my head under his chin. "Me either."

I want to sob into his shirt. Why didn't this happen before he moved in? I curse the questions left unanswered, allowing them to refuel my resolve. Yes, Shane is almost perfect and ridiculously hard to resist. But there's so much I don't know about him. He's resistant to discuss anything meaningful about himself. I'm often left thinking our conversations are superficial, just to pass the time. That always leaves me feeling cold, far worse than the wind currently stinging my cheeks.

I force myself to pull away. "Okay, what should we eat?"

There's a furrow in his brow, but he smooths it soon enough. "Figured your sight was set on something."

I give a lazy shrug. "I have a lot of favorites."

"Such as?"

"Tell me yours, and I'll share mine," I sass.

He smirks. "I've never been here before."

That familiar comfort settles between us, and I grin. "Let's make it fun. Do you prefer mini donuts or caramel corn?"

Shane considers this. "Mini donuts?"

"You sure about that?" I ask and he nods. "Great. Those are sold at the booth I was heading for."

"Let's go." He smacks his lips, and I giggle.

When we're standing in line, I point to the menu. "Hot chocolate or apple cider?"

"I like both, but hot cocoa."

"Solid choice," I say and offer my palm for a high-five.

He rolls his eyes but slaps my hand. "You act like we're so

buddy-buddy."

I bump into him lightly. "Because we are, Rooks. I really like being with you."

"As friends?"

Shane questions our relationship often enough that I know he'd prefer taking things further. But I'm the one holding back.

"Yeah? I think it works for us."

He shifts his stance, staying quiet. The familiar tension prickles up my neck, but I ignore it and order my food. Shane does the same and seems fairly unaffected. I try to brush off the disappointment.

The pinch in my belly steals my appetite, but I take the funnel cake when it's ready. I break off a massive bite for nothing more than something to do. We head for an available picnic table and sit down. I lick sugar off my thumb and hear Shane groan. When I glance over, his teeth are clenched.

I point to his donuts. "Not good?"

"That's not the problem," he grinds out. I lift a brow, and he leans forward. His finger swipes across my face, and he lifts it for me to see. "You had some extra there," he explains and sucks the digit into his mouth. Now it's me who's trying to trap a moan.

And just like that, we're back in action. I'm on a see-saw of emotions with this man. We finish our cocoa and Shane tosses the trash away.

I clear my throat and point to a craft tent. "Scarf or mittens?"

"Scarf," he says without hesitation. "You?"

"Mittens. Mostly because I can knit a scarf."

"You can?"

I rub my chin. "Yep. I made scarves for everyone last Christmas."

"Not me," he mumbles.

I bite my lip, then rub his shoulder. "Sorry, Rooks. We didn't really know each other then. I'll make up for it this year."

The light returns in his brown eyes. "Yeah?"

"And then some. I can make you a hat, too. If you'd actually wear—"

"I would," he insists.

"Okay, it's a done deal. When's your birthday?"

"April twenty-sixth."

I hum. "That's your golden, right?"

His lips twist adorably. "Uh, what's that?"

I poke his dented cheek. "Your age and birthdate are the same number."

"Oh, right. Then yes." He ducks his chin, trying to hide a smile.

I shimmy on my seat. "I'll make sure to spoil you."

His honey stare locks on me. "Not sure I deserve that."

"That's for me to decide, huh?"

Shane studies my expression, and I flush under his intense focus. These flirty moments make my barriers weak beyond belief. I sigh and drag my gaze off his handsome face. Signs for the variety of attractions around Fall Haze snag my attention.

"Hay ride or corn maze?" I ask.

"The guys at Jacked Up were talking about the maze. Might be cool to check it out," he suggests.

"I'm good with that," I say.

He sweeps his arm out. "Ladies lead."

The corn maze ends up being a very good choice. There's random trivia posted in designated areas, which is a reprieve from the lingering stares and heated moments. For the most part, Shane and I laugh our way through until finding a way out.

I'm still giggling while we stroll toward the carnival area. "Who knew that Pteronophobia is the fear of being tickled by feathers."

"Not us, apparently." His fingers dance up my forearm, and I squeak.

"I shouldn't have given up my sensitive spots," I admit.

Shane grips my pinkie, squeezing gently. "Rookie move."

I wink at him. "Takes one to know."

He grunts and keeps walking. Is it possible for my face to hurt from smiling too big? I think that's what is happening. We stop in the center of the game booths, and I lift a brow in question. "Darts at balloons or test of strength?"

Shane doesn't hesitate, striding toward the attendant holding a sledge hammer. He lifts it over his head with ease and immediately swings it down in a perfect arc. The bell clangs out, announcing his win. Shane glances at me over his shoulder and winks.

The booth worker waves across a row of small prizes. "Your pick."

Shane nudges me. "Choose what you'd like."

"Oh my gosh. Look at that bear," I gasp out.

He looks up where I'm pointing. "The one covered in sequins?"

"Yes! How cute. She's a bling bear."

Shane lifts his chin at the attendant. "How much for that one?"

The guy sighs. "You have to ring the bell again."

Shane laughs. "Challenge accepted."

I swallow roughly. If he strikes that thing again, I'll have to change my thong. I glance at the bedazzled stuffed animal, then at Shane's bulging arms. Wait, why was I trying to avoid this?

Even through the cotton of his shirt, I can see his back muscles bunch and flex as he lifts the hammer again. With expert precision, Shane strikes dead center and clangs the bell without blinking. I exhale all dreamy and almost fan my face. Totally worth it.

Shane grabs the bling bear and gives it to me. He looks taller somehow, a megawatt smile stretching his lips. I just about tip over from the swoon.

"Come here." I motion him closer. "Take a selfie with Blingy and me." He loops his arm around my hips, and we pose for the camera. I bring the phone closer so we can see the picture.

Shane stares at the screen intently. "Should I go for something bigger?"

I shift my legs and clutch the sparkly stuffed animal tight. "Nope, this is exactly what I wanted."

His honey eyes gleam. "Good, me too."

I lift a brow. "You wanted a sequined bear?"

"Nah, just seeing you happy."

My chest cinches tight, and I swear my heart is trying to escape. I breathe out choppy and just stare at him. What the eff do I say to that?

Shane saves me by hitching a thumb over his shoulder. "I gotta use the can. You okay staying here?"

His question is unnecessary, but I appreciate it all the same. I take a look around, noticing a few girls from work close by. I nod toward them and say, "Myla and Britt are over there. They'll keep me company."

He shuffles his feet but doesn't move far. "You sure?"

I laugh and start backing away. "Yes. See you in a bit."

Shane still seems reluctant, but turns for the bathrooms way across the field. I wander up to my friends, and they smile.

"Hey, girl. Fancy seeing you here," Myla greets.

"And you already won the best prize," Britt adds.

For a moment, I think they're talking about Shane. Then I remember the enormous bear I'm holding. "Ah, yeah. Shane actually got it for me." They share a look I'm far too familiar with. I roll my eyes. "Don't even start," I say.

Britt holds up her hand. "Addy, you better be hitting that soon or he's free play."

I glare at her. "You wouldn't."

She flips her black hair over a slim shoulder. "Duh, but I'm not who you need to worry about."

A huff pushes from my pursed lips. "Oh, whatever. If Shane wants to date, he's free to do so."

Britt grins. "Yeah, right. I'm gonna get a beer to wash down that bullshit. Want one?" She makes a chugging gesture. We both pass, and she bounces off.

"She's just trying to make you jealous," Myla says.

"Reverse psychology at its finest right there," I mutter.

"Britt might be onto something."

"Ugh, not you too."

Her smile spreads. "You hump that hunky roommate yet or what?"

I frown. "No, thank you very much. We're just friends."

She sticks out her tongue. "Still using that excuse?"

I bump her with my hip. "We've managed to keep things G-rated. The original boundaries are still intact."

"You don't sound so happy about that."

I shrug. "It's my fault there's limitations, but I'm not the only guilty one. He should have made a move before making the move. So, I shouldn't have been so quick to slap a label on us. He should have called before we became roommates. We screwed ourselves over."

Myla snort-laughs. "Oh, that's priceless. Have you talked to him about this yet?"

"Nope, and not sure I will. There's a lot beneath the surface, and I'm afraid to make waves."

"What if he's the one to do it?"

I cross my arms. "Unlikely considering I've already been waiting for months."

"To be fair, you stuck him in the zone. Now he's being respectful, Addy. I doubt he'd push you into anything. You told him the new arrangement and he's following orders. So honorable," she coos.

"Wish he'd be a little less so," I reply.

"It's not too late at all. How long has he been living with you? A month?"

"Six weeks," I correct.

Myla giggles again. "But who's counting, right?"

I roll my eyes. "Yeah, yeah. I pay attention to him."

"Show him you're interested in more. You established the rules, time to break them."

"I dunno. We have a good thing going. I love hanging out with him. Shane seems to get me." I comb through my hair and yank on the ends. "Why does he have to be so great? He loves everything I do. And I don't think it's a ploy to get into my pants. Shane genuinely enjoys watching HGTV and making the coffee in the morning and cleaning up after himself and playing silly games."

Myla tilts her head. "I'm confused as to where the problem is?"

"Adding more could ruin everything."

"Don't tell me you're using the 'I don't wanna destroy our friendship' excuse. You'll never know without trying, Addy. Maybe he's desperate for you, too."

I scoff. "Doubt it."

She shoves me lightly. "Stop being naïve. That man wants your ass."

"You sound like Delilah and Raven."

"Because we're right."

I cross my arms. "So, why doesn't he take me?"

Myla rubs her temples, the frustration clear. "You specifically said off-limits."

I tilt my face to the sky. "Gah, why did I do that?"

"You were being safe and careful. I get it. But the time for caution is over. Throw that shit to the wind," she demands.

Before I can answer, the gravelly voice I'm falling for calls out, "I hope you're not gossiping about me, ladies."

I twist toward Shane and smile. "Never. Nothing but the truth."

Myla waves at him. "Hey, Shane. Addy and I were just discussing Halloween."

We were?

He opens his mouth but closes it again. I twirl a lock of my hair, deciding to roll with it. "Uh, yeah. Dagos is always swamped." At least that part is true.

"On that note, I should get going. Nice chatting, Addy. See you at work tomorrow," Myla says and dashes off without another word.

Shane chuckles. "So, Halloween? More planning ahead?"

I squint at him. "Huh? For what?"

"Not important."

"Well, since we're on the subject, what're you gonna be?"

He scratches his neck. "Not sure, I guess. I don't have a costume, never dressed up for it in the past."

The need to know more burns on my tongue, but I bite it back. "Oh, okay. You'd make a hot cop or security guard."

"You like a man in uniform?"

I nibble my bottom lip. "Maybe."

If it's Shane wearing it, abso-freaking-lutely. Not sure my nether region will be able to handle that after the strength test display. He's way too sexy

His brown eyes do a slow sweep of me, scorching heat following close behind. "Sounds like I better find a badge." Shane's bicep bunches under my hand, and I suddenly realize I've been stroking him. I yank my fingers away and mutter an apology. He chuckles and shoots me a panty-melting grin. "I didn't mind that one bit, Adds. Never be sorry for touching me."

Sandpaper scratches my throat when I gulp. "O-okay."

Shane's hand brushes across my lower back. His palm settles there, a white-hot brand marking me. I love the idea of him staking claim, fantasy or not. "What's next?"

I can't take my eyes off his. "How about some rides?"

"Ferris Wheel?" he suggests.

The image of more teasing touches pops into my mind. "I'm definitely down for that."

CHAPTER 9

SHANE
Tempt

The Keurig gurgles and spits out a final few drops of coffee. Right on cue, Addison staggers out of her room. She's sleep-rumpled and sexy as fuck. Her hair is a wild mess of red and my fingers itch to smoothen out the knots. Creases from the pillow crisscross along her cheek, and I want to rub the lines away. She's wearing an extra large Dagos tee that almost reaches her knees. I picture her in one of my shirts, and the thought almost sends me rushing to grab one. Damn, I'm fucking losing it. Addison's bleary eyes land on me, and she smiles lazily.

I've jerked off more in the two months living here than all of last year. This picture of perfection is why. Thinking about her costume from Halloween only adds fuel to the fire. My dick was hard all night—hell, it still is days later. There're times I think she's tempting me on purpose. But I've done my fair share of pushing the limits. I adjust myself behind the counter, blood pumping far too fast before nine o'clock.

"Hey, Adds," I murmur.

"Morning," she mumbles.

"Vanilla hazelnut." I pass her the steaming mug.

She takes a deep inhale before sipping slowly. The satisfied moan she gives makes my dick too happy. I'm already sporting a semi and don't need further encouragement.

"You're a saint," Addison says quietly.

"That's what you always say," I reply. And each time, it strikes a bittersweet nerve. I don't deserve that title.

"I mean it, Rooks. I'd be lost without you."

"At least until caffeine gets in your system."

Her foot nudges mine. "For real, you're the best."

"It's nothing, really." I shrug and shove my hands deep into my pockets.

I stopped asking if she'd like a cup weeks ago. This is her routine, and I've wedged myself into it. Addison pays me back with wistful smiles and shy blushes. I can tell she likes the small ways I'm taking care of her.

"Anything going on tonight?" I ask.

She looks away. "I'll probably just come home after work."

We tend to tiptoe around touchy subjects, never landing a direct hit. Something Addison doesn't like talking about is her plans. Or lack thereof. She's been coming straight back here more often than not. I like to think it's because of me. To test my theory or because I'm a glutton for punishment, I tell her, "There's a marathon of House Hunters on. Or we could keep binging on Stranger Things."

Addison's face lifts back to mine. I'm rewarded with her signature smile. "That sounds perfect."

These moments are my favorite, when she's warm and soft, no barriers in sight. There's been plenty of close calls where we toe the line. The fragile structure we've created is growing more unstable by the moment. One wrong move will topple the tower, but would that be so bad? Her effect on me is steadily taking over. I'm helpless to fight the bundle of burning lust building in my gut. I want her with every fiber of my being. My desire is a rabid beast demanding action, but I won't force this.

Addison seems set with our arrangement, frustratingly so. I can tell Addison wants me as more than a friend. There's fire in her eyes, heat trembling in her limbs. But she hesitates. There's something stopping us, blocking our path to that next step. And it's more than her initial reasoning for keeping things strictly platonic. Something else holds her back. I have no fucking idea what that is, and it's making me twitchy. I could just ask her, of course. Will I? Absolutely not.

No rocking the boat and all that shit.

I peer down the hallway, remembering something. "What's all over the bathroom counter?"

Addison's freckled cheeks bunch when she smiles. "Oh, it's my new makeup. I'll go put it away. I was too lazy last night."

I grip her hand so she doesn't leave. "I don't mind."

Her fingers wiggle against mine. "I have a bit of a lipstick addiction if you didn't notice." I watch her tongue slowly trail across her lower lip.

"I do, too."

Her giggle knocks me from the trance.

"I mean, uh, on you."

Addison blushes. "Thanks, Rooks. You're sweet."

"Just for you," I murmur.

She lifts her chin, those green pools swirling with something I can't quite grasp. As if pulled, I take a small step forward. Her pulse flutters wildly in the base of her neck. My hungry gaze bounces between the frantic beat and her searing stare. I swallow roughly over the boulder in my throat.

Addison tilts her head and blinks. "Whoa. That was… intense." She rests a palm on her forehead. "I think we should go running now."

I stay silent, but the need to disagree almost drips off my tongue. There's so much more I want in this moment. I imagine hoisting her up into my arms. We'd crash into the wall in our haste to get naked. Our skin would ignite and blaze, roaring flames gaining power when we kissed. I'd drink from her mouth, and Addison's thighs would clench around me. We'd tumble and fall and become one.

The fantasy vanishes when Addison pulls her palm away. The loss of touch allows me to breathe, and clarity rushes in. I need to get a fucking grip on this shit. I press on my temple in an attempt to drill that indisputable fact straight through.

Addison turns for the hall, and I slowly follow. We go our separate ways to change, the distance growing. Our rooms share a wall that I want to knock down every day. It's like a fist slamming into my chest each time I stare at that barrier between us. But I cherish the schedule we've built. Jogging is one of the many things we do together on weekend mornings, and I won't take it for granted by pouting like a petulant toddler.

My body is already burning so I toss on shorts and a thin tee. When I walk into the living room, Addison is stretching behind the couch. She might be covered neck to toe, but the tight-fit clothing does nothing to hide her seductive figure. The thermal leggings and sleek pull-over mold to her like a second skin. When she spreads her legs and bends over, I get a prime view of that delectable round ass. What I wouldn't give to palm those luscious globes and squeeze until she moans.

My dick twitches to life, and I grip the hardening shaft. Fuck. Running with a boner is horribly uncomfortable. I dash into my room to throw on another layer for moral support. Clearly my cock can't be trusted. Not that I'm doing much to control the innate reaction.

I snap my waistband and prepare for the embarrassment. I'll be limping along beside her with this third leg dragging me down. Maybe I should have jacked off first. Too late now.

Man, the fuck-up, I scold. I'm acting like the pansy Trey accuses of me being.

Addison knocks on my door. "Ready?"

I turn toward her. "Yup," I croak.

She studies me closer. "You sure about that?"

I'm nodding too fast. "Definitely. Let's go."

Pounding the pavement should alleviate this excess pressure mounting inside of me. Maybe I'll go out again after Addison leaves for work. I'll keep running until the only thing left on my mind is sleep.

I fill up our water bottles while Addison grabs the keys. We hop down the stairs and set off along Main Street. The weather has been relatively pleasant considering it's early November. The sun is shining bright in the cloudless sky, but the blast of frigid wind is keeping foot traffic light these days. We don't have to fight through any crowds while making our way to the designated paths. Leaves crunch beneath our sneakers as we cross onto the trail that loops the lake.

Our pace is steady and easy, but Addison is puffing. I've noticed the cold is harder on her. Soon I'll suggest exercising indoors until the temperature turns around. I glance over at my jogging partner and immediately get distracted. Even with a sports bra, her perky tits bounce, and I can't look away. Out of the corner of my eye, I catch sight of a branch. I duck at the last second and stumble.

She laughs, but it's more like a gasping pant. "Watch where you're going, Rooks."

I purposely slow down my speed. "Good advice," I mumble.

We go for another mile before Addison taps my arm. "Can we walk for a bit? My lungs are screaming."

"Shit, of course."

She leans forward, hands on her knees, to catch some much needed breath. "Thanks. Sorry for being a wimp. Before you came along, I only ran occasionally. I'm still acclimating to the rigor of your workouts."

Her back rises and falls rapidly, drawing my attention. I rub up and down her spine, trying to soothe her. After a few moments, she straightens, and the bright flush is fading from her skin. Addison shakes her bottle and finds it empty. I pass mine over, watching too intently as she sucks on the mouthpiece. Chugging water has never looked so erotic.

She grins at me. "What would I do without you?"

"Jog lightly on a treadmill?"

We both laugh.

There're a few drops of water on her bottom lip that are currently stealing my focus. I wait for her tongue to sweep away the moisture, but it doesn't happen. I brush my thumb along her plump flesh and collect them for myself. In a rare show of boldness, I suck the droplets off my skin. Addison inhales sharply, the air catching in her chest. If it wasn't for these compression briefs, the tent in my gym shorts would be obscene.

She lifts a slim brow. "You're not playing fair, Rooks."

I move closer until I'm hovering in her space. She smells like sweet sweat and spiced apples, exactly what I'm craving. I dip lower so my mouth is at her ear. "It was never my idea to play in the first place. This is your game, Adds. I'm waiting for the rules to change."

Addison trembles and grips the front of my shirt in a small fist. For a second, I believe this is it. Then she says, "Why now?" Her breath breezes against my neck, causing my entire body to tense in response. I want to read her expression, but won't sever this connection. She takes my silence as a nonresponse and huffs. "Figures you don't answer."

Her flat tone stabs into my gut, but I'm unsure what to say. Addison releases her hold on me and shoves several feet of distance between us. She turns to face the lake, and it's as if concrete fills my limbs. What the actual fuck just happened? I frown and walk toward her.

"Adds?" When she doesn't reply, I try again. "Talk to me. Don't shut me out."

When Addison spins around, her familiar smile is back in place. "Forget it. I'm not thinking straight. This overexertion cut off the oxygen supply to my brain." She makes a small circle near her temple.

I shake my head, not buying that shit for a second. "Be honest, Adds. What did I do to upset you?"

She presses her lips together and shrugs. "Nothing. I mean, everything is fine, and we're good. Super-duper friends, right?"

I clench my eyes shut and trap the defeated growl begging to escape. I want to kick myself for causing her to clam up like this.

Dammit, I fucked up. Again. Just like always, but I deserve this failure. I lower my gaze and concentrate on the scattered yellow and orange coloring of the landscape.

Addison pats my shoulder. "Don't worry, big guy. We're still buddies. I just got weird for a hot minute, but that moment has passed." She sighs. "You coming to Dagos later?

I grunt, still averting my eyes. "Is that even a question?"

She nudges me. "Well, there's a little bit of pumpkin shandy left. I've been saving it for you."

I cringe. "Gross, Adds. How can you drink that shit?"

"It's delicious, duh."

"Then I'll buy you a tall one."

She points at me. "With a sugar rim?"

"Obviously."

"You're so *good* to me," Addison coos.

I wave off her words, acid continuing to churn in my gut. "Yeah, yeah." She has no idea how *bad* I want to get.

She hums happily, and the noise is a relief. "That's all I ask. Should we go home?"

And just like that, we're back on solid ground.

CHAPTER 10

SHANE
Never

I grab the remote and click on Netflix. I scroll the options while lifting my feet onto the table, ready to relax and unwind. Tension from this morning has slowly been melting away. The beer in my hand is definitely helping, and I take another swig. My gaze automatically seeks out the clock and I smile. Only twenty more minutes until she's home.

After Addison scampered off to Dagos, I took care of the relentless throb in my cock. I treated myself to another sprint around the park followed by a cold shower. Mitch called and joined me at the bar for dinner. He gave me shit for not making a move on Addison yet. I asked him how his unrequited crush was going. That shut him up real quick. I ate the signature tater-tot hot dish, tried a new microbrew, bought all the remaining pumpkin ale in stock, and came home to wait for Addison to finish her shift.

So far, it's been a great Saturday. Tonight will be even better.

I rest my head against the cushions and stare at the ceiling. I'm on my third drink and feeling looser than usual. The lack of strain in my muscles is a pleasant change. My lids are getting heavy, and I stop fighting to keep them open. When a key slides into the lock, I snap to attention in an instant.

Addison pushes open the door, an award-winning smile shining on her face. "Hey, you." She glances at the paused television. "Am I interrupting something?"

I laugh off her implication. "Hardly. Just been hanging out."

Addison steps into the room and unzips her coat. She makes an obvious show of looking at my lap covered by a blanket. "I can't tell."

I toss the covers off and nod toward the frozen screen. "You think I'm watching porn?" That possibility is inconceivable. Addison provides more than enough material to feed my fantasies.

Her giggle echoes across the distance between us. "I'd hope not. We share that couch."

I pat the spot next to me. "Been keeping it warm for you."

She lifts a brow. "I'm not convinced."

"There's a six-pack of shandy in the fridge. All for you."

Addison licks her lips. "You know the way to a woman's heart. Hold that thought, though. I'm going to slip into something more comfortable."

Under different circumstances, her meaning would be seductive and a huge turn-on. However, we've been in this situation often enough for me to be well aware of what she's changing into. I'm not at all surprised to see the familiar tattered hoodie and threadbare sweatpants when she reemerges. Addison detours into the kitchen for a beer and takes a long sip. Then she prances over and plops down on the empty space next to me.

"So, what's the feature presentation this evening?" she asks while snuggling under the quilt.

I scratch my chin. "It's a toss-up between a *Fixer Upper* marathon or we can start the second season of *Stranger Things*."

Addison's head swings back and forth. She's wavering, it seems. "Or we could play a game," she suggests and takes another swig of her pumpkin delight.

"What'd you have in mind?"

Her tongue slowly rolls along the top row of her teeth. "Never Have I Ever?"

When her thigh brushes mine, I press closer. My heart kicks up automatically, preparing for an overhaul. "Not sure I know the rules."

Addison's green eyes gleam. "I'll go first." She swallows another mouthful of beer. "Never have I ever repaired a car."

I blink at her. "What part? The engine? Or a flat tire?"

She shakes her head. "Doesn't matter. I haven't done it. Don't think so hard. The point is to find stuff you haven't done that I have. Then I drink, and vice versa."

I nod, the meaning sinking in. Does she realize how much shit I haven't done? This game was meant for me. "All right. Never have I—"

"You've gotta drink," she interrupts.

I do gladly. Her positive energy is infectious, and I'm getting high off it. The alcohol doesn't hurt.

Addison points her beer at me. "Okay, you're up."

"Never have I ever worked in a bar," I say with a smirk.

She gives a glare but pairs it with a beautiful smile. "Touché." Addison's lips wrap around the bottle as she tips it up. Her throat bobs with graceful swallows, and I follow the movement. She catches me staring.

"Be careful, Rooks. Keep looking at me that way, and I'll get the wrong idea." Her tone is light and bubbly, but the meaning bangs out like a drum. She doesn't give me time to respond before throwing out, "Never have I ever gone to community college."

"Never have I ever attended kindergarten," I volley back and take a long swig.

Addison lifts a brow. "How is that possible?"

"Is that question part of the game?"

She crosses her arms. "We can pause a moment for story time."

My gaze skitters away, unease swooping in like an inky cloud. "Where I come from, public education wasn't an option. I was homeschooled."

Addison must read the change in my mood and lightly nudges my shoulder. "That's something I've never done."

I glance at her. "Should I drink?"

Her laugh chases the storm off in a split second. "Duh, we're still playing."

I get up to grab a fresh beer. "Need one?"

"Better bring a few. The night is young."

I reach for her empty after she finishes it off. Addison smiles, and her cheeks are rosy. Would her skin be warm if I brushed my fingers along it? Would she lean into my touch? I shake my head and hurry to the fridge, needing to cut off those desires before they gain power. I don't want to rock the boat. We've been sailing smoothly through this roommate agreement, and I intend to keep it that way. Unless Addison makes a move. Then I'm likely to lose my ever-loving mind.

I pass her another pumpkin shandy, and she hums happily. "Thanks for getting these. I was worried they'd be gone by the end of my shift." She sniffs the sugary brew and makes another satisfied sound. I laugh and drop down into my spot.

"It was obvious how much you wanted them. And Grayson was glad to get rid of them," I say with a shrug.

She rolls her eyes. "If it was up to him, we'd only serve Coors and Pabst. Myla takes my side on offering more choices for those with a dignified preference."

I chuckle. "Ah, is that what you call it?"

Addison pops her lips after taking a sip. "Absolutely. Now, whose turn is it?"

"Mine, I think." I search for something simple and glance around, settling on her feet. "Never have I ever owned a pair of colorful socks."

"Oooh, good one," she commends. Addison leans against the armrest and swings her legs onto the couch. She relaxes into the cushions and exhales heavily.

"Long day?" I ask.

Her toes wiggle against my thigh and I start massaging. Addison noticeably tenses. I almost stop, but in the next beat, she sprawls out and practically shoves her foot in my grip. I dig into her arch, and she moans.

"Oh, yes." The sound is indecent and is a straight hit to my dick. Addison doesn't seem to catch my reaction, her lashes fluttering in pleasure. "Keep going, Rooks. Ah, right there," she purrs.

I'm ready to crack from the pressure in my groin. I use a pillow to hide my erection and plop her feet on top. My fingers roll over her heel and spin her ankle slowly. I keep rubbing, she continues groaning, and something has to give.

I pull at her orange sock. "Halloween was last week, Adds. October called and wants their Jack-o'-lanterns back."

"Very funny. These bad boys are timeless. I can wear them year-round."

"Does that mean your naughty nurse costume will make another appearance soon?" I suck on my bottom lip while recalling her sexy outfit. The white patent leather dress stuck to her like glue, and I wanted to peel it off. She paired it with high heels and fishnet stockings and looked good enough to eat. My filthy imagination feasted on the sight. This stroll down memory lane isn't helping with the problem in my jeans. I cough into my fist and refocus on her soles.

She leans forward and pinches my forearm. "You like that getup."

"I sure do," I admit freely.

Addison catches my heated stare, her jade eyes latching onto mine. We're suspended together, and time floats on without reason. All logic evaporates as I inch closer. I want to kiss her, lick the red stain off those pouty lips. Her breath fans against my jaw. I wrap my fingers around her calf and tug lightly. Just a little further.

Her phone beeps, and she jerks back. Our moment is lost in a puff of smoke. Addison sits upright, her feet leaving the cradle of my hands. Frustration lashes through my chest, surpassing the ever-present lust.

"Hot date?" I ask and jut my chin toward her screen. I'm certain it's not another man, but hearing her confirmation feels necessary.

Addison rolls her eyes. "Hardly, it's just D. They're at Boomers."

"Do you want to join them?" I'm silently begging her to tell me no. We're having fun in the comfort of our living room.

"Not even a little bit. We're having fun in the comfort of our living room."

I want to wipe my brow in relief. "Okay, good."

"Cheers." She taps her bottle to mine, and we drink. "Okay, no more distractions. Let's keep playing."

I point at her. "Go ahead."

She chews on her nail, giving me a sideways glance. "Never have I ever had a threesome."

Beer almost comes shooting out of my nose. "Holy shit, I wasn't expecting that," I rasp.

"Well?" She lifts a brow and gestures to my brew.

"I haven't done that." I want to laugh at just how far off that possibility is.

Addison snaps her fingers. "Crud, that's a bummer." Then she gulps down several swallows of shandy.

"Why'd you drink?"

"Because it was a bad question. If neither of us has done it, that means I drink by default."

"All right, that makes sense." I peel at the bottle's label, my concentration beginning to scramble. I shove away the depraved visions desperate to break free. The right thing to do is steer us onto safer topics. "Uh, never have I ever broken a bone."

"So tame." She winks at me and takes a sip. "Never have I ever shot a gun."

I finish off my beer and open a new one. "I've never been outta state."

Addison gawks at me. "Where the heck did you grow up? A deserted island in the middle of Minnesota?"

"Something like that," I mumble and run a palm down my face. Is the room tilting slightly?

She downs the remaining booze in her bottle, reaching for another on the table. "I haven't owned a truck." Addison's eyes have a glassy gleam, and I chuckle.

"Feeling your pumpkin spice?"

She holds up her thumb and forefinger, a sliver of space between them. "Maybe."

Now that I'm thinking about it, my movements are getting sluggish. There's cotton in my brain that's starting to clog good sense. My inhibitions are slipping, the alcohol unlocking those hidden cravings. I slump into the couch and let my eyelids droop. Addison laughs, the twinkling sound curling around my dick. I smile, and it feels crooked. So much for being suave.

"Glad I'm not the only one affected," she says.

My head lazily lolls to the side. "I haven't owned anything pink."

She giggles again. "You're good."

"Thank you?"

"I've never had a penis," Addison blurts and bites her lip.

I grunt out a chuckle. "Ah, that's how you wanna be?"

Her arm bumps into mine. "Well, duh. I'm trying to win."

"And how do we determine the winner?" I sit up, my competitive side stirring from this groggy slumber.

Addison seems to ponder that. "Whoever gets the biggest shock value," she stage-whispers.

Pretty positive I've got this in the bag. I wasn't planning to rock the boat, but she's upping the stakes. I chug more beer for liquid courage, but at this point, I'm not sure I need it. It's confession time.

Here goes nothing.

I turn toward Addison, not shying away. "I've never had sex."

She sputters on her sip of shandy. "What?"

"I'm a virgin."

"H-how is that... nope, no way." She squints at me, one eye closing to get a steady look. "You've never slept with anyone?" The question is a garbled mess.

I shrug off her shock, used to this reaction whenever the topic comes up. "Nope."

Addison combs through her hair, tugging on the wavy ends.

"Welp," she says with a slow nod, "I declare you the winner. There's no way I'm beating that. But you've gotta tell me more."

Prickles dot my skin, and I scratch at the irritation. "I have a lot of experience with controlling my urges."

"Consider me impressed. Is this related to your mysterious hometown?" She rests her chin on a closed fist, apparently preparing to listen.

I can't avoid the topic of my past forever, I guess. Might as well spit it out, at least some of it. "It's kinda complicated to explain. I grew up in a very... restrictive community. We were raised to abstain and avoid temptation. I rarely left my family's farm so opportunities to even speak with girls were rare. Sharing a bed with a woman was inconceivable," I admit.

Addison blinks at me. "So, you're super religious?"

I glare at the colorful rug beneath my feet. "I'm not sure about all that anymore. I didn't conform as ordered. That's the easiest way to explain it."

When I glance over, she's rubbing her temples. "There's an enormous tale for you to tell, but not right now. I'm sleepy."

Any hope of us finally getting on the same page snuffs out in an instant. After all that, she's shutting me out. I groan long and loud into my hands, burying the shame along with my face. The buzz I have going heightens my disappointment, leaving me somewhat adrift.

"What's wrong, big guy?" She rubs my shoulder.

"Nothing," I mutter.

"Upset about spending another night alone?"

LASS

What the fuck? Is she making fun of me? I peek up at her when she stands. Addison's green eyes sparkle like gemstones, and she holds out an open palm.

"That can be fixed." She wiggles her fingers in invitation.

I grasp her waiting hand and rise from the couch. I stare at her, waiting for the meaning to sink it. When that doesn't happen, I stupidly mumble, "Huh?"

"We can be bed buddies," Addison suggests like it's the easiest solution.

It's my turn to choke and struggle with breathing. My tongue is sticky and can't pronounce words. How drunk am I? Is she actually suggesting we sleep together?

She points at me. "No funny business—snoozing only."

I'm suddenly alert with crystal-clear awareness. "Okay."

"Your bed is a big beast. I can sleep on the opposite side and maintain our boundaries."

I'm nodding along as she talks. I'll agree to anything at this point to have her lying next to me. "You're right. There's plenty of room for you."

"And don't think this conversation about your history is over, Rookster. We'll talk more tomorrow. M'kay?"

"Yeah, sure." Even the mention of my past can't dull this moment. I'll deal with it in the morning.

She hitches a thumb to the hallway. "Shall we?"

The rapid beat of my heart threatens to crack a rib, but a broken bone isn't a concern right now. I shuffle forward and settle my palm on the small of her back like it belongs there. I guide her to my room and sweep an arm through the open door. "After you, Adds."

Forget smooth sailing. I'm ready to capsize.

CHAPTER 11

ADDISON
Truth

Why am I so warm? I try to kick off the blankets, but my legs are tangled—between another pair of legs. I continue taking inventory of my situation and smile. My face is resting against bare skin, a very naked chest to be specific. Someone ditched their shirt during the night. I keep my eyes shut and nuzzle against my cuddle partner. Might as well take advantage before he wakes up.

Shane makes a great pillow.

Well, so much for staying on my side of the bed. Not that this position was a conscious decision. I was minding my own dreamy business and harmlessly rolled over, latching myself onto a source of body heat. I snuggle closer, so toasty and comfortable. Is there anything better? I think not.

I blame the deprived lady-bits, but let's be honest, this was my idea. And I'm not budging until he kicks me out.

Shane moves slightly and his super-impressive morning wood prods into my hip.

Down, boy.

My thighs clench and I might bump him on purpose. He shifts and the solid-steel in his shorts stabs me again. I pop my eyes open and try not to gasp. Shit, he's huge. That bad boy is likely to break me in half. My hand has plans of its own and begins to trail down his side. I gain some much needed clarity just before my fingers reach his pelvis.

That's a no-go, Addy. Shut it down, I scold my horny alter ego.

Shane stirs and stretches against me. I trap a moan from escaping, but damn, he feels good against me. The ridges of his sculpted abs dance along my belly when he arcs further.

Suddenly he stills, freezing in my grasp. I speak up before things can get too awkward.

"Hey, bed buddy," I rasp hoarsely. Jeez, could my voice sound any more like a phone-sex operator?

One of Shane's palms is stuck to my ass, and I swear he gives me a pinch. "Morning, Adds." His gritty timbre scrapes along every inch of me, and I shiver.

I dip my chin, which causes me to take a direct hit of his woodsy scent. Why must he smell so good all the time? Can't a girl catch a break? I clear my dry throat and attempt to power through this clusterfuck. I start by slowly peeling myself off him, trying not to whine at the loss.

"How'd you sleep?" I ask and prop up on an elbow.

"Extremely well, and that never happens." Shane is quiet for a beat, swallowing hard. "To be honest, I've never felt so well rested." His dark hair is disheveled in that effortless way guys pull off. There's a rosy hue on his cheeks, and the sight is endearing, making this mountain of a man appear soft in some small way.

"Beer helps with that. I hit the pillow and conked out," I tell him.

Shane gives me a lazy smirk, his eyes hooded. "Nah, that's not why." His arm is still around my waist, and he flexes. "It was the company."

Flutters go wild in my lower stomach. "Someone's being forward."

"Gotta take a chance. Not sure when you'll be lying beside me again."

I recall his admission from yesterday, still trying to comprehend how he's a virgin. I mean, has he looked in the mirror? Is it weird that I'm extremely turned on by his apparent lack of awareness? Because I totally am.

"We gonna make this a habit?" I toss out with a laugh, not wanting to appear too serious.

He raises a brow. "Are you just using me for my bed?"

I shrug. "I won't deny the perks of this agreement. Ever since you moved in, I've been waiting to test this baby out. It's like a memory foam hug while floating on puffy clouds. Absolutely worth the wait." I give a little bounce on the springs.

Shane groans. "You're killing me, Adds."

I stop moving, realization dawning. "Sorry. I didn't mean—"

"It's okay." He chuckles and motions to his covered bottom half. "This is my fault."

"Pretty sure that's a natural reaction, right? You can't control it."

He laughs again. "Oh, there is a very logical explanation."

"No action between the sheets?"

Shane rubs his torso. "That definitely doesn't help matters."

"I can't believe you've never done the dirty deed."

"Why? I'm giving off the impression of a lady's man?"

I yawn, my tongue scratching like sandpaper. I slap a palm over my mouth. "Can we press pause for a second?" I ask through slightly parted fingers. Shane gives me a funny look so I rush to explain. "I don't want to poison you with my dragon breath. Let's take care of bathroom business quick and resume this chat, 'kay?"

He agrees with a slow nod, and we dart off in separate directions. It's odd how rejuvenating peeing and brushing my teeth feels. I suppose the events of this morning have me a tad sideways. But whatever the reason, there's an added pep to my step as I stroll down the hallway.

Shane is sprawling out on his massive mattress when I walk into the room. He pats the space I vacated moments ago, those drool-worthy dimples winking at me. There's no second-guessing before I'm sliding in next to him.

"Better?" he asks, and I catch a whiff of minty freshness.

"Much. Now, where were we?"

"You were shocked by my lack of experience."

"For real. How?"

He peeks over at me. "You want all the reasons/details now?"

A few secrets slipped off his tongue last night. Maybe he's ready to tell me more? "I won't push, Rooks. Tell me to quit being nosey if you don't wanna share."

Shane stays silent, and I think he's taking the out I give him. Then he exhales roughly and curses a blue-streak. When he's done swearing, his brown gaze finds mine. "It's fine. I need to get this shit off my shoulders. I just… dammit"—those pools of warm honey plead with me—"I don't want you to see me differently."

"Whatever you have to tell me won't change my feelings or opinion of you. I'm here regardless of what's stashed away in dark corners. You're my… friend. I know who you are, Shane." I brush the hair off his forehead, and he sighs.

Shane readjusts and fidgets, tucking an arm behind his head, until he seems set. "I'm not ashamed of how I was raised or where I grew up. But it's difficult for me to talk about. Maybe because it feels like a betrayal since I left without their blessing. I couldn't stay in that suffocating environment a moment longer. The walls were closing in, becoming smaller and more confining with each passing day. I love my family. That isn't the issue. But disagreeing with their strict convictions created a huge rift." A muscle jumps in his jaw, and he exhales harshly.

"Like, spiritually?" I ask with wide eyes. My experience with this sort of thing is zilch, but listening to him is captivating.

He offers a slow nod. "Yeah, sure. Not even sure what denomination you'd call it. Pastor Raines preaches a little of everything, but in the end, going against his word is the worst crime. I was faithful to the church and my family. Above all, I worshiped and obeyed the good Lord above. I've spent my life trying to conform and be the man everyone expected. But in many ways, I fail and fall short. I want so much... more than what was planned for me. Even though I was born into that world, it never seemed like my place. I didn't belong, and it only got worse. I wanted to explore outside of my family's compound and find adventure. The first time I mentioned these dreams to my parents was the last. They didn't take it well. My mother was devastated, called me wicked and depraved. I'm a sinner and likely damned, but that's the price I'll pay."

I lace our fingers together and give him an encouraging squeeze. "I think you're noble."

Shane smirks at me, the expression strained.

"You haven't heard it all yet." He glances at our locked hands and some of the tension melts away. "When I turned twenty-three, they tried to force me into a situation. Would you believe me if I said it was an arranged marriage?" Shane grunts, his molars grinding. "But that's what my parents wanted, to follow Pastor Raines and his commands. It sounds crazy, even more so after I moved here. I refused, not believing that was my path to take. It didn't feel right deep inside. When the date got closer, the pit in my stomach grew until it was this uncontrollable need to escape. I want a wife who loves me, not assigned out of duty or because the elders order it. I hardly knew the girl chosen for me. I was supposed to take her hand, yet we'd never had a conversation. I'm sure this type of situation can be successful, just not for me. That was the last straw, I guess. I was shunned and forced to leave, which wasn't entirely bad. It sucks I can never go back and visit, but those are the stakes."

I blink away the quickly forming tears. My heart hurts for this man, the pain a piercing ache I've never felt before. I brush my thumb over the calluses on his palm. Shane is so genuinely good. Does he realize that? I wipe under my lashes and give a wobbly grin. "I'm not sure what comfort to offer in this moment that could make up for what you've suffered and lost. You're so strong, Shane." His fingers flex against mine, and I drag our joined hands against my chest. "I'm in awe of you," I tell him honestly.

He stares at me, those soulful brown eyes shining. "You shouldn't be."

"But I am--"

Shane doesn't let me finish. "I left my younger sister behind. It makes me sick to think about what will happen when she turns eighteen."

"Oh, my," I murmur. My mind spins with possibilities, none of them pleasant.

I feel him nod, the openness in his features shuttering, a gate slamming shut. "Fucked up, right? Far too much dread for this early in the morning. I should make you coffee." Shane starts to pull away.

"Hey." I tug on him. "Don't go."

"How could you want to me stay after that?" His wild gaze searches mine, begging me for something. Maybe forgiveness or a reason to believe again. I think about the nights I've heard him through the wall. Nightmares keep him awake, leaving him tossing and turning. The noises speaking of pain and sorrow. His distress finally makes sense.

I suck on the inside of my cheek. "I'm sure you did everything possible for her."

Shane groans and flops down on the bed, arms spread wide. "I tried to bring her with me, but she wouldn't abandon our family. She wants to be there."

"Then you send her all the best."

"Why are you being so supportive?"

"I believe in you."

He beckons me closer, into the nook I fit so snugly in, and I return to his waiting embrace.

I won't deny what's clearly meant to happen. I'm done fighting us.

"You're so brave, Rooks. Most would cave under the pressure and probably do. It takes serious guts to leave everything and everyone you know," I say against his collarbone.

"They didn't leave me much choice," he grumbles

"Doesn't matter. Maybe they lit a match, but you could have extinguished it before real damage was done. Instead, you walked away and let their twisted plans burn. Your dignity remains intact." My lips dust over the hollow of his throat, and he trembles slightly.

"You're making me sound like some hero."

"Because you are. Give yourself some credit."

"I don't deserve it."

I poke him in the ribs. "Knock it off. Don't be so hard on yourself. If you hadn't left, we never would have met. How's that?"

His body tenses beneath mine. "Don't even think about shit like that."

"See?" I gulp down a bundle of nerves and wade into uncharted territory. "Do you like me? As more than a friend and roommate?"

He snorts. "What was your first clue?"

"Well, that python in your pants is giving me a massive hint."

His upper body shakes with a hearty laugh and jostles me. "Why are you so adorable?"

"I think the term you're looking for is obnoxious."

"I said what I meant." He strokes a finger down my blazing cheek. Static sparks in my chest, and I'm finding it hard to breathe.

"Should we go to breakfast?" I blurt.

His smile collapses with my abrupt jump in subject. "Uh, sure."

"Don't go sounding too excited about it," I mutter.

"You have a knack for shutting me down whenever we're getting to good parts."

"Is that so? What'd you have in mind?"

Shane glances at my mouth and licks his bottom lip. "A taste of something new. Maybe a slice of forbidden." He lowers himself slowly until his handsome face hovers an inch from mine.

I shudder and need that sliver of distance erased. He's destroying my defenses, but I don't need them anymore. Surrender is inevitable. I'm more than ready to give in. My stomach growls, but food can definitely wait.

"Kiss me," I murmur.

CHAPTER 12

SHANE
More

I don't hesitate, diving toward her like a starving man. Fuck breakfast. I'll feast on her until we're both satisfied. I comb through Addison's hair and grab a fistful. My hold is gentle but it anchors her to me.

Thunder rumbles from my chest and echoes around the room.

"You're so beautiful," I murmur against her freckled cheek. I drag my nose along the blushing skin before pulling back a little. Addison must see the determination in my eyes. She sucks in sharply and her nails dig into my shoulders.

I drop my mouth over hers and press softly, testing the waters. She pushes into me, giving permission and seeking more. I loop my arm around her waist and yank her closer, eliminating the last space separating us. My large paw almost spans the entirety of her narrow midriff. I'm a giant in comparison to her slight form. Protective instincts rise up, and I tuck her even tighter against me.

Addison licks my bottom lip and a moan tumbles out. I open for her, matching each teasing sweep with one of my own. She tastes like peppermint candy, and I have a serious sweet tooth. Our tongues slide together, lost lovers reuniting, and the silken heat sets me on fire. I use my hold on her to steer our position, changing the angle to get deeper. I'm plundering and drowning and never want to come up for air. Suffocating in Addison is one hell of a way to go.

Her palms roam up until she's scratching my scalp. The pleasurable sensation gets me harder, and I grind into her thigh. One leg hitches around my hip, granting me better access to her center. I take a chance and slide my pinkie under the waistband, drawing tiny circles on her skin. Addison wiggles, and my dick is the happy recipient. She's wearing too many clothes. I want her pants off, but maybe that's too much? I'm not sure how far she wants us to go.

When Addison sucks on my lip, I'm momentarily distracted from stripping her naked. I delve into her mouth, ravenous for more. I've been envisioning kissing her since we first met. My one-sided fantasies seem foolish and flat as raw footage reels in. Nothing could prepare me for her petal-soft lips and tantalizing moans. Each sound cinches around my cock and squeezes, dragging me closer to the edge. I rock into her, driving myself to the brink faster. Molten lava floods my gut and I'm melting for her.

This is only a kiss, but far more than a simple form of affection.

The floodgates are opening wider, an exchange of breath, tempting touches shooting me higher. I tug and she pulls, my fingers digging into her supple curves. My hand roams further, brushing over her ass and settling in the dip of her tailbone. She feels so good, velvet engulfed in salvation. I haul her pelvis into mine, grinding her against my aching dick. She gasps into my mouth, and I swallow her mewls.

"You feel me, Adds?" I ask with a punctuating thrust. Her tiny body is molding to mine, cementing our bond—barriers be damned.

"Yes," she moans. "Y-you're so big."

Her breathy pant is enough to make me bust. I don't need to hear more, capturing her pleasure between my lips. Her body tells me all I need, pliable and bending to me. She's what I imagine Heaven to be. Why did we wait so long? I drift under her shirt, over the expanse of bare skin.

Shit, she's not wearing a bra.

I'm so fucking hard, painfully so. How easy would it be to flip over and demand she strokes me? To take away the ache only she causes? I'm growing hazy with need, bordering on insanity just for her fist around me. My body screams for her, and she seems willing, yet I hold back.

Fucking pussy. Trey's familiar taunt circles round, driving me crazy in a different way. But I shove that bullshit away and stay lost in Addison's kiss.

She claws down my back while swiveling those sinful hips. She rolls against me, a liquid wave I attempt to catch. Our mouths fuse as an endless loop, slick lips parting for lapping tongues. I inhale

Addison's apple spice scent and trap each succulent morsel in my lungs. This craving for her body is a never-ending need. I want it all, anything and everything she has to give, like a selfish bastard. It's obvious I want more, but even this lust fogging my brain can't turn me into a barbarian.

Then her hand slips into my briefs and all bets are off. Addison's tentative fingers dance over my ass, and I buck against her. My eyes cross, and I'm dizzy as fuck. The lack of blood flow to my brain gives opportunity to my filthier desires hovering on the sidelines. My cock is leading this show and taking full advantage. All too soon there's a telltale tingling at the base of my spine.

Dammit, I don't want to blow in my shorts. How fucking embarrassing that would be. But pulling away and stopping this seems impossible. Screw my pride. The mess is worth it. I screw my eyes shut and rock into her, ready to tip off the ledge of sanity.

Addison makes the choice for us. She rips away from me with a pitiful groan and snap of elastic. I barely register the sting against my lower back, too focused on the flush racing up her pale neck. Our chests rise and fall in a frantic rhythm, syncing with paired precision. Panting breaths bounce between the small gap separating our mouths. I want to go back for seconds, and thirds, but she's slamming on the brakes.

She presses two fingers to her swollen pout, blatant evidence of my kiss. The heavy-lidded daze clouding her eyes makes me feel like a king.

"Whoa," she murmurs.

"So good, Adds." My lips ghost over the hollow of her throat, and she arches closer. I'm ready to plunge in all over again, until she scoots back and creates a definitive gap.

"Enough of that." She points an accusing finger at me. "Keep touching me like that and I'll end up jumping your bones."

"How is that bad?"

Addison fiddles with her sleeve, avoiding my stare. "I, uh, don't wanna rush into anything. Your first time should be with that special someone."

I pinch the bridge of my nose. Is she crazy? Doesn't she realize how much I want her? The blanket is covering my erection, or she'd see how badly I want to continue. My dick strains against the thin cotton of my briefs, and I grimace. This set of blue balls is going to be a bitch.

But this is about more than sex. The furious pounding of my pulse speaks of our deeper connection, and she must feel that. If not, I'll keep proving myself until she finds me worthy. Lord knows I have plenty of shortcomings.

I rake through my messy hair and exhale heavily. I'm still teetering on edge and swallow a ball of fiery lust. When I glance over at Addison, she's ogling my bare torso with her tongue peeking out. That's definitely not helping. "We should've done this sooner. Why'd we wait so long?" I ask the question still circling my mind. I run a finger from her temple to jaw, tracing an especially straight line of freckles.

Addison leans into my waiting palm. "Why don't you tell me?"

Her question is one I've been expecting. I've been secretly pining over this woman for years, yet never made a real move. I ruined the few chances she gave me by second-guessing everything. "Other than my lack of experience?"

She huffs. "I could care less about that. Why'd you ghost me for so long? I thought we had a connection."

I scratch over my rough stubble. "Fuck, Adds. It was never my intention to make you feel otherwise. That's just one more example of how I fail. I'm a shameful embarrassment."

Addison props up straighter. "Definitely not, Rooks. Don't talk about yourself like that. We all make mistakes. Just wish I'd known why."

"Considering my background, I was clueless. How could I ever gain your interest? I collected countless pick-up lines that would make Ricco Suave jealous. But when it came to actually using them, I'd turn into a stammering idiot."

She raises a brow. "Lay it on me, Rooks."

My dick twitches at that name, just when shit was starting to relax. But I get a little hard whenever she calls me that. Lying in bed with her? Dynamite detonation. I clear my throat and attempt to rein the arousal in.

"How you doin'?" I drawl in my best attempt at a New York accent.

She giggles. "More."

I tug on her sweats. "Are these pants made of Windex? Because I can see myself in them."

Addison wrinkles her button nose. "So bad. I want another."

I dig into the recesses of my mind, searching for the perfect one. "Are you a server?" She nods eagerly. I lower my head and whisper in her ear, "Can I come in your section?"

She shivers and grips my bicep. "That's a good one."

"Would it have worked?"

"Absolutely," she purrs.

I follow my gut and kiss her, just a soft peck. Addison sighs against my mouth, and her hold on me tightens. I pull back after a few beats, not wanting to push my luck.

"That makes me a bigger fool than I thought," I murmur and nip at her bottom lip. "I figured the odds of you liking me were very low. You're so far out of my league, Adds. Guys fall over themselves for your attention, me included."

She's quiet for a minute. "Remember Holi-Daze last year?"

I think back to the rowdy crowd and waiting for Addison to notice me. More than that, I recall the assholes giving her a hard time. "What about it?" I grumble.

Her smile holds a secret. "Something clicked for me that night. After you got rid of those douchebags harassing me, I took a long look at my savior. How'd I miss you before? I had this epiphany, or something super weird. Then we went to the racetrack and out dancing. I figured you felt the same way. But you didn't call me." Her voice is unsure, and it drives a sharp blade into my chest.

After Addison gave me her number, I couldn't dig up the courage to text. Each time I was about to push send, something would stop me. I'm done being the incompetent ass. But fuck, old habits die hard. My Oaklain roots are thick and gnarly. Try as I might, they're almost impossible to destroy completely. Bile bubbles up my esophagus returning to that place.

She strokes down my arm. "You okay? We can talk about this later. There's already been a lot of… unexpected events."

I grunt, lacing her fingers through mine. "I was treated like a sinner for wanting certain things. I often dreamed of a life outside the compound. I craved unspeakable acts, was cursed with an insatiable sexual appetite. If I ever told my mother what fantasies plagued me, she would have locked me in the basement."

Her eyes blow wide open. "Really?"

I chuckle at her expression, but my stomach clenches at the truth. "Eh, maybe? I didn't stick around long enough to find out."

"Thank goodness for that," she mumbles.

I squeeze her hand. "Garden Grove is a whole new world. I had no idea what to expect, but this place is straight out of a fairytale for a guy like me. And meeting you? The prettiest lass in all the land? It all makes sense because of you."

Addison's cheeks turn a beautiful shade of red, and my palm tingles to touch the blush. "You make me feel like a supermodel or something."

I scoff. "They all pale in comparison."

Her toes dance up my shin. "You do have all the right lines."

I press gentle kisses to each of her red fingernails. "I love how you tempt me. It's extremely gratifying to find the source of my madness. I was taught to turn away from perversion, block out all vices that weren't holy and pure. You're my deepest, most sinful desire. The feelings you evoke within me are far from redeemable. My craving for you is unforgivable, but I don't give a damn anymore."

"That's kinda... romantic, in a slightly twisted way." Her tone is too hesitant for me.

"You're my sweet corruption, Adds. There's no doubting my feelings for you."

"You're making me sound a little devious. I don't wanna be a bad influence." She scoots away, encouraging a game of cat and mouse. I'll definitely chase.

I shake my head, immediately following her. I cinch an arm around Addison's waist and pull her into me. My throat is dry when I gulp in her apple spice. "You're delivering only good. Not sure you're capable of the alternative. At least not for me," I murmur into the crook of her neck. "Fuck, am I screwing this up?"

Addison won't look at me, but I can tell she's blushing something fierce. "Does this make me your harlot?"

"Do you want to be?"

She bites her lip. "Maybe."

I wrap her tighter in my embrace, providing no means of escape. I kiss the soft spot behind her ear and she trembles. "Don't you see? I was nothing before you. I literally had no purpose until I stumbled into Dagos. You're the greatest thing to ever happen. You give meaning to my life."

She lifts her chin, that green gaze blazing hot into mine. "Do you really mean that?"

I nod against her. "I used to imagine my other half, the possibility of what was waiting for me in this existence. But I didn't dare believe reality and fantasy could be the same. I was always looking for something, or maybe someone. I couldn't be satisfied. Now? I'm well aware of who I want. I picture her in every scene, fantasize explicit things. I want one girl. There's only one who can break those chains from my past."

Addison's signature grin is firmly set, and I exhale slowly at the brilliant sight.

"Jeez, Rooks. You're turning into quite the charmer. How will I ever resist you?"

I place a gentle kiss to the corner of her mouth. "Easy—you don't."

CHAPTER 13

ADDISON
Ladies

I take another sip of coffee while scrolling the latest article on my favorite fashion blog. Burgundy and blush hues are making a comeback this season. Shopping will be in my very near future. I glance up from my phone and the hazelnut flavor suddenly tastes like ash. My appetite is in the mood for something far... meatier.

Shane emerges from the hall in all his shirtless glory, freshly showered and mouthwatering. Sometimes I think he's pretending to be allergic to cotton. Or he's walking around half-naked for my benefit. Either way, his lack of clothing is much appreciated. Those warm honey eyes are focusing intently on me, and I try not to squirm. His cropped hair is wet and glistens in the light. I grip the cup tighter, my fingers jumpy with want to comb through the longer lengths on top. I'll attempt to tame the unruly strands, but really just use it as an excuse for getting close to him.

My thighs clench when Shane scratches the dark stubble covering his jaw. That reflexive habit of his always gets to me, even more so lately. I have whisker-burn chafing the lower half of my face, evidence of the scruff-effect. Do I complain? Nope, just the opposite. I relish each rough scrape of those coarse bristles against me.

He's too darn sexy, but I no longer hide my appreciation of his body. As Shane prowls closer to the couch, I admire his predominate Adonis belt and flexing abs. Those low-slung sweats give me an excellent view. I hide the gawking behind my ceramic mug, but I'm certain he can see my reaction a mile away.

Shane plops down onto the sofa, throwing a bulky arm over my shoulder. I fold into his side and inhale crisp pine soap. Damn, he's delicious. He tightens his hold and murmurs in my ear, "You left a pair of underpants on the bathroom floor. How am I supposed to control myself with those sexy scraps littered around?"

I almost spit out my drink. "What did you call them?"

"Underpants?" His tone is hesitant but serious, and he clearly doesn't understand why I'm laughing.

I set my coffee on the table and twist toward him. "Are they tighty-whities or big enough to be a parachute?"

Shane's expression pinches. "I'm confused. What's so funny?"

"No one calls them that."

"What would you say instead?" This man, he's so adorable.

"Panties or thong."

His cheeks bloom bright-red. "Ah, I see."

"Hotter, right? No one wants to sleep with a woman wearing underpants. Well, unless they've been married for twenty-five years and couldn't care less," I explain.

Shane licks his lips. "I hope you're still wearing whatever those lace strings are on the floor in twenty-five years."

I wiggle my brows. "Such a charmer. Maybe you'll be around to find out."

His palm clasps the back of my neck and tugs. Our mouths swiftly meet, and I open for him. I suck on his upper lip while he nibbles on my bottom one. We adjust and tilt in opposite directions, getting a better angle. My tongue darts out and drags along his. I'm about to hop in his lap, but he holds me off. Shane groans and pulls away, resting his forehead against mine.

"I'll always be around, Adds," he murmurs softly.

"Uh-huh, good," I reply and attempt to make another move.

His hand locks on my waist and traps me in place. "I gotta go to work. If I show up with a semi, the guys will never forget it."

I giggle and dip down, licking across his pec. Shane shudders so I add another quick swipe. "Maybe you should call in sick."

"W-what'd you have in mind?" he stammers as I get dangerously close to his nipple. Serves him right for not putting a shirt on.

My mouth smacking off his skin echoes around the room. I prop my chin on his sternum. "I could put on some skimpier underpants."

Shane glares at me. "Such a tease."

I wink. "Pretty sure you admitted to liking my temptation."

"And you don't even have to try. You're sexy wearing a winter coat. Doesn't matter what we call those under-things. You constantly turn me on."

He's been dishing out variations of this line all week.

My red lipstick drives him wild.

The tight sweaters make him hard in a snap.

Whenever I touch him, he pictures me naked.

I'm definitely noticing an increase in the sexual undertones department. With each passing day, he grows bolder and pushes further. Not that it's a huge shock considering we've demolished the boundaries between us.

Well, kind of.

I'm not one hundred percent sure where we stand. I try to avoid making assumptions, but Shane pretty much laid it out for me last week. I'm fairly certain he has the serious hots for me. I'm *the one* he's referring to. After sharing our first kiss on Sunday, we've been locking lips like addicts. Can't leave out the dry-humping. He never got to experience making out just for the point of kissing, so I'm catching him up to speed. I haven't slept in my bed in six days, ever since he invited me in to share his. I'll never turn that opportunity away.

Even though we're getting closer each day, I'm still holding off. I don't want to ruin anything. To Shane, we're covering new territory on the daily. Once again, a conflict is forming and knotting my stomach. I want to have sex with him more than my next breath. But the pressure of being his first? This great, special love he's chasing? It's intimidating as hell. Maybe I'm being stupid. I'm sure Raven and

Delilah will say as much when they show up in a bit. If I even decide to tell them. I'm kind of enjoying living in this secret bubble with him.

Shane shifts beneath me, and I shake myself out of this weird musing. I smile at him, and he returns the expression.

"You good?" he asks and strokes down my cheek.

I nod into his touch. "Yup, just need more coffee. The girls are coming over soon."

He balks, turning into a stone pillar. "I better get dressed."

I muffle a snort. "Now you wanna get decent?"

Shane pinches my butt, and I yelp. "I'm modest, Adds. This"—he gestures across his bare chest—"is just for you."

Cue the swoon and dopey grin. I feel my lids get hooded, too. I shiver against the flutters attacking my gut. Good grief, he knows just what to say to cause a full-body onslaught. My fingers skip down his torso and tantalizing happy trail. He sucks in sharply, and I'm playing with a combustible spark. If I keep going, who knows what precarious position my friends will find us in.

I yank my hand away and leap off the couch. "I, uh, better get ready. You know, they'll be here soon."

A protruding bulge tents his pants, and I avert my gaze. At least, that's the story I'll retell. In reality, I shamelessly watch Shane adjust the monster between his legs. He catches me leering, and I shrug helplessly.

He groans. "See what you do?"

I snap my jaw shut. "Um, yeah? I mean, that's not all my fault. We were just... eh, talking? Yeah, nothing was going on. You need to control all that," I say and wave at his lap.

Shane chuckles and stands, moving toward his room. "So long as you're near, that's not happening. I'll do my best, though." He winks at me over his shoulder, and my knees get a little weak.

For the thousandth time—how is he a virgin?

As if purposely interrupting my dirty downward spiral, there's a knock on the door. I walk over to open it and let my friends inside. A chilly blast of late fall welcomes me and I shiver.

"Hey, ladies," I greet and motion them past me.

They shuffle forward as a huddled clump. "Why is it so cold already?" Delilah complains and unwraps the thick scarf around her neck.

Raven covers her wind-blown cheeks and shudders. "I feel like summer and winter decided to bypass autumn this year. We hardly got any perfectly cool days."

I nod and stash their coats in the closet. "Right? This weather has been brutal, and it's only mid-November. Imagine how December will be.

Delilah smiles. "One perk is people rush into Jitters for a hot beverage to keep their shopping spree going. We've been pretty busy."

Raven's nose is in the air, sniffing around. "Have you been baking, Addy? I'm kinda offended."

"Uh, no." I hide my face to cover the flush. "That's coming from the candles over there," I say and blindly gesture toward the mantle.

They're both studying me with a suspicious glint in their eyes. "It smells stronger than usual," Raven points out.

"Did you put a few more in the mix?" Delilah asks.

I purposely avoid their questioning expressions. "Shane really likes the apple pie ones. I've been buying more of them."

"Does he now?" Raven's suggestive expression is fit for bad reality television. She belongs on a billboard or something.

Delilah's eyes sparkle. "Where is that naughty stud?"

I shush them. "Jeez, turn your voices down. He's changing for work, right in there." I hitch a thumb in the direction of his room.

"He's not joining us for an impromptu gabfest?" Delilah asks.

I cross my arms. "Oh, is that what you two are really doing here? Want to inspect the living situation?"

Raven giggles. "You mean, the love nest? Um, duh."

Delilah elbows her. "Just for a little bit. Then we're hitting Main Street. We have Maisey on the clock today while we get our girl-time on."

"I master-baked all morning to make sure she's stocked up. She won't run out of anything unless Marlene and Betty throw a surprise gathering at the senior center," Raven says.

"For how much those old ladies complain, they're great customers," Delilah admits.

I usher them toward the couch, and we all settle in. "This town would be far more boring without their gossip and skewed updates."

Delilah *tsks*. "Sad, but true." Her attention darts straight ahead. "Is this a new table, Addy?"

I beam while recalling the adventure involved. "Yep, Shane and I found it on Marketplace. We drove to North Breck last weekend."

Raven pets the gleaming wood. "Very pretty. Vintage?"

I nod. "And handmade."

"You're so good at finding deals. If I ever convince Zeke to start his own contracting business, you should be in charge of any decorating jobs. I'll continue pushing both of you until it happens," Delilah warns playfully.

Giddy tingles prance across my skin. "That's something to consider. It'd be fun."

Raven makes an arc through the air like a banner. "Making the dreams happen." She mock-gasps, fingers fluttering over her gaping mouth. "Speaking of magic, I heard a certain server was awful cozy with someone sitting in her section."

I laugh. "Seriously? That's nonsense. I'm very professional at Dagos."

Delilah snorts. "Puh-lease. You play favorites hardcore, not that I'm complaining. I'm happy to see more sway in those hips."

I shove her lightly. "Lies, both of you."

We all break into a fit of giggles, but when Shane enters the room our cackling cuts off in a hot second and the following silence vibrates with unpredictability.

"Hey." He drags the word out and lifts a brow at me. Shit, it's so obvious we've been talking about him.

"Hi, Shane," my friends sing-song simultaneously, and I smack my forehead.

He chuckles and smiles wide, showing off those irresistible dimples. "How's everyone doing?"

"Great," Raven chirps. "We're just chatting, totally innocent."

Delilah nods quickly. "Yup, yup. We'll keep your girl occupied while you bring home the bacon."

I make a strangled noise and whisper through clenched teeth, "Shut. It. Down." Three sets of eyes latch onto me, and I wince. "Uh, tell Jack we say hello."

Raven tacks on, "And Trey."

He tilts his head and squints at us. "Um, all right. Will do."

I want to bury myself beneath the blanket to avoid this entire exchange. Instead, I slap on a too-big grin and say, "Hopefully it's not too crazy at the garage."

Shane rubs his temple. "Thanks. I'm sure it'll be a fairly steady Friday."

Delilah slaps a palm over her mouth to stop the laughter from bubbling out. "Maybe we'll catch you later."

He nods and slowly strides to the foyer. Shane sends me a lingering glance, and my feet get itchy to race over there. I shrug and give him a finger-wave. With my thumb and pinkie, I signal that I'll call him later. He looks like he wants to say more but leaves after another tense beat.

Delilah fans her face. "Wow, that was intense."

Raven joins in, squeaking loudly. "Forget the frost, there's a heatwave coming."

Delilah nudges me. "You're a brat. Thanks for telling us you're having sex."

My gaze bounces between them. "Because I'm not?"

Raven coughs and sputters, "Bull crap. I could see the static-cling between you two. If we weren't here, your clothes would be in a heap on the floor."

"Wait, for real?" Delilah's features tighten. "How's that possible?"

I pick at my chipping nail polish and think of a diversion. "We might have to add manicures to the daily agenda."

"You're not getting out of this," Raven mutters.

I don't want to share anything too personal, especially where Shane's involved. "I'm, uh, not ready."

Delilah smacks her lips. "Girl, you're jonesing like a junkie needing a hit. How long has it been?"

Is it too early for wine? This conversation calls for it. I twirl a stray lock of hair and attempt to calculate my extremely long dry spell. "Is that really important?"

"First, you've been single for who knows how long. High school? Second, you're sharing an apartment with a guy who clearly wants to change your status. Third, why the heck not?" Delilah makes an imaginary check mark after each item.

"He's insanely hot," Raven says.

I point at her. "I'm telling Trey."

Her blue eyes twinkle. "Do it. I'll probably get a spanking."

I cringe. "Ugh, never mind. I don't wanna think about that."

She rubs my shoulder. "I'd be more than willing to share all the filthy details if it gets your motor revving."

I jerk away from her with a laugh. "Oh my gosh, stop. Please don't. Those sordid tales will scar me for life." I plug my ears for added effect.

Delilah tugs on my arm. "Ride that pony, Addy. What's the holdup?"

"Biatches", I snap and hold up a palm. "It's in progress, 'kay? Can we move on?"

Raven purses her lips, and Delilah watches me closely. I stay quiet and wait them out. After what feels like an hour, they both crack up. I shake my head and feel the prickle of irritation fade.

"Okay, let's go," Raven says, and we all stand.

"Where should we start?" Delilah asks.

I follow behind them, remembering the article from earlier. "Donna's Digs has new stuff. I saw some great burgundy leggings in the display window."

"Oh, and Poppy Petals has these adorable ornaments I wanna check out," Raven says.

"We can have lunch at Maggie's," Delilah suggests.

I realize too late that they're suddenly very quiet. They catch me zoning out, my spacey daze focusing on the path to Shane's bedroom. I drag my eyes to them and search for an excuse. Delilah beats me to it.

"Who needs an oil change? We should swing by Jacked Up," she says.

My responding smile is obnoxious, and there's no point trying to hide it.

"I totally called it," Raven stage-whispers to Delilah.

The two blondes exchange a look, and I huff. "Yeah, yeah. I'm totally screwed."

CHAPTER 14

SHANE
Official

I spin the keychain around my finger, watching the chrome pieces glint with each turn. I thought it was clever making something for Addison out of a nut, bolt, and screw. I found the stray parts at the garage earlier and fastened them together on a ring. I thought the gift would be symbolic of our arrangement, but doubt is creeping in the more I'm thinking about it.

Why would Addison want leftover junk? The significance makes it more special, though. Right? I scoff and glare at the ceiling. I'm probably fooling myself.

When she enters the kitchen, I straighten against the counter. The metal in my palm is momentarily forgotten when she smiles.

"Hey, Rooks. Whatcha doing?"

Addison looks stunning in a green sweater and dark jeans. Her red hair is tied up in a messy bun, a few tendrils framing her freckled face. Sinful red stains her pouty lips, and I want to lick the color off. I tug her forward by a belt loop and drop my mouth onto hers. She grants me this luxury, and I'm a lucky bastard. Cinnamon apple invades my senses. I'm famished beyond reason. I groan and she mewls and we deepen the caress. My tongue strokes hers once, twice. I have to force myself away after a third.

I nibble up her jaw and she leans closer. "I missed you," I whisper in her ear.

Addison collapses into me. "You're so sweet. My shift dragged on forever without you there."

"Work always gets in the way." I press my lips to her cheek, and she shifts to stand straight.

"But we're free now. What're we gonna do?" She winces. "I mean, if you don't already have plans."

I chuckle at her adorable expression. It's Saturday, and by some miracle, we both have the night off. "Obviously we're hanging out, Adds. I've been waiting for you," I tell her.

Her green pools sparkle. "I was hoping you'd say that." She glances at my hand. "Oooh, whatcha got there?"

I let the keychain dangle off my thumb, an offering of stupidly small proportions. I almost toss it in the trash until Addison gasps.

"This is amazing, Rooks. It can hold the key to our love nest." Her expression freezes as the words tumble out. "Um, our apartment. Yeah, just this very standard, not overly fluffy place we live in.

Together." Her bumbling attempt at backpedaling makes me laugh.

"Love nest?" I ask with a smirk.

Addison grimaces and won't look at me. I tip her chin up, and she peeks up through long lashes.

"I'll happily refer to this as our love nest," I say.

A deep flush races up her neck. "It's something silly Delilah started. The name just slipped out," she rushes to explain.

I wrap my arms around her waist and pull until she's snuggling against me. Her face nuzzles my chest, and I sigh, allowing the calm to wash over me. Hugging her is a simple pleasure I'll never take for granted. We just seem to fit, more so over the last week than ever. Since my lips first touched hers seven days ago, everything makes more sense. I nearly combust while the vision of us truly joining as one enters my filthy mind. Of course my dick leaps on board, twitching awake with Addison pressed against me. I slowly peel her off my chest and shove necessary space between us.

She sighs happily, unaware of my discomfort. I suffer this pain alone, and somewhat silently. It's becoming far more challenging to bury my perpetual longing. In these weak moments, I focus on how fast we've bonded. I can't be upset about that.

Needing a distraction, I tug at the hem of her sweater. "Is this new?"

"Yup." Addison pops her P. "I got it yesterday while out with D and Rave."

"How fun," I say.

"Sure was," she replies. Addison was busy with her friends all afternoon until heading to work. They stopped by the garage to bring us lunch, the surprise making my entire week.

I lift a brow. "Anything else... interesting happen?"

She chews on her lip, hiding a smile. "Maybe."

I study her expression as she fidgets, recalling their chattering in our living room. If they were trying to hide the topic of their conversation, it didn't work. It was a dead giveaway when I walked into the room and their voices all cut off.

I don't mind, though. I want Addison talking about me. Pride and pleasure surges through my veins believing she's whispering about me. Hopefully her friends are encouraging that next step so she latches onto me. There's still a frustrating blockage she's using to keep her distance. I don't know why, and that's driving me a bit madder with each second.

"Maybe you'll share those secrets with me," I prod.

Addison's green gaze burns hot on me. "Someday."

I exhale heavily, accepting that. For now. "So, what's our agenda?"

"Happy hour?" she suggests.

"And dinner?"

She giggles. "Well, yeah. That was implied. Where should we go? You love Dagos, but I'm there enough. Let's try somewhere else."

Her comment makes me pause, and I scratch my temple. "Uh, I don't go there for the food and drinks, Adds. It's not the establishment I like."

"No?" Her eyes are so open and honest.

"Nah, the service has me coming back for more," I murmur.

Hasn't she figured this out by now? I guess our status isn't that stable. Are we officially dating? Or still *just* roommates who happen to share a bed? Fuck, I suck at this. This uncertainty needs to dissipate and quick. Tonight I'll make my intentions clear, lay a solid foundation, and tie up loose ends. No more faltering.

Addison's giggle breaks apart my confusion. "The surprises never stop with you, Rooks."

"Is that a good thing?"

"Very. I figured you really love the tater-tot hot dish."

I smirk. "Well, I'd never turn it away. But there's something I'll always want more."

Her, only her.

Addison blinks at me. "Wow, um, all right. That's really… uh, exciting." She concentrates on the floor, cabinets, fridge, and pretty much anywhere that's not me.

Shit, this woman is irresistible. I kiss her softly because my words aren't computing. I tack on a few more for good measure. "I've never been able to stay away."

She tugs at the collar of her shirt. "Jeez, okay. Turn down the heat, Rooks. Let's go to Alma Grassa before I burst into flames."

Imagining her freckled skin smoldering beneath my palms gets me buzzing. That's a bad idea. I shift my stance and glance down. "That fancy spot off the lake in Rove Maple?"

She nods eagerly. "Uh-huh. I've always wanted to go there for date night."

How can I resist that?

My nails are still lined in grease. I'm wearing faded jeans and a plain Henley. I wasn't planning for anything extravagant. "Should I change?"

"You look perfect."

I scrape my teeth along my bottom lip. "Ready?"

Addison shimmies her slim hips. "This is gonna be so great. Our very first official date." She laughs. "And I've got rhymes. Better watch out, Rooks. I'm the entire package."

I settle a palm against her back and lead us to the closet. "Trust me, I'm well aware."

She gives me a lingering look and zips her coat. "Damn, you're on fire with all this game."

"I'm just getting warmed up, beautiful," I say and usher her outside.

The drive to the next town over takes fifteen minutes. Country music floats from the speakers, drowning any silence between us. Not that there is any. As I drive, my truck eating up the miles, Addison chatters away about anything and everything. This fall has been unseasonably cold. She wants to find a new trunk for storage and has a few saved on Marketplace. A hollow ache forms in my chest with the news she's working a double shift tomorrow. Guess a lazy Sunday together is out of the question.

I nod and provide short replies when it fits. Otherwise, I'm more than happy listening to her ramble. A few short months ago, I was unsure and awkward, afraid to say the wrong thing. I'm hardly the same man, fueled with confidence and comfort thanks to the girl sitting beside me. Addison puts me at ease in a way I didn't believe was possible. Whenever she touches me, the worry and frustration melts away. Her smile is like a pure shot of bliss.

Don't be such a fucking sap, I scold. I scoff and glare out the windshield.

When I glance over, Addison is beaming at me. An easy grin splits my lips, and just like that, I could care less about being soft. I'll be anything for her.

I fiddle with the temperature settings to keep my hands occupied. Addison hums along to a popular song, and I tap my thumb on the steering wheel. This moment surrounds me, soaking into my skin, and it feels so… good. We're clicking into place like I always imagined.

Addison bounces in her seat, pointing at a brick building cloaked in white lights. "There it is. They've decorated it for the holidays. How pretty, right?"

I don't care about the structure in front of us. My eyes are locked on her. "Gorgeous."

She turns to look at me and tucks some hair behind her ear. "Oh, you. Cranking up the swoon, eh?"

I reach for her hand and thread our fingers. "Been waiting for you to notice." Her breath catches when I kiss her wrist, my tongue darting out for a taste.

Addison's lips part as she stares at me. "I see you perfectly."

"That's all I've wanted." I jut my chin toward the restaurant. "Shall we?"

She nods, and I get moving, rushing over to the passenger side. I open the door and help her out. We stroll toward the entrance wrapped around each other. The sidewalk is icy, and our shoes crunch in the snow. Winter isn't far off. We get inside and wait by the host stand.

Addison sighs wistfully. "If I didn't know better, I'd think you read my diary."

I gawk at her. "You have one of those? I thought they were a myth."

Her peal of laughter is a whimsical melody. "I stopped writing in it during middle school. It was all about happily ever after and Prince Charming and finding true love." She shrugs. "Pretty fluff-puff, just like a twelve-year-old girl."

My heart takes off in a sprint, and I tuck her into me. It doesn't seem possible that her sacred childhood dreams would be available for me to see.

"I'd love to read it," I whisper in her ear.

She scoffs but leans closer. "I bet you would. Too bad that's never going to happen."

I let the subject momentarily drop as we're led to a table. We slide into opposite sides of the booth, and the glossy wood separating us seems massive. I stretch across the cavern and capture her palm against mine, squeezing gently.

"Tell me about your wishes back then. I've told you about mine."

Addison bites into a breadstick and munches away, leaving me hanging. She chews slowly and methodically as if trying to test my patience. Apparently she's still learning that I'm a master at waiting. After she chugs some water and swallows it all down, Addison dabs the corner of her mouth with a napkin. Then proceeds to say nothing at all.

I raise my brows. "That was quite a production at stalling. Now spill."

She wrinkles her nose. "It's so silly. I've wised up an awful lot since those immature musings."

"I've learned a lot about you since we've been living together. But there's so

much more waiting below the surface."

"I feel like you know all the good stuff," Addison murmurs.

"Not true. I want it all."

Her soulful gaze bounces all around the quiet restaurant as a blush colors her cheeks. "Well, jeez. Some of the more... sensitive subjects come with time. And experience."

"We're always dissecting my past. I want to hear more about yours," I push.

Addison huffs. "Well, I'm not nearly as interesting."

"I beg to differ."

She laughs. "Um, okay. Ask away, Rooks."

I glance at a passing server, knowing we'll be interrupted soon. "Just tell me one thing you really want out of life. Whether that's love, a great career, wealth, independence… whatever."

Addison tilts her head, mulling it over. "I want to find my person, the one I'm supposed to be with forever. My parents have that. Then we'd move into a house with a wraparound porch and a white picket fence. I'm an only child and always wanted siblings so we'd have at least two kids. The romantic dream, you know? I grew up imagining my perfect match, that soulmate connection. So, to answer your question and be extremely cliché, I wanted to find that one who'd love me unconditionally. I dreamed of a handsome boy sweeping me off my feet. He'd treat me like a princess, and we'd be completely crazy for each other." She giggles and rolls her eyes. "Told you it was silly."

I have lump in my throat. "Is that past tense?"

She licks her lips and silently shakes her head.

Before I can prod further, our server stops by. The menu holds Italian fare, which suits me fine. We order a bottle of wine, mostly for Addison, and a double portion of pesto cavatappi to share.

"Too bad the noodles aren't longer like spaghetti. We could have reenacted *Lady and the Tramp*," Addison says when we're alone again.

"Not sure I like being called a tramp. You're a fine lady, though."

She winks. "I just want an excuse to kiss you."

"All you have to do is ask," I tell her and move to her side of the booth. In the next moment, we're aligning, sliding into place and just right. My lips dust across hers like a feather, and she trembles. We part before even getting started, aware of the public setting.

Addison cups my jaw. "You're going all out this evening."

"No more messing around."

"I didn't know that's what we were doing."

"We're not. That's just it."

Her green eyes expand to saucer-size. "You wanna be?"

How do I explain this without sounding like a douche? A wild beat bangs in my ears, making it even more difficult to find the correct direction. Definitely not helping that it's a sauna in here. I wipe over my damp brow and dive in.

"I was thinking"—I gulp loudly—"that we could make things official this evening."

Addison opens her mouth, then snaps it shut. Her forehead

pinches. "Like boyfriend and girlfriend?"

"Aren't we already in a relationship?" I take this opportunity to solve my earlier conflict.

"Okay." She drags the word out. "What do you mean then?"

"Sex, Adds."

"Shane!" Addison gasps and flattens a palm to her chest. "I'm scandalized."

I jerk away as if she's burning me. "Fuck, Adds—"

She grips my arm and yanks me into her. "Where are you going? I was joking. Well, mostly." She peeks up from under her lashes. "I don't put out on the first date."

I immediately want to argue, the plea waiting on my tongue. We've hung out countless times since I moved in with her. There must be a sliding scale somewhere, dammit. How do I show her this is very serious for me? She's the beginning, middle, and end. Nothing really existed before her. I'm positive she's the solution to any problem, the answers to my prayers. How do I prove that without appearing desperate and spilling my guts?

Addison must catch the war waging on my features. Her nails tap along my skin, soothing my spiraling mind.

"Hey, I just think we should wait until you're sure," she whispers. I sputter at that, and she holds up a finger. "Maybe you don't hold your first time up on a pedestal, but I don't want any regrets. It might be different for a guy— what do I know—but this is something you'll always remember. That's a lot of pressure for me."

A steel pipe strikes my gut and I want to double over. Fuck. "Are you ashamed? Do you wish I had more experience?" I manage to force out.

Addison is vehemently shaking her head. "No, not at all. I'm insanely turned on by you being a virgin, to be totally honest. Apparently this is some subconscious fantasy or something. It's so hot for me, and I'm crazy attached to you." Her words are full of conviction, leaving no room for doubt. Plenty creeps in regardless.

"Then why?"

"I want this to be the experience you've been dreaming of."

"Adds," I groan. "I've been sure for years. If you're involved, that's it."

She laughs, but the sound is shaky. "Someone's overly eager."

I can see the indecision on her crumpling features. It's obvious I'm pushing it. That's definitely not how this should be. I grind my molars but shove out what needs to be told. "Let's wait until we're both ready. And feeling one-hundred percent sure about us. I don't want you second-guessing anything. Once I have you, that's it for me."

Addison's throat bobs with a thick swallow. "Yeah? Really?" I give her a nod and she exhales for what seems like a full minute. "Okay, good. I'm actually glad we talked about this, awkward as it might be. It's been kinda weighing on me."

"Uh-huh, me too." Guess that answers my questions about her lingering hesitation.

She sweeps my hair away, her fingers the smoothest comb. "Will you settle for keeping this above the belt for a bit longer?"

"Whatever you say, Adds," I force out and swing my gaze to the ceiling. This girl will be the end of me all right. And I'm going to love every blue-ball minute.

CHAPTER 15

ADDISON
Peep

I finish applying the ruby stain and slick on a layer of clear gloss. I inspect the new shade—o the Extreme—and smile. As always, the bright color pops against my fair skin and gives me the desired effect. I blow a kiss at the mirror and start sweeping my hair into a ponytail.

I wonder if Shane will like it. An exaggerated eye roll immediately follows that train of thought. I don't need to go fishing for compliments. He loves anything red, especially on me. If last night is any indication, his preference is far more favorable than I thought. Why did I shut him down?

Last night was magical, a date I've always dreamed of. After a delicious dinner, we went to the movies and caught an action flick. It was Shane's turn to choose, and I was happy to oblige. We shared popcorn and lifted the armrest to snuggle. I can still feel the electricity pulsing between us. But when we got home, nothing else happened. A few stolen kisses and wandering touches ended the evening.

Why did I open my big, cock-blocking mouth? I'm kicking myself across the room for holding off on sex.

I don't put out on the first date?

I scoff all over again at my lame excuse. True as it might be, Shane is a very different story. I would have stripped him naked back in May at the racetrack if he'd given me the okay. Now I'm a coiled spring ready to attack at the slightest brush of his hand. It's so going down later.

Too bad I work a double shift today. Eff that. By the time I get home, my body will be in desperate need of a massage. A good long soak in the tub is my typical cure. Maybe that's a great way to jumpstart the filthy shenanigans.

I quirk a brow at my reflection. I'm ready to crank up the heat with Shane. No more chickening out. I'll invite him to join me in a bubbly bath for naked fun. He can rub my back and I'll stroke his front...

A low moan interrupts my dirty plotting. I perk up and twist toward the hallway. Another muffled noise greets me, and I shuffle closer. I glance at the clock and bite back an expletive. Where does the time go? My shift starts in fifteen minutes, and I need to leave, but there might be something wrong with him. I won't be able to focus until proving he's okay.

I creep into the hall, following his gruff groans. The shower is running and overpowers Shane's painful sounds, but I can still hear them. I press my ear to the door and wait.

"Adds." My name is garbled and stretched out. I get flustered at Shane's gritty tone and stumble back.

Is he hurt? Or just the opposite? I glare at the kitchen, then at the dark wood in front of me. I'm being pulled in two directions, unsure what choice is best. I knot my fingers and bounce on my toes.

Screw it.

I tentatively turn the knob and poke my head into the bathroom. Even through the foggy glass, it's crystal-clear what Shane is doing. His powerful arm strokes up and down, back and forth, the movement rhythmic and stealing every bit of my attention. His breathing is shallow, each pant forced from him. He doesn't notice me, too lost in whatever fantasy he's imagining. I could leave without him knowing any different. But I stay rooted in place.

The slap of skin bounces around the small space and my empty core squeezes. I'm suddenly damp and needy, burning up where it matters most. I've never witnessed anyone pleasure themselves until this moment. It's really erotic and extremely arousing. I shift my stance, the evidence becoming painfully obvious.

I blink quickly and guilt slithers up my spine. I shouldn't be spying on this intimate moment. I'm slowly moving away when a low growl escapes Shane's mouth.

"Fuck, Adds. Yeah, baby, just like that." The rumble strikes in the molten center of me, and I reach for the counter to balance.

Holy shit, he's getting off to me. How can I possible leave? If anything, I should join him.

Shane's pumps become more uneven and sloppy. He seems

hurried, rushing to reach that pivotal peak of pleasure. The effect on me is a raging inferno, and I'm helpless to avert my stare. I lean harder on the cool ceramic beneath my palm. All circuits are misfiring, and I couldn't move if the apartment was on fire.

Hot fucking damn.

I want to take over, wrap my fingers around his thick length. He'd throb and pulse in my tight grasp. I'd revel in each thunderous curse spilling from his lips.

Shane bows and his abs ripple, shredding apart my willpower to remain a bystander. He's jerking his dick with an urgency I feel in my lower belly. I want him sliding deep inside me. Right the hell now. I'm preparing to rip off my pants when his voice calls out again.

"You're gonna make me bust, Adds. Is that what you want?"

I gasp and the spell is broken. Everything stills with that tiny noise, then takes off at warp speed. Shane's head whips toward me, and I'm totally busted. I feel my eyes blow wide open and trip backwards.

Oh, shit. How am I going to explain my voyeurism?

Shane rips a towel off the bar and rushes forward. "Fuck, Adds. I'm sorry. I thought you'd already left. Dammit," he rakes through all that wet hair, "you shouldn't have witnessed me like that."

My ears are ringing as I try to formulate a response, or do anything other than gawk at him. His muscular torso glistens, and I want to drink the droplets trailing sinfully low.

"Just give me a chance to explain. Shit, I'm such a fool. What you must think of me," he mutters.

Wait, he's embarrassed? I was the one leering like a creeper. My lips open with a squeak. "Uh, I'll just give you some, um, privacy," I stammer.

In the next second, I slam the door closed and press against it. My pulse is hammering too fast, and I inhale deeply. How the heck am I going to function normally after that? I'm still trying to get my lower half to stop vibrating. And what about Shane? While I'm getting really turned on by the sight of him, he's trying to get off. I ruined it for him. That lack of release when he was so close is going to hurt.

Maybe I should just go to work and forget this happened. Un-freaking-likely. I want to laugh at my stupidity. The vision of him jacking his massive dick will be forever etched in my memory. I roll my forehead against the cool wood and send Shane a silent apology.

The steady surface disappears, and I topple into his arms. He's still dripping and water immediately soaks into my shirt. His massive form is covered by a small scrap of terry cloth and the sight should be comical. All I can do is drag my eyes across the expanse of toned maleness I'm pressing against. The probability of drooling is definite.

At full height, my head rests at the base of Shane's neck. He dwarfs me, but we're perfectly matched. I allow his strength to seep into me, letting the tension evaporate from my limbs. I feel safe and protected, cherished and treasured. Maybe even loved. I berate myself for the last one. It's a crazy notion. We're just—

I stop short. How do I finish that sentence? Our potential is growing exponentially by the second.

Shane wraps around my waist and pulls me in tighter. I return the gesture, looping around him like a starving vine. We remain quiet, allowing the events from the last several minutes to speak. His hugs are warm comfort, giving me a natural buzz no substance can offer. I find myself in ecstasy from the sweet flavor, replacing the craving for something much spicier. This is home and peace and everything good.

I never want to let go. Hopefully he doesn't either.

His chin drops onto my crown. "You were just gonna run off?" I shrug and he grips me harder. "Fuck that, Adds. Talk to me."

"I didn't mean to walk in on you... doing that," I murmur.

"Masturbation is normal, Adds." His tone is defensive. I immediately want to soothe his concern.

"Trust me—there's nothing wrong with what I just witnessed."

"Then why flee?"

I tilt up, and his scruff rasps against my cheek. "What would you have me do? Sit and watch you finish?"

His honey eyes spark with unadulterated lust. "Join me."

I gulp when his hard length jabs into me. "Now?"

He kisses my forehead. "Doesn't your shift start soon?"

"Maybe."

Shane chuckles against my balmy skin. "I want you so fucking bad, Adds. Not sure I could make that more obvious. But I don't wanna rush, not after waiting this long. I have plans to savor every inch of you."

"Oh, wow. I'm so ready for that." If he wasn't holding me up, I'd probably collapse.

His palms smooth up and down my sides. "You fit so good against me, baby. I can't wait to really feel you."

I swallow the pooling saliva, forcing it down my dry throat.

"What are you doing to me?" I whisper.

"A little temptation goes a long way, Adds. Now you'll be thinking of me all day," he purrs into my neck. "And only me."

Doesn't he realize I already do? This is serious overkill and bordering on torture. "Maybe I should call in sick."

Shane cups my ass. "Naughty girl, you don't really wanna do that. Grayson would be pissed."

I currently have a single goal in mind, and it isn't Dagos. "Not sure I can walk away," I whisper and squeeze him with all my might.

"You gonna make me decide, Adds? Not sure I'm strong enough to resist, no matter how right or wrong."

I exhale heavily. "Okay, okay." He releases me and I step back. I take a good, long look at his flexing muscles and sigh again. "Damn," I mutter.

On impulse, I smack a loud smooch to the center of Shane's pec. The outline of my lips in bright red marks his skin when I pull away. I grin at my handiwork, glad he has a piece of me branding him.

"How's that for a tease?" I murmur. Two can play at this game.

A rumble brews in his chest, and I'm positive he's about to pounce. "That's the hottest fucking thing, Adds. Might have to make this kiss permanent."

"I'd love to see that." I wink at him.

Shane plants his mouth on mine, sucking the air from my lungs. "Better get going, beautiful."

I slump against him with stars in my eyes. How is he real? I inhale deeply, trapping his scent in every part of me. Then I peel myself off him for the umpteenth time. "Until later?"

He smirks. "Damn straight. We'll do it right."

"Promise?"

"Oh, Adds." His chuckle is pure sex, and my thighs tremble. "I can guarantee your ass is mine tonight."

I force my feet to move and strut toward the foyer, shaking my butt for added impact. "Bye, boyfriend," I call over my shoulder.

"Better save me a seat in your section," he grumbles behind me.

I send him a saucy smile. "You can count on it."

CHAPTER 16

SHANE
Blush

I take another swig of beer and seek out Addison in the crowded bar. Every man in this place seems to have his sights set on my girl. Not that I blame them. She's the definition of irresistible. I find myself unable to look away for more than a few moments, drawn to her more than ever.

As if she feels my stare, Addison peeks over at me. Her secret smile hits me square in the gut, and I suck in a sharp breath. I send her a smirk and pat the spot she kissed earlier. Her lipstick is staining my skin, and I never want the evidence to wash off. A flush colors her freckled cheeks, and she smiles wider.

Every glimpse is a tease, those lingering glances driving straight south. I adjust my aching cock and beg for relief. My desperation for her is driving me mad. I thought it was bad before. This is much worse. I can almost feel her body beneath mine, encouraging moans spilling from those lips. All her freckles and shades of red are alluring. This bone-deep desire is clawing at me and getting more intense the longer I sit here.

I've been holed up at Dagos all afternoon, sulking like a sullen child who's told to wait a bit longer. Addison has hours left on shift. This is a true test of patience, and an unfortunate reminder of my extensive experience waiting. The numbers on the clock mock me, ticking like frozen molasses. My body is strung so fucking tight, I'm liable to snap at any unlikely source. Whenever she passes by my table, a few whispered words are all it takes to get me revving harder. As if further provoking is necessary, especially after this morning.

I fling a few popcorn kernels into my mouth, munching roughly, and attempt to shake off the lingering shame. I'm positive my face is still red from embarrassment. How could I be so careless, letting her catch me jerking off? But Addison wasn't mortified, which is baffling. Why isn't she disgusted by my actions? My addled mind tries to calculate her reaction, but comes up short. Even in my wildest dreams, she would take off running and screaming. Imagine my dumbfounded shock when she told me watching that was a turn-on.

Could she be more amazing?

My focus follows Addison across the room, and I let loose a string of expletives. A stranger strolls up to her and leans far too close. Why is he invading her personal space? I force my ass to remain glued to the stool, recalling her scolding from thirty minutes ago. She's at work, and I can't barge in each time a man talks to her. I've been hulking around like a barbarian, pounding on my chest and chasing off any potential competition. Isn't it my job to protect her?

I tense when the guy edges in further. But I hold myself back, confident Addison will handle his unwanted attention. She's mine in all ways that matter. The connection between us is strong and continuing to gain power. She's in my bed each night, curling up against me, sharing intimate feelings and promising more. Our lives are weaving together as one. How do I make it permanent?

After guzzling the rest of my drink, I search for a distraction. As if hearing my summons, Trey enters the bar with Mitch trailing behind. I wave and they amble over, wearing matching smirks. This ought to be good.

Mitch grips my shoulders and gives me a shake. "Hey, man. How the fuck are you?"

I shrug him off me. "Uh, fine. Why?"

"Heard you might need reinforcements," Trey says.

I bunch my muscles. "For what?"

Pretty sure Trey's eyes are sparkling, and it's creepy as hell. "Why don't you tell *us?*"

"I'm just enjoying a relaxing Sunday at the bar. Not sure what you're referring to."

I lock my jaw, preparing for him to give me shit about masturbating with Addison at home. She wouldn't rat me out, though. I'm being paranoid, and these two are digging for dirt.

Trey grunts. "This place is a zoo and is only getting worse. I was told to keep you entertained before someone gets punched out or something."

My chuckle is forced. "Real funny."

Mitch hoots and points at me. "Dude, you look ready to cause damage."

"Whatever." I grumble.

Addison stops by and drops off a round of beers. She shares a look with Trey and Mitch, proving my suspicions.

I lift my chin at her. "You called them to keep me occupied?"

She pats my cheek. "Sweetie, you're scaring away my customers." Addison dips down and whispers, "I know you're hot and bothered. The feeling is very mutual. But there's nothing we can do about it right now."

I inhale her cinnamon apple scent, and a calm wave washes over me. My pulse slows, and I take a deep breath. "Yeah, I'm aware."

She straightens and gives me a wink. "Good. I'll be done real soon. Until then, spend time with your friends."

As if on cue, Trey and Mitch give me cheesy smiles. Fuck, I'm really losing my cool if these two were sent to deal with me.

"Okay," I say.

Addison flounces away, and the guys bust out laughing. I groan and cover my face.

"Holy shit, you're so pussy-whipped. You've been a grouchy asshole all week at the garage. Even Jack made a comment about your bitching being louder than mine. But one touch from her and you're a totally different man. Wow." Trey whistles.

"That's rich coming from you." My voice resembles a growl and I swallow roughly. Maybe I need to rein it in, at least a bit.

Trey shakes his head. "You're not turning the tables on me. What gives?"

I comb through my hair, searching for a plausible cause. With the holidays approaching and bringing more traffic, Jacked Up is busier than usual. I glance around Dagos, people packing in wall to wall, and realize Garden Grove in general is experiencing the influx. "Uh, the garage has been a madhouse lately. Guess I'm more bothered than usual. The tickets never seem to quit."

That's feasible, right? I'm not about to give him more ammunition when it comes to Addison. The limited amount of time we have together has been dwindling. My urges are a monster that hasn't been fed. Our date last night was supposed to be it, consummating all I am with her. That fell fucking flat. Now she's untouchable for twelve hours. I had to take matters into my own hand, quite literally. My patience is a fraying rope, and I feel like the asshole Trey is accusing me of being.

Trey's features tighten. "Fuck, we're all feeling that added pressure. Holi-Daze will be here soon. It's gonna get worse before it gets better."

I grin and cover it with an exaggerated yawn, hiding the reaction that goes against my words. I'm actually looking forward to the winter festival this year. After rolling my neck, I say, "Yup. That's what I mean."

Trey scrubs over his mouth. "You know the best cure?"

"Exercise?" I guess.

He steeples his fingers. "More specifically, getting laid."

"Oh," I mumble stupidly.

Trey tilts his head, picking up on my flat tone. "Addison isn't giving you the goodies?"

Mitch chokes on his drink, and I bang a fist on the table. "Shut up, Sollons. Don't talk about her like that." Placing any blame on her leaves a bitter bite in my gut.

He just rolls his eyes. "Take a fucking chill pill. Honestly, you're worse than Raven on the rag. What's got your briefs in a bunch this time?"

"Let's drop it," I demand.

Trey squints at me. "Need some pointers? I can recommend a few moves."

I chug some beer to keep myself from agreeing. It's so fucking juvenile to admit I've never had a girlfriend until now. Most days, I feel decades behind these two with plenty of experience. If I'm honest with Trey, he'll laugh in my face.

"Just loosen up. She'll come around eventually. Look at how much progress you've already made," Trey points out.

"I think you've got it backwards," Mitch tells him, and I glower.

Trey motions him on. "Well, spit it out. Apparently we're here for moral support or some shit. Might as well make it interesting."

Mitch shrugs and gestures to me. "Your story."

Ah, fuck it. Why not?

"We haven't had sex yet," I mutter under my breath.

Trey almost falls off his chair. "What was that?" He scoots closer.

"We've been… waiting for the right time," I say.

"You gotta make a big move, dude," Mitch offers.

I cross my arms. "Don't you think I've tried? Addison wants to be sure. I mean, we both do."

Trey snorts. "She nervous about popping your cherry?"

I don't respond, keeping my expression neutral, but his assumption is dead-on. I have zero attachment to my virginity, at least since meeting Addison. She gets all of me, and I'm ready to tear her clothes into shreds.

Mitch makes a noise of agreement. "Chicks are weird about that shit. What's the big deal, right?"

Trey snorts. "Too romantic at heart, the lot of them." He studies me and says, "I'm almost impressed you lasted until twenty-five. Not really sure how that's possible. And I also feel really bad for your dick. You moved to Garden Grove two years ago? In all that time, I never saw you out with any girls. Makes it pretty damn obvious you're a one-woman kind of guy. No offense… Nah, scratch that, you can be offended. I'll be the first in line to congratulate you after it happens."

I want to bang my head against the table. "Why are we still talking about this?"

"Because we're fucking bonding, rookie. Grit your teeth and deal with it," Trey mutters.

I've never hated that nickname until this moment. My skin is tight and itchy. I need a kiss from Addison to take the edge off. She's at the server station loading up her tray with drinks. Some douchebag is hovering nearby, watching her, probably hoping to get a moment of her precious time.

Addison tips her head back and laughs. The guy keeps staring, captivated by the sound. I recognize the expression covering his face. Hell, I wear the same look of stunned wonder almost constantly. He reaches for her, looping an arm around her slim waist. Addison tries side-stepping out of his hold, but he tugs and she falls into him.

Bold fucking bastard. That was a big mistake.

A brick of dynamite detonates and I jump to my feet. The stool crashes to the floor, but I barely hear it over the roaring in my ears. That's the fucking line, and he just steamrolled over it.

I storm toward them, one goal in mind. No one else gets to touch her that way. I'm the one to make her laugh and blush and fidget. That's my job. Addison is *my girl*. The list bangs into me with each pounding footfall.

She's escaped his grabby palms when I arrive in front of them. Addison notices me first, eyes wide, and shakes her head.

"Rooks, I'm fine--"

I don't let her say more. I haul her against me, staking my claim like the caveman I've turned into. "It's most certainly not fine," I rumble dangerously low, my glare centered on the moron who put his paws all over her.

He holds up his hands. "Yeah, man. She already told me off. Didn't mean any trouble." Before I can argue, the stranger disappears into the crowd.

Addison's startled gaze meets mine. "Shane, what the hell? We discussed this exact thing not even--"

"We're going home," I interrupt.

Her brow furrows. "I'm in the middle of a—"

"Doesn't matter. We're taking care of this right the fuck now." Then my lips are on hers, drowning the rest of her resistance. Addison melts against me, opening for me like a blooming rose. Her immediate surrender gets me harder than a steel pipe, and I groan out loud. Sharp nails bite into my back, her rough handling solidifying my decision.

I rip away from Addison's mouth and smirk when she dives back for more. Instead of giving in, I hoist her over my shoulder in one swift move. She squeaks and begins protesting, but her weak murmurs get swallowed by the rowdy patrons.

I spank her lightly. "This ass is mine," I say loud enough for her to hear.

She shivers and exhales a breathy, "Oh, my."

My chest shakes with a rumble. "Is that a yes?"

Addison nods quickly. "Uh-huh."

"That's my girl." I kiss her blazing cheek.

I rush to the door like my feet are on fire, Addison secured in the fireman's hold. Hoots and hollers ring out behind us, but Trey's are the loudest. "About damn time, rookie. Go get some."

In-fucking-deed.

CHAPTER 17

SHANE
Bang

I bound up the alley stairs, flames licking my spine. Addison flops on my shoulder and giggles louder with each step. I'm being reckless, not handling her with nearly enough care. I should be gentle and considerate. But that part of my brain has officially vacated the premises.

My boots are a blur as I race forward. I barge inside the apartment without pause. The door crashes against the wall, but it hardly registers with me. All my energy is spent on the redhead vixen clinging to me. I beeline for my bedroom, which is really ours now. Even more so once we truly claim one another.

"You can put me down," Addison murmurs.

"Not a chance. You're precious cargo." I tighten my hold for emphasis.

She pinches my ass in response, which gets me hustling faster. I toss her onto the mattress, and she bounces with a laugh. Addison splays out like a starfish, arms and legs scissoring wildly. I stand tall at the foot of the bed, so damn hard my zipper is about to bust open. Fueled by adrenaline and animalistic need, I move lightening quick. I ditch my shoes and socks, tug my shirt off, and get started on my jeans.

"You wanna flirt with other guys?" I growl.

Addison balks and shakes her head. "I wasn't—"

I cut off her protest. "Laugh at their jokes? Let them brush up on you? Give them a signal you're enjoying the company? Let me watch them get way too close all day long?"

The concern melts off her face, and she grins. "Maybe I was trying to make you jealous."

I smirk and shift onto the bed.

"You need attention?" I remove her heels and throw them over my shoulder. "Get that from me. I take care of you. All your smiles are mine. There's no need to provoke me, Adds. I'm right fucking here, waiting for a sign you're ready."

Addison gets the hint and shimmies out of her leggings. She whips off the Dagos tee, leaving a red lacy bra and panties. Those sinful scraps of silk will be gone soon enough, but I enjoy the view for a moment.

"I only want you, Rooks," she purrs and stretches out further.

"You're incredible," I say and take her in. The urgency dissipates while I gorge on the sight.

Addison releases her hair from the ponytail and long waves

tumble out. A sea of auburn cascades down and blankets the pillow. Twinkling green eyes beckon me, ruby lips part and sing a seductive tune. The slender column of her neck bobs with a long swallow. Her luscious tits are almost spilling out of those confining cups. A narrow waist leads to flared hips, a flawless expanse of smooth flesh. Toned thighs clench and spread wider, calling me in. Her painted toes dig into the sheets when she squirms under my hungry gaze.

I'm distracted by the endless array of freckles—those little dots showing me the way. Starting at her forehead and sweeping to her soles, her skin is a map of countless landmarks. The tiny circles create unique designs in every direction, and I have every intention of exploring them all. I trace a route down her arm. "You're so beautiful."

Her speckled nose wrinkles. "I've never liked my freckles."

"I'll love them for you." I'm concentrating on the little trio leading into the waistband of her thong. Addison must feel my searing stare and her fingers flit down that path, dipping under the silky material.

"I'm more than ready to let you. What're you gonna do with me?" she whispers.

I lift her ankle onto my shoulder, tracing a line up her calf with my nose. I inhale her sweet apple scent and lock my jaw to stave off the need boiling from within.

"Find my salvation," I moan into her satin skin. My tongue carves a path up until I'm kissing those tempting speckles. "You smell so damn good."

"You always say that," she rasps.

I drag her panties down, my mouth exploring lower.

"This is different," I murmur against her bare center.

Addison's fingers spear into my hair and yank. I lift my gaze to her wide eyes. "I need you. Now," she demands.

I'll never deny her. Especially not this. I shove my briefs off, blindly chucking them into the discard pile. My naked body covers her, and I prop up on an elbow. My blood pumps way too fast. I fear this will be over before we begin.

Addison shivers under me.

"You're so hot." Her nails lightly graze the grooves of my ribs.

I follow her lead, my palms wandering up until reaching the closure of her bra. My eyes rake over the red fabric covering her tits. I snap the elastic strap and ask, "Did you choose this color for me?"

She nods, her lips brushing my collarbone. Her "yes" escapes as a long sigh.

I open the clasp and slip the silky material off her. Addison arches up, her bare chest brushing against mine. Our hips bump, and my dick slides through her slickness. I see stars and almost lose my grip on reality.

"Fuck, you're so wet," I groan into her ear before sucking gently on the lobe.

She trembles and bows into me further. "I want you so bad, Rooks. Do you feel how much?"

Her knees lift and lock against my legs, trapping me against her. She clings tighter to me, and I can almost hear the desire crashing into her. I rock forward and back, coating myself in her. The molten heat between us sets me on fire, and I never want to cool down.

"Adds, you're gonna make me lose control," I warn.

She swivels and my tip hits her opening. The noise that rips from me is indecent, and I repeat the sound immediately. I can see the erratic pulse thrumming through her veins, echoing my want. But she voices it to be sure.

"Please," Addison begs. "Make love to me."

This close, I catch the golden flecks in her green eyes. I drown in the hypnotic thrashing and press my mouth to hers, sealing our fate. When I slide into her, everything I knew before ceases to exist. It's a full-body awakening, this prickling sensation swarming my entire being. She's snug and tight and fucking perfection. I break away from her lips and watch as she gives me this gift. Addison's expression morphs, the pleasure blooming across her flushing face and escaping from her mouth.

"You're so big," she whimpers. "I think you'll tear me in two."

"Never, baby. You're made for me." I thrust into her further for emphasis. "We're bonding as one. Do you feel that?"

"Oh Lord, yes. I want more," she pleads.

Her body welcomes mine, not fighting the intrusion. Her arousal makes this easy for me, the glide effortless, and I'm quickly sunk to the root.

"If this is a sin, send me straight down," I chant. She's totally worth it.

"Nothing this good could be wrong," she moans.

"You're my Eden." I sink deeper, her body greedily accepting mine. I demand, and Addison gives, offering herself as a sacrifice.

If this is what sends me to eternal damnation, I'll willingly go. She's worth any amount of purgatory.

I punch forward and manage to reach even further, desperate to live inside her. A roar almost rips from me when Addison clamps around my cock.

"Harder, Rooks. Give it all to me," Addison breathes. She wants to be consumed? I'll give that word new meaning.

And I do, pounding faster until the headboard is knocking into the wall. I stare at her pink nipples and latch onto a pebbled peak. I suck hard, pulling the tip between my teeth. She mewls when I lap at her and speed up my punishing thrusts. Her fingers roam from my neck and shoulders, digging into my back. I imagine the marks she's clawing into me, bright red and raised. The color resembles her nails, lipstick, and hair. But it's the exact shade of my burning lust.

"Yeah, Adds. Brand me," I hiss. "I'm fucking yours."

"You're making me high," Addison cries. "So damn high on you." She bucks up and meets my fluid strokes. Her eyes seem unfocused, proving her words. She nips at my jaw and licks away the sting. Her legs cinch around my waist and squeeze until my vision gets fuzzy. Now we're both soaring in another dimension. That need propels me on, finding another level to meet.

I slam my mouth onto hers, needing to be connected in every way. The kiss is messy, a sloppy exchange of tongues and lips and teeth. This is ravished possessiveness flooding me. That's what happens when a man waits twenty-five years to find nirvana. I didn't realize how euphoric sex would be. Her lips drinking from mine, our bodies aligning as one, will be seared into my brain for eternity.

"Does it always feel like this?" I withdraw before pushing back in, plunging further with extra power in my hips. I waste no time repeating the process. Our movements are on a smooth loop, I push and she greets me with a pull.

"No, never. Something very different is happening," she whispers.

"This is special between us," I tell her with a slow slide in and out.

"Uh-huh," she mumbles.

"I'm already addicted," I say.

"Me too. So much. You've never done this before? Really?" She asks between gasps.

"Why's that hard to believe?"

"Because you're insanely amazing," Addison pants.

I nibble up her neck, feasting on the tender flesh. "I promise you're my first." And last, I add silently.

Her response is another throaty moan. She rests her forehead on mine and clings harder as if there's any chance I'm letting go.

I'm pistoning fast, in and out. I'm going to explode any moment. Telltale tingles zip up my legs. Heat gathers at the base of my spine, and I know what's coming. I'm right there, my balls tightening in warning.

"Adds, I can't hold back much longer. Tell me what to do."

"Touch my clit," she instructs. Addison places my hand where she wants me, showing me the circular motion that gets her moaning louder. The rough pad of my thumb finds purchase on her hard nub, rubbing and adding pressure when she asks.

"Yes, like that. Ohhh, oh, it feels so good," she wheezes.

Addison's vise-grip on my dick contracts like a fist. Sparklers ignite into flames, roaring out of control across my skin. My teeth scrape along her lips, sucking the bottom one into my mouth, then dipping in for more. I'm dizzy as uncut ecstasy pumps into my veins and sends me spiraling. I should do so many things in this moment—slow down, take a breath, make sure Addison gets off—but none of them happen. There's no more avoiding this looming climax, and I dive into free-fall. I barely register Addison spasming beneath me because my limbs are convulsing. My release seems to go and go until I'm wrung dry with seizing lungs. My arms give out, and I collapse, gasping and breathless.

When a semblance of my wits return, I check on my girl. With a bit of effort, I manage to prop myself up. Her lazy smile screams of bliss, but my imagination could be playing tricks on me.

I return her grin. "Holy shit, gorgeous. That was..."

"Incredible," she finishes for me.

"Yeah. Fuck, Adds. You ruined me."

She laughs. "It wasn't that rough. I only bit you once. By accident."

"No, I didn't mind one bit. I mean, there's no better feeling than what we shared. I'm destroyed forever."

"You don't sound disappointed about that," she says.

"How could I be? You're everything."

Addison's cheeks turn my favorite shade of red. "Such a charmer."

I nuzzle into the hollow of her throat. "Anything for you."

"Ohhh, my." She fans her eyes. "Talk about getting ruined."

"Better get used to the swoon, Adds," I murmur into the crook of her neck.

Her chest vibrates with a happy sound. "You won't hear me complain. Should we take this party to the shower? I probably smell like—"

"Mine. You're mine, Adds." I inhale deeply while skimming my nose up the slope of her jaw. "And you're not going anywhere."

She shivers. "You're so damn hot being bossy. I love this alpha side of you."

"More than the sweet?"

"Nothing is better than your sweet," she murmurs.

"Hey," I start and sweep some hair off her face. "I'm sorry the end came too soon, quite literally. That's been bottled up way too long."

She traces my spine. "Don't apologize. I got mine. And next round will be even better." My dick jerks inside her, and she giggles. "Which is starting real soon, I guess."

I kiss her softly. "Fuck, yes. Why wait?" I begin moving again, testing out my stamina.

Addison stills my hips, halting the slow slide. "Easy, cowboy. Give the lady a minute for recovery."

I quirk a brow. "I wore you out?"

She scoffs playfully. "Already cocky?"

"Absolutely." I buck forward, and she chokes out a cough.

"Okay, yeah. You're already a pro. And we'll only get better with practice," she says.

I lightly pinch her nipple, and she squirms. "I've always been somewhat of a perfectionist."

Addison hums. "I'll be your study, Rooks. Use me."

"I'm trying," I rasp against her lips.

She taps my hip. "Roll over."

I follow the order immediately, flipping us without slipping from her warmth.

"Impressive," she sighs and adjusts her position.

"Timeout over?"

Addison nods. "Giddy-up, Rooks. Our night is just getting started."

CHAPTER 18

ADDISON
Pump

I crack my eyelids open and stretch languidly. I'm deliciously sore in all the right places thanks to my sexathon with Shane. For a recently dethroned virgin, that man has killer moves. I smile thinking about the countless orgasms he granted me. Shane is a giver, and I'm one lucky lady.

My brain begins functioning normally as the fog fades. I glance around the room, taking stock of the morning. The sun is barely rising over the horizon, signaling the early hour. I should still be sleeping. Why aren't I?

As if on cue, an obnoxiously loud snore startles me out of my lazy state. I think the windows are rattling from the intensity. I turn toward the source of my premature wake-up. A long sigh escapes me as I study Shane's relaxed features. Dark lashes fan his stubbled cheeks and twitch ever so slightly. He must be lost in dreamland. I comb through his thick hair and cup his jaw without alerting him. He's so freaking hot. I gobble up the opportunity to just stare at him. I softly brush the smooth skin between his brows and digest the fact he's all mine.

My gaze slithers down his marble torso to the sheet covering his lower half. The thin material is tenting over his lap, and my thighs squeeze on reflex. Pretty sure he's always hard, even while deeply unconscious. This trouser snake refuses to lay dormant, and that suits me fine. I'll be the one reaping those constant benefits, like right now. His thickness is hardly concealed by the flimsy fabric, and the obscene outline is very visible. All the erotic possibilities slam into me, and I scoot closer.

I backpedal almost immediately. For a second, the valuable lesson I learned yesterday evaded my erotic musings. I shove those dirty desires in a dark corner until Shane can be an active participant. I don't want to traumatize the guy.

My bladder pinches with nature's call, and I snap to attention. A shower is definitely in order, especially after our filthy fun. That will be a good distraction until Mister Handsome wakes up. With a lingering glance at my bedmate, I determine he's out cold. Later we can share that bubble bath I was planning.

After a super-fast rinse followed by all my bathroom duties, I find Shane still snoring away. I shake my head and check the time, realizing it's not even seven o'clock yet. What's a girl to do? With giddy fizz in my belly, I reach for my phone and click on the Kindle app. There's a steamy romance with my name on it. Maybe it'll give me some new inspiration.

I snuggle into bed and dive into my book. The minutes tick by without notice as I get more engrossed in this sexy CEO story. His new employee is giving him a very *hard* time and I like it. I'm well into chapter four, and this scene is heating things up. I feel a flush coming on when Shane stirs next to me.

"Adds?" He rubs at his eyes. His sleepy gaze scans my wet hair and oversized tee. I barely looked in the mirror and can only imagine what he's seeing. I attempt to fluff my damp locks and tug at the shirt's hem. Why am I suddenly modest? He's well acquainted with all my lady-bits after last night.

I give him a quick peck. "Hey, you."

"Why are you so far away? And dressed?" The pout on his lips is endearing, and I erase some of the space between us.

"Better?"

He kisses my cheek. "Why are you wearing clothes?"

I laugh. "It's just something I slipped on after showering."

"I was hoping you'd still be naked."

"Well," I start and bite my lip. "Someone woke me up early, and I figured why not get started with the day."

Shane goes a little pale. "Was I talking in my sleep?"

I wipe away the worry from his creasing forehead. "No, just snoring."

Now he gets a little pink. "Oh, uh, that's weird. Was it loud?"

I nod with a wince. "Just a bit."

"Shit, I'm sorry. I had no idea that was an issue for me."

"Don't fret, it hasn't been. Maybe you're stuffed up, or lying in a weird position."

"How long have you been up?"

"Uh"—I glance at the clock—"a few hours."

Concern dents his expression. "Why didn't you shake me? Cover my mouth and pinch my nose?"

I rub his bulky shoulder. "You looked so peaceful."

"I was thinking of you," Shane murmurs.

"Nude?"

"There might have been some reenactment of last night."

I fiddle with the blanket. "Do you have any regrets?"

He shakes his head wildly. "Absolutely not." He links our fingers together. "Only that we didn't have sex sooner."

I peek at him from under my lashes. "I wanted you to be certain, Rooks."

Shane presses his lips to my temple. "I've never been more sure of anything, Adds. Now more than ever, I know we were meant to cross paths."

"Yeah?"

"Undoubtedly, baby. You're part of my grand plan."

"So romantic," I mumble against his jaw. He's been calling me beautiful, gorgeous, and baby more often. Adds will always be my favorite, but the other names send a new thrill through me. I caress his shin with my toes, feeling treasured and cherished. I'm such a sap.

His nose brushes mine before he pulls away. "So, what were you doing before I woke up? You were blushing, Adds."

I dip my chin and giggle. "Um, I was reading."

Any remaining doubt thaws from his expression, and he peeks at my screen. "Anything good?"

"Well, Bastian—the hero—was just about to have his way with Athena—the heroine. You interrupted me at a peak moment, so to speak."

"That sounds promising." His gravelly tone scrapes along my heated skin, and I quiver.

My voice is all breathy when I say, "It really is."

Shane's fingers roam up my thigh, finding me bare under the cotton tee. "Guess you're not hiding too much."

"Those pesky barriers aren't necessary."

"Naughty girl. Hoping for another round?"

I toss my cell off to the side. "I was optimistic."

Shane continues lifting my shirt until it's a heap on the floor. "Much better."

He tugs me against him, his ever-present hard-on begging for attention. Now that the initial rush of having sex has settled, I'm ready to explore other options. As if there's a better idea with a willing Shane in bed. I drift my hand across his pecs and purr when the muscles flex. His touch is also wandering, each brush a tease to my hyper-aware system. His finger scrubs over a spot on my boob, and I glance down.

"You stinker," I gasp and bat him playfully. "I have a hickey."

Shane's gaze moves to my neck, and he smirks. "More than one."

My hands fly up and cover the offended area. "No way. People at work will see." I can already imagine what Marlene and Betty will spread around about this. How did I miss them in the mirror? Easy—I was too busy thinking about this guy.

He chuckles. "So? I made it pretty obvious what was going down last night. A few love bites aren't the most noticeable factor."

My lower belly heats recalling Shane's caveman tactics. "There's something about you all growly that gets me going." I bite my lip and let the fiery coals burn hotter. "Speaking of, we did things a bit backwards and missed some important milestones."

"Oh, yeah?"

"Uh-huh", I mumble and let my palm roam down his flexing abs. "Foreplay is really fun. Can I touch you?"

"Please do."

I push on his chest. "Lay flat and enjoy."

Shane doesn't hesitate, crossing his arms behind his head and relaxing onto the pillow. Massive biceps bulge, and I'm utterly distracted by the chiseled boulders. I want to nibble all around that perfectly defined man-meat. I'll get to that part later. There's another piece of his male anatomy that I want to become far more familiar with first.

There's a bottle of lotion within reach, and I pump a few squirts into my palm. "How convenient," I say and wink at him. Shane wags his brows and settles deeper into the mattress. I walk my fingers down his stomach, removing the sheet along the way. "I've been thinking of this since catching you in the bathroom."

"I told you to join me," he rasps.

"Next time. We'll start with this." I wrap my palm around his straining cock, coating him until he's slick. His hard length jerks in my grip, and I set a steady rhythm. I glide up and down, watching him disappear in my fist. He's steel sheathed in velvet, and the combination is mouthwatering. I tighten my grasp around his flared head before stroking along the shaft.

Shane snaps his neck back, corded muscles bunching. "Fuck, Adds. That feels too good."

"Is that a thing?"

"I'm gonna come embarrassingly fast," he hisses.

I rotate my hold and pump him faster. "That's the greatest compliment, Rooks." I kick it up another notch, his groan spurring me on. "Not to mention a huge turn-on."

"Fuck, baby. Oh, shit," he moans.

In the next beat, Shane's release coats my hand. The white ropes keep pulsing out, and the sight is so freaking erotic. In this moment, I want him covering all of me. He curses long and low, punching his hips up and up as the euphoria takes over. I know that high and shift my legs with residual effect. All too soon, Shane floats back to reality. He blinks lazily at me, his honey eyes bleary.

"Damn, you're good at that," he chokes out.

I hum, still fondling him. "It was just a few flicks of my wrists. Nothing fancy... yet."

That earns me a slow smile, dimples included. "It was everything, Adds. And I can't wait for more."

"Me either."

Shane grabs my discarded shirt and helps wipe off my palm. "Damn, that was a lot. Sorry, beautiful." He kisses me softly, and I suck on his bottom lip.

"I didn't mind. But that tee might need to be replaced."

He quirks a brow. "Maybe you'll finally wear one of mine."

I click my tongue. "Would you like that?"

"Fuck, yes."

"It'll go great with my hickeys."

Shane growls deep in his chest. "I love you talking like that."

"You wanna possess me, Rooks?" I shiver at the thought, enjoying it far too much.

His thumb traces around the marks on my neck. "Only if you allow it."

I lean into his touch. "Does that go both ways?"

Shane's eyes flare, igniting into roaring flames. "I've always been yours for the taking."

"That's so sexy," I murmur against his mouth.

Then he's on me, pushing my body into the memory foam. His big body settles between my legs, and I arch into him. He licks down my throat, heading straight south.

"Your turn, Adds."

CHAPTER 19

SHANE
Woof

I end the call and pocket my cell. My smile feels like it's overtaking my entire face. Addison is going to be surprised and hopefully excited. If all goes well, this will be one more step that solidifies our future together. But hey, I'll settle for another blowjob.

Adjusting myself is mandatory after thinking about her red lips sucking me off. Addison's mouth around my dick has to be the sexiest fucking sight. Hot fucking damn. She gives herself to me so willingly, over and over. I had zero comprehension of pleasure until Addison came into my life. Now I'm tapping into euphoria on the daily, and she's in the driver's seat. I'm constantly thanking the heavens and stars above for showing me the path to her.

I should probably be seeking forgiveness, but there's no guilt weighing me down. I can't find an ounce to be sorry for when it comes to Addison. The shackles once holding me captive have released, and I'm free from the burden. I've never been more grateful.

The day is ours for the taking, and I'm ready to get moving. My other half isn't quite with me, though. I plop down on the couch and prepare to wait. Addison wanted to change after her lunch shift, which gave me a chance to confirm my plans. I've been meaning to do something special for her. She's already done so much for me. I'm hoping this will step things up a notch or ten.

Addison walks into the room, and my breathing stalls. Will I ever get used to this sight? I'm betting not. She's left her hair down, maybe for me. I made my preference obvious by continuously playing with the silky strands. It's become an automatic response when she uses me as a pillow after we have sex. Over the last ten days, my fingers are buried in her luscious locks more often than not.

Of course she catches me staring and flips a few waves over her shoulder. "Hey, Rooks."

"Looking good, Adds." I stand and meet her near the kitchen. I dip my mouth to hers, unable to resist getting a taste of those red lips. "In the mood for a little drive?"

Her green eyes light up. "Did you find another trunk on Marketplace?"

I chuckle and shake my head. She loves her bargain finds, especially when it comes to furniture and home goods. Scouting out random items with her is something I've come to enjoy. But not today.

I tug on her belt loop. "I thought we could check out Furry Tales."

"The animal shelter in Rove Maple?"

"Yeah, that's the one."

"Why?" Suspicion paints Addison's tone.

"A new adventure?" My words hold more truth than I'm letting on.

She squints at me. "I used to volunteer there."

"Oh?" I keep my expression blank, attempting to play nonchalant. The lady on the phone told me Addison was their best worker.

"Uh-huh, in high school. I loved it."

"Why'd you leave?"

She shrugs. "I started full-time at Dagos and couldn't keep up with both."

"Do you ever go back?"

"It hurts my heart." She winces. "I want to take them all home."

I draw her into me, and Addison nuzzles against my chest. "You never did?"

"My parents wouldn't let me. These days my schedule is too erratic and unpredictable."

I kiss her forehead. "Well, let's go visit."

She offers a half smile. "All right, Rooks. If you're trying to make me cry, we could just watch that Humane Society commercial."

My gut clenches and I suck in sharply. If she cries, I'm hoping they're happy tears. Maybe this isn't such a grand idea.

Addison nudges me. "We going now?"

"Um, sure."

She laughs. "I'll be fine, don't worry. I'm not gonna burst into a puddle. If nothing else, it will be nice to see Donna and snuggle with some pooches."

I spoke with the director earlier, and her glee practically burst through the speaker. This will be a glance into Addison's past I wasn't expecting when starting down this path.

"We can leave if you're too sad," I suggest. I'm really banking on the opposite being true.

Addison waves me off. "It'll be fine. We can eat dinner at the Tavern. It's this adorable little restaurant and my favorite small-town dive. Don't tell Grayson." She laughs. "They serve an avocado cream cheese sandwich and it's so delicious."

Stopping there might be more challenging than she thinks, but I agree. I shrug into my coat and help Addison slip hers on. We lock up the love nest and head out to my truck. I'm familiar with the drive after our date at Alma Grassa.

She reaches for my hand, and I lace our fingers together. "Thanks for thinking of this."

"Something new for us to do."

Addison winks at me. "Guess we can't always be having sex."

I nibble on her knuckles. "I'm sure we can find an abandoned storage room somewhere."

"That sounds promising."

"Yeah?"

"Expand our horizons."

I chuckle. "Is that what we're calling it?"

"Yup, being creative is the best way to keep things fresh in a couple. I don't want you to ever feel like things are getting stale."

Now I'm full out laughing. "Adds, I had sex for the first time last week. We can do it missionary for a year and I won't be bored. But trust me, we can be plenty inventive."

Her green eyes sparkle from across the cab. "Okay."

And I'm getting hard. I blow out a heavy breath and think of puppies. The tingling heat in my lower half subsides, and I steer the conversation onto non-naked activities. "Are you excited for Thanksgiving?"

Addison chews on her nail. "Uh, yeah, but I'm not prepared at all. Raven assigned me to appetizers, and I've been stalking Pinterest for the best recipes."

We're celebrating the holiday with her friends in a few days. Trey was surprisingly agreeable to hosting at their house. Apparently his fiancé offered up some special cupcakes, just for him.

I squeeze her hand. "How about Norwegian sushi?"

"I need something more than pickle rollups."

"What about those little cranberry puff things?"

Addison nods. "Yeah, those looked interesting. I'm planning on at least four dishes."

"You know there's only six of us, right?"

She shoves my shoulder lightly. "Yes, smarty pants. But this is the first Thanksgiving my parents won't be in town, so I'm trying to make it special."

I kiss her wrist, trying to ignore the pressure in my chest. "I'm sorry, Adds. We'll make it a celebration to never forget."

She gives me a wobbly smile. "Thanks, Rooks. I know you will."

I want to tell her we're family now, but maybe that's too much.

One day I hope that's the case, to soothe this remaining ache. And the sooner, the better. What I feel for her is only getting stronger, this visceral bond well established inside of me.

We pull into the shelter's parking lot, and I cut the engine. I touch Addison's chin, and she leans closer, brushing our lips together. I drag my tongue out and taste the apple gloss she has on. After sucking a little more off, I pull away before things get out of control.

"There's a bit more to this experience," I whisper into the small gap separating our mouths.

Addison hums, her eyes closed. "Is that so?"

I brush my thumb up her jawline. "Yeah, baby. It's a big surprise."

Her jade gaze pops open wide, and she reaches for the door. "Well, let's go."

I grin and let her joy wash over me. My girl loves this stuff. I nod toward the building. "After you."

Addison practically sprints inside, ice coating the pavement or not. Donna is waiting at the entrance with her arms spread wide. The women share a hug and warm greetings. Their easy affection is a reminder of more I've missed. I don't have this connection with anyone from my past. I rub at the sting in my throat and avert my gaze, giving them a moment to catch up.

"And you must be Shane." Donna extends a hand, and we exchange a quick shake.

"It's nice to meet you," I start. "Thanks for setting this up."

Addison looks at us with a raised brow. "I'm out of the loop."

"Answers are right this way." Donna gestures down the hall.

We follow close behind, Addison almost vibrating beside me. I slide my palm against hers, and she relaxes slightly. Donna leads us into a private room with a large pet crate in the corner. She walks over to it and opens the metal gate. An adorable ball of wiggly fur tumbles out and darts toward us.

"He's an—"

"Australian Retriever," Addison finishes for me. "How did you know I love them?"

"Adds, it's no secret you often seek out this breed in your random searches."

She shrugs sheepishly. "I suppose. She bends down and scoops him up. He's so precious. Look at this face."

I offer an amused grumble. "Should I be jealous?"

Addison elbows me. "You're hilarious. Thank you for this. I've only seen this cross in pictures."

"You like him?"

She nods into his speckled fur, their freckles blending. "How could I not? He's so sweet."

"Good, because he's yours."

She freezes, but her gaze jumps to mine. "What's that?"

"You've always wanted a dog," I begin.

"Well, yeah, but—"

"Adds, I know you have an inconsistent schedule working at a bar," I cut in, well aware this is her typical reason. I have bullet points prepared, more than ready to argue my case. "But I live with you now. Jack said the pup could hang out at the garage while I'm there. He thinks having a cute dog will help bring in more customers." We both laugh at that. "He can join us on our runs and get plenty of exercise. There's a dog park five miles from our place. Plus, he needs a loving home. He came all the way from North Carolina, the only survivor from his litter."

She blinks moisture from her eyes. "That's quite the speech. You've been thinking a lot about this."

"I have. I think this little guy is a great addition to our love nest."

She sniffs. "He really is. What should we name him?"

"How about Dustin? Dusty for short?"

"From *Stranger Things*?"

"They have similar hair," I point out.

Addison ruffles the curls. "Dustin is perfect." She snuggles him tighter, and he licks her face. She giggles, and he squirms higher, using her tit as a step stool. Smart dog.

I hold my hands out. "Pass him over." I take my turn petting Dustin until Donna returns.

"All settled?" she asks.

"Yes," we answer in unison.

"Great." She claps. "I'll just take him for a final check-up and meet you out front in about twenty minutes. Feel free to hang out in here or grab a coffee in the lounge."

After a group hug, with Dustin squished between us, we let Donna take him away. Addison stays cuddling against me. "How will I ever repay you for such a gift?"

"You already have."

She looks up and grins. "You've made me very happy, Rooks. Maybe I can think of a new way to make *you* happy."

I swallow roughly. "Getting creative?"

She swipes along her lower lip, stained in ruby-red. "Should we find out how smear-proof this color is?" She tilts closer to whisper in my ear. "Maybe on your dick."

White spots dot my vision from the instant blood loss to my brain. "Now?" I choke.

"We're about to be preoccupied with a puppy. Better get our kicks while we can. It'll be fast," she promises.

"Oh, I have no doubt about that." My imagination is already running wild, and I'm harder than a steel pipe. I might come from the thought alone.

"Are you up for it?"

I'm nodding so fast my neck might snap. "Yes, absolutely. Yup, this is an excellent idea." I glance around the small space, searching for an alcove or more discrete area.

"There's a very private bathroom down the hall," Addison purrs. "There's even a couch."

I tug her to the door. "Then why are we still standing in here?"

She laughs. "I knew you'd have a pinch of kinky."

I bite her earlobe. "I've been dreaming about that red lipstick all over my cock."

Addison grips me through my jeans. "Me too. Looks like our wish is coming true."

CHAPTER 20

ADDISON
Festive

I extend my arms to get more warmth from the crackling flames. Nothing screams December like a winter bonfire, at least in Garden Grove. They're a seasonal staple and thrown into the festivities with Santa and his reindeer. Everyone who is anyone around here has attended at least one by the first weekend of this month. I've already been to three. What can I say? I've got the holiday spirit.

Charcoal and pine fill the air, infusing my system with more cheer. I have a candle that smells similar, but nothing beats the real deal. Nostalgia sinks into my bones, and I smile despite the cold wind swirling around me.

We're all gathering at one of the designated spots in Grove Park and make quite the bunch. This is a town-sponsored event open to the masses, and there's enough bench-seating to host us all. A few more people join the circle, adding to the impressive turnout. Some folks are passing out apple cider and marshmallows. Others dole out extra blankets. It might be below zero, but we hardly seem to notice.

The fire is massive but controlled. We take safety very seriously around these parts. I huff and shake my head, hearing an echo of my dad repeating those words. He's probably on some beach drinking a margarita instead of ankle-deep in the snow. I'd say he's missing out, but my grin wilts into a frown.

"What's wrong, Addy?" Delilah asks from beside me.

I offer a limp shrug. "Just thinking about my mom and dad. I doubt they're coming home for the holidays, which kinda sucks."

Raven rubs my shoulder. "I'm sorry, friend. We can be parentless together."

"Your mom isn't stopping by?"

She scoffs. "And leave her European villa? I won't hold my breath. I'm used to this, and it's better for everyone."

Delilah nods. "Yup, we can start our own traditions. Thanksgiving was a hit."

Raven sighs wistfully. "Trey won't admit it, but he enjoyed having the house full. I think it reminded him of celebrations with his family."

"Ohhh," I coo. "What a softie. Next he'll be after you to fill the rooms with babies."

Raven coughs into her fist, steam rising from the effort. "Uh, I dunno about all that."

"Oh, whatever," Delilah says. "We'll all be barefoot and pregnant soon enough."

"Speak for yourselves," I mutter.

She elbows me. "Don't pretend. You and Shane have been bumping uglies for a month. You're a smitten kitten." Delilah bites the air, and we all giggle.

"Am not." I dip my chin, feeling a flush rising. Of course they notice.

"She's already in love," Raven stage-whispers.

"Called it," Delilah adds.

I clear my throat and shift slowly. There's no point in denying the obvious, yet I don't need to come right out and admit it. Dusty is curled up on my lap under a blanket, acting as my personal heating source and perfect distraction.

Delilah points to the puffy lump. "Seriously, he's the best present ever."

"Right? My man did good," I reply.

Raven claps her mitten-clad hands. "See? He already gave you a baby of sorts. Counts for something."

I roll my eyes. "Yeah, I'll settle for this fur-baby."

"Not sure how he'll top it for Christmas," Delilah says.

"Probably ask her to marry him," Raven replies.

I shake my head so fast, the knit hat almost falls off. "Ummm, no. Didn't we just go over this? We haven't even said the L-word."

Delilah waves my words away. "That doesn't matter."

I poke her arm. "Does to me. I want to make sure we're forever. I only plan to be engaged once."

They share an eye roll. "Pretty sure that's everyone's plan," Raven points out.

Delilah nods. "Yeah, it's not like anyone wants a divorce."

"You're proving my point. Marriage is not on our radar. I'm fine living in non-matrimony," I say and try to inject confidence in my voice. The truth is, I'm falling crazy hard for Shane, and he's my one. I feel that fact down to my roots. He fulfills all my needs, and I've never been more satisfied. I clench my thighs until they burn. Shane should be off work soon, then the real fun begins.

"Okay," Raven starts. "Let's plan Christmas. Who knows when we'll all be together again with Holi-Daze starting next week."

Delilah rubs her temples. "Oh, man. I'm scared, Rave."

Raven pats her knee. "You're a boss, D. We've got this. No festival can defeat us, even the busiest one of all."

"My feet hurt just thinking about it," Delilah complains.

"I found these gel-pad inserts that fit in any shoe, even heels. They save my ass every shift, especially the doubles I'm gonna be pulling. I'll get you both some," I say.

Raven sends me an air kiss. "Thanks, boo."

"That would be magical. And Zeke promised to help out with the rush at Jitters." Delilah's comment seems mostly for her own sake.

"Just think of the funds," I say, and we all hum happily.

Delilah does a little dance. "We can take a vacay. All six of us."

"Oh, yes! There's this cabin resort up north, and it looks stunning. The layout is massive. We'd all get our own wing. It's nestled in the middle of nowhere so plenty of privacy. A perfect winter retreat," Raven says.

"We could go in January after things slow down," I suggest.

"That will give me enough time to secure coverage for Jitters. I'll train Emery while she's on break from college." Delilah fist-pumps at her brilliant plan, and we laugh.

"Is she sticking around until classes resume?" I ask. I haven't seen Delilah's sister since summer. It'd be nice to catch up with her.

"Yup." Delilah pops her P. "Zeke is trying to make a love connection happen for Ryan. Second chances and all."

"Oh, that's sweet. Will Emery go for it?" He's had a crush on that girl since high school. I take a sip of hot cocoa, and the flavor bursts on my tongue. Delicious.

Delilah shrugs. "She's still in her wild phase. If she ends up moving back to Garden Grove, I give them a decent shot."

"Only time will tell," I murmur, and flutters erupt in my stomach. There's so much truth in that simple saying. Dusty wiggles on my legs, and I readjust.

"He's a good sleeper," Delilah says.

I slide my hand under the blanket and stroke his soft fur. He licks my palm and nuzzles into me. "Dusty is such a good boy. I think he had a traumatic start to life. Now he's finally able to relax."

Delilah taps her chin. "Maybe I should buy Zeke a dog for Christmas. We used to talk about getting one someday, but that was eons ago."

"You should. He or she can be the Jitters mascot. And we can go to the dog park together." I almost bounce in my seat thinking about all the pup-fun. I swing my gaze to Raven. "Does Trey want a pup?"

She tilts her head. "Um, maybe. We have a nice backyard for one. You're quite the doggie-dealer, Addy."

I laugh. "Having Dusty is so great. I want you both to have that happy, too. Have you finished Christmas shopping?"

Delilah sticks out tongue. "Ugh, no. Not at all."

"I'm getting a lot of stuff online, but Trey wants this special toolkit from Farm Fleet. I'm hoping to get out there tomorrow," Raven says.

"I don't know what to get Shane," I whine.

"Make him a coupon book," Delilah offers.

I imagine crafting some X-rated options and giggle. "Oh my gosh, that's hilarious." Hurt flashes across her expression and I cringe. "I was just envisioning the possibilities. That's a really cute idea."

"I gave Zeke one in high school. He never used them all." Delilah shrugs.

"Was there an expiration date?" I ask.

Her brow wrinkles. "No."

I snap my fingers. "Tell him to dust that bad boy off and get redeeming."

She purses her lips. "Very funny. Why don't you make Shane a keychain for the love nest? Return the favor."

I dig in my pocket, fiddling with the bolt and screw. "I could try finding something at Dagos, where we first met."

Raven blinks quickly. "So romantic. I like it." She grabs a stick and spears three marshmallows. She holds them low over the embers and asks, "S'mores?"

Delilah and I nod. I watch the white gooey-goodness cook, and my thoughts drift to Shane. I tap on my phone and send him quick text.

Me: Hey, I miss you.

His response is immediate.

Shane: I was about to message you. I'm about done. Miss you lots, Adds.
Me: You still coming to the fire?
Shane: Yup. How's our guy?
Me: He's taking a nap, curled up in my lap.
Shane: Lucky mutt. :)
Me: Maybe you'll steal his spot soon.
Shane: Damn straight. He can keep it warm until then. XX
Me: OO

Delilah nudges me. "Remember when he wouldn't answer you?"

I glare at her. "Hardy, har. Thanks for the reminder, D."

Raven finishes assembling the s'mores and hands them over. "I'm sure glad you got that crap sorted. We have an awesome sixsome."

Delilah cracks up. "Wow, that sounds crowded. I've never even tried a threesome."

Raven scowls. "Such a dirty bird."

I take a big bite of melty chocolate perfection and moan. "That's why we love her, the filthy entertainment. You provide the sugary snacks. Seriously, how do you make this taste better than any I've ever made?" I say with a full mouth.

Raven finishes her s'mores and brushes off her shoulders. "It's all the love. Plus, I snuck in a mini peanut butter cup."

"Genius." I suck the leftovers off my fingers.

"Best in the business," Delilah brags.

"Thanks, friends. It's all about being inventive and trying new things," Raven replies.

My cheeks heat thinking about my recent exploits and adventures. "Trying new things is definitely exciting."

"Not sure I wanna know. Let's talk about Christmas plans instead, with our sixsome," Raven says.

Delilah raises her hand. "I volunteer."

"Don't you spend it with your family?" I ask.

"We always celebrate on the eve. I'm wide open on Christmas Day," she informs us.

"That's what she said," I say.

"Nice one." Raven holds up a hand and we high-five.

Delilah grins. "I'll be here all night. Anyways, we can definitely host. I'll set up dinner in the apartment, then we can go down to Jitters for some masterbaking."

Raven points at me. "Bring more pickle rollups. Those things are so yummy."

"That was all Shane." I giggle. "I figured they were too basic."

"No way. I couldn't get enough. You can be in charge of appetizers again," Raven says.

"Okay," I agree. "Done and done."

"Speaking of pickles, how's the sex?" Delilah asks.

I nearly spit out my drink. "Way to be blunt, D. Jeez, give a girl some warning."

"You know that's not how I play. So, was all the waiting worth it?" she prods.

I can't control a dopey grin from spreading across my face. "Uh, yeah. We're very compatible." They hoot loudly, and I shush them. "Marlene and Betty are over there. For old ladies, they have supersonic hearing. Be quiet."

"Puh-lease." Delilah grins. "Let them listen. Maybe it will give them a joyful boost."

I cringe. "Gross, no. They can get their kicks elsewhere."

"So, you've been busy making up for lost time?" Delilah wags her brows.

"Have you?" I shoot back.

She rolls her eyes. "Yeah, yeah. Aren't we all."

"Everything is going great, thanks for asking. It's going to be a holly and jolly holiday," I laugh.

Raven fans her face even though it's freezing outside. "Yes, girl. Welcome to the happy lady-bits club."

Strong arms wrap around me from behind, mindful of the pooch on my lap. My favorite woodsy cologne filters into the air, and I inhale greedily. I snuggle deeper into his embrace and sigh.

"What are you girls talking about?" Shane murmurs.

My friends go quiet, and I laugh. "Isn't it obvious?"

He leans closer and whispers in my ear, "Are you telling them all my secrets?"

I lick my dry lips. "Maybe."

"Guess we'll have to make more."

"Starting now?"

Shane chuckles, and the gritty sound shoots straight to my lower belly. "I wouldn't want to interrupt anything."

Delilah gives me a light shove. "You're not. Take her away and have fun. Make *love* all night." Her emphasis on that pesky L-word has me wincing. She reaches for Dusty and cuddles him close. "I'll watch this cutie-pie so he doesn't get traumatized."

I laugh and allow Shane to scoop me off the bench seat. He leads me toward the table piled with food. "I'll at least take you to dinner first."

I pinch his butt. "I'll save extra room for dessert."

CHAPTER 21

SHANE
Bonus

I slam the hood closed and exhale roughly, scrubbing over my weary eyes. I've lost track of what number car this is for me today. We're like a damn assembly line this week. I finish one, and the next comes rolling in. Fuck, even my fingernails are tired… and pitch black.

After grabbing a rag, I wipe off some excess grease. I adjust my hat, flipping it backwards. For being the middle of winter, it's hot as hell in here. The only thing keeping me going at this point is the clock, the overtime pay is rolling in. The extra funds will let me spoil Addison a little more.

I force my feet forward and drop the paperwork off on Jack's desk. I scan the check-in log and smile. One more job to go and I'm done. That gives me an added boost to get this shit over with. Then I get to see my girl.

"What the fuck are you so happy about?" Trey calls from across the garage.

I hitch a thumb toward the lot, where a blue Ford should be parked. "Last one for the day."

"Sucks to be you. I'm outta here."

"Looks like I'll be getting employee of the month," I joke.

Trey grunts. "No such thing. I'd settle for a bonus. Jack should be able to afford it after this month."

A vision of the gift I want for Addison flashes in my mind. Another big check would get me one step closer to buying it. "I wouldn't turn it down."

"Well, no shit." He flips through the list of tickets on our main clipboard. "Did I tell you so or what? This is so much worse than a few weeks ago. Fortunately for both of us, we live with our women."

I kick at the stained concrete. "Yeah, but that's not enough. Addison is busting ass at Dagos. Other than sleeping in the same bed, I feel like we're barely crossing paths."

"Oh, poor rookie. Getting laid isn't enough?"

I flick him off. "Fuck that. It's about more than sex." Stolen moments between the sheets isn't nearly enough. It feels rushed and cheated.

Trey shakes his head, but he's smiling. "Yeah, yeah. Feelings and mush, I know. I put a ring on it."

"Set a date yet?"

He scratches the back of his neck. "Some weekend in June. I told

Raven I'd be in charge of the booze."

I chuckle. "How helpful."

Trey dusts off his hands. "Do what I can."

"Lucky Raven," I say with another laugh.

"I hear no complaints." He crosses his arms, not making a move to leave.

I take a step toward the door, making the decision for us. "Gonna grab that car."

Trey clears his throat. "Hold up. Whatcha doing Sunday?"

I tilt my head and study him. Trey has been more chummy lately, which suits me fine. Must be Raven's continued influence. Doesn't hurt that I'm a part of their group now. I'm hoping to be a permanent fixture.

"I barely know what's happening tomorrow. Why?"

"Jack insists we take the day off, jobs piling up or not."

I shrug, my pulse picking up thinking of the possibilities. "Probably spend time with Adds."

Treys rolls his eyes. "Duh, rookie. I'm aware you prefer to be inseparable. You two should come ice fishing."

"You have a house?"

"Jack set his up last weekend. He gave me the keys."

I whistle. "Nice. I'm down for sure. Can all six of us fit?"

He laughs. "Yeah, Jack doesn't mess around. He's got the deluxe trailer."

"Tell me when and where."

"It's on Grove Gulley. We'll figure the rest out later. I'm beat and gotta get home," Trey mumbles.

"Good plan. Take it easy," I say.

"Later, rookie. Don't work too hard."

Trey strolls out, and I follow close behind to fetch the vehicle. The ramp buzzes as I get the car lifted. I'm opening the valves when Jack walks in.

"Hey, boss. Didn't know you were hanging around."

"Just got back from a tow. About to head out for the night." He pats my back in a very brotherly gesture, or how I imagine close family behaves. His warm acceptance always does something funny to my soul. It's nice to feel like I'm part of the clan.

"I can close everything up," I offer.

"Final job?" He spins the tire.

"Yup. Shouldn't take more than an hour."

"Good. It's already late. I really appreciate you guys going above and beyond. I couldn't run this shop without you. Having reliable workers to count on means everything."

Jack's words make me stand a little straighter. "Thanks, boss. Happy to have this job," I tell him honestly.

He knocks on the car's frame. "Your dedication shows. Hopefully you don't quit after this long haul."

I shake my head. "Nah, can't get rid of me that easily."

"Good." Jack squints at me, the corner of his eyes crinkling. "How's your roommate, rookie?"

"You know she's more than that." I smirk while thinking about my girl. She's closing the bar tonight, which means I won't get more than a few words with her until much later.

LASS

"Like razzing you. The love is clear across your face." I flatten my expression and he laughs. "No use hiding it, Marlene and Betty caught wind. They'll probably help plan the wedding."

He's joking, but the suggestion sinks in, and I don't mind it one bit. Jack is the one person I can talk to about this. "I've, uh, actually been thinking of asking Addison. Do you think it's too soon?"

He pats my shoulder. "Nah. When you know, you know. Time is just a number. Don't waste it wondering if enough has gone by."

"So wise," I say.

His sharp chuckle echoes off the concrete. "Most would tell you different."

"Not sure I believe that."

"Water under the bridge, I suppose. Anyway, I'll leave you to it. Don't need to keep you longer than I already have."

I notice the dark circles under his eyes and the wrinkles marring his forehead. "You okay, Jack?"

He brushes off my comment. "Don't worry about me. This is just a tough time of year, too many memories."

I inhale a ragged breath, his meaning resonating deep inside of me. I rub at the ache in my chest and smear oil on my coveralls. "Wanna meet for a beer in a bit?"

Jack smiles, but it doesn't reach his eyes. "Dagos?"

I look at my feet and shrug. "That's my plan."

"Sure, rookie. I'll meet you there." He saunters off with a wave.

I dive into my toolbox, ready to get this shit done. A few moments later, the bell in the lobby rings.

"Forget something?" I call out.

It's silent for a beat, and I turn toward the door, ready to investigate.

"You, Rooks."

I gape at Addison draping herself against the doorframe. Her sultry pose gets me hard in a split second. There's no use trying to hide my reaction, the sparkle in her green eyes says she's well aware.

"W-what are you doing here?"

She slowly unzips her coat and steps into the garage. "Am I interrupting?"

I feel my eyes bulge at her low-cut shirt. Her tits are on full display, and my tongue lolls out. Hard nipples poke through the thin red material, and it's obvious she's not wearing a bra. She's wearing a skirt and stockings, both molding to her curves in a seductive package. Holy shit, am I dreaming?

She giggles. "I take it this is a good surprise."

I'm nodding fast. "Yup. Still not sure this is actually happening."

Addison saunters toward me, and her heels click on the floor. Each soft tap reverberates against my ribs, and it's difficult to breathe. She drags her nails up my sides, locking those wandering fingers behind my neck. "Oh, I'm very real." She kisses my throat, and I shudder.

"How are you here?"

"Myla wanted to switch shifts. I couldn't agree fast enough. Raven let me borrow her keys." She plays with the ends of my hair, tugging lightly. Her fingers roam up until she knocks the hat off my head. Fuck, that feels amazing.

A rumble escapes me, and I clench my fists tighter. "You're too good for me. What did I do to deserve this?"

"You're so pure," she whispers. "My saint."

I shake my head. "I can't claim that title."

"You can for me." She sways back and forth, rubbing against me in all the right places. I tremble when she bumps her pelvis against mine.

"Well, you're my blessing. My angel."

"No," Addison murmurs with red cheeks. "You give me too much credit."

"I don't give you nearly enough," I confess.

Her lips lift, smiling against mine. "You make me so happy."

"At least I'm doing something right."

"Touch me, Rooks. I don't like this distance."

I flip my palms over, showing her the grime. "My hands are filthy. I'll get you covered in grease."

"I don't mind getting dirty."

"Fuck, I love you." I wrap my arms around her and haul her against me. Addison clings to me and tries to burrow even further.

"Really?" Her voice is far too unsure for my liking.

I tip up her chin so she's looking at me. "I love you, Addison Jaymes. I was ready to tell you that first day at Dagos, crazy as it would have been. But that's the honest truth."

"Hmmm." She collapses into my embrace. "That's good because I'm crazy in love with you."

Those three words are a balm to my scars, healing the past and feeding the future. She loves me. My chest expands and threatens to crack wide open. I want her to reach in and take my heart into her hands. That beating organ hasn't belonged to me in years.

I press our lips together, sealing the promise between us. My hips rock into her, and I need these clothes stripped off five minutes ago. "I'm gonna show you how much."

"I was hoping you'd offer that," she murmurs and stretches her neck. I drift my nose up that silky column, adding nips and nibbles along the way.

"Always. I only wish we were somewhere else. It'll be hard to properly express myself while covered in grit."

"But these coveralls are sexy," she says against my mouth.

I swallow roughly, nearly choking when she cups me through my pants. "Yeah?"

"So hot. My pure saint all grungy and rough."

My knees almost buckle. "Jesus, Adds. Someone's feeling frisky."

"I couldn't wait for you to get home. The love nest was getting lonely," she pouts.

I grip her thighs and lift until she cinches her legs around my waist. "I'm so fucking glad you came, Adds. You're always welcome here."

She bites my earlobe, and I squeeze her ass. "Maybe you should show me the break room?"

I chuckle against her jaw. "We don't have one, baby."

Addison looks over her shoulder. "That table will do. This should be fast."

I hustle over to the flat surface and clear it off with a sweep before setting her down. Her spread center is at the perfect height. I pull at the spandex covering her lower half. "How do I get this shit off?"

She brings my hand to her covered pussy. "Rip the seam," she instructs and bows into me.

I don't hesitate, and the flimsy material tears under my strength. Addison yanks open my coveralls and dips her fingers into my jeans. With a flick of her wrist, my dick is in her tiny hand, and I'm dizzy with need.

"Fuck, Adds. Take me out," I beg.

She does, listening to the lust coating my words. The cool air stings my scorching skin, but I ignore it. In another second, I'm sliding deep into her warmth, and the cold is instantly forgotten.

"Oh, oh," Addison chants. "Yes, right there."

I'm pounding into her, not giving either of us a chance to adjust. I'm going full fucking speed ahead, racing to the finish line. "You're so fucking wet, Adds. Been thinking about me?"

"All day, so much. I need this," she whines and bucks into me.

"I'll always fulfill your needs." I jerk her shirt up and confirm my suspicions.

"No bra? You're my naughty angel."

"I love driving you crazy."

I thrust faster, and the table crashes into the wall, rattling a shelf of tools. I sweep my palm up her stomach, leaving a black trail behind. I pluck her nipple, and Addison clamps down on my cock. Her tits smeared in grease is my undoing, and I lose the grip on my control.

"Yes, Rooks. There, there!" she wails.

I'm spilling inside of her tightness while she pulses around me, milking me of everything. Our moans fill the otherwise silent space, giving away our bout of exertion. I draw Addison into me and kiss her temple. Her forehead rests on my pounding chest.

She releases a long sigh. "Wow, it just keeps getting better."

"Just imagine what happens next."

Her green eyes lift to mine. "I'm ready."

CHAPTER 22

ADDISON
Whoops

I reel in the slack and check the bobber, waiting for the slightest dip. I watch the fishing rod for any movement, but there's not even a wiggle. With a sigh, I prop it up in the cup holder. The guys left us in charge and ran to get lunch. Big surprise, we haven't been very successful. The fish haven't been biting, enjoying a lazy Sunday like the rest of us. But this experience has been a blast, regardless of our lack in catch.

Jack's ice house is small but cozy. The heater in the corner is doing a great job keeping us warm. The three of us are huddled on the futon under a wooly comforter. Dusty is curled up by our feet, taking a snooze. That pup knows how to weekend like a boss. I pop another chip into my mouth and munch away. Almost immediately, another painful lash sears through my chest, and I wince.

Delilah scoots away from me. "Seriously, what's your deal? Hard gas?"

I shove her and stick out my tongue. "You're a brat. I'm having heartburn."

"I didn't know you have that," Raven says. "My mom used to have bad episodes especially after really spicy or salty foods." They both stare pointedly at my snack.

I lift the bag. "Dill pickle chips are life. I've been craving them like crazy lately."

Delilah lifts a brow. "Yeah, I can tell. You've almost polished them off."

"I'm hungry, okay? The guys need to hurry up with real food. Then I'll put the bag down."

"If there's any left," Delilah whispers to Raven.

"Hey," I snap. "Be nice."

Raven tilts her head. "You feeling all right, Adds? You seem a little... testy."

I shove more chips in my mouth and chew loudly. "Other than this acid reflux, being super tired and cranky from working nonstop, PMS, and my friends ganging up on me? I'm dandy."

They wince and remain silent. Good, maybe I can catch a quick nap. I scoop up Dusty, settle deeper into the cushions, and lean my head back. Just as I'm dozing off, a putrid stench wafts over to me.

I slap a palm over my mouth, trying not to gag. "Ugh, what stinks something fierce? I might barf." Nausea roils in my stomach, and I take a few deep breaths.

My friends sniff the air, seeming to feign indifference. "It's not so bad," Raven says.

"It's the same dead-fish aroma we've been stewing in for hours," Delilah says.

I wave a hand in front of my face. "No, this is something really nasty. Like rotten eggs mixed with vomit."

Raven wrinkles her nose. "Ew, that sounds gross. I don't smell anything, though."

"Maybe it's all those dill pickles," Delilah suggests.

I swallow the rapidly pooling saliva and cough roughly. "Very funny, biatch. I might need to step outside."

"It's five degrees," Raven reminds me.

"I'll risk it," I toss back.

Raven passes me a bottle of water. "Maybe you're dehydrated."

I chug some down, and my stomach settles slightly. "Thanks, that helps."

Delilah pats my back. "Hopefully it doesn't come back."

"No kidding, that was foul. I hate throwing up, and it was a close call." I tug at my collar, the temperature spiking suddenly. Good grief, what's the issue with this place? I finish the rest of my water and burp, cringing as the pickle flavor makes a second appearance. Something passes between them, then they look at me.

"What?" I eye them.

"When was your last period?" Delilah asks.

"I dunno. When was yours? We always sync up," I reply.

She purses her lips. "Aunt Flo paid me a visit last week."

"Hmm, weird. I guess we got off track." I shrug.

Delilah taps her chin. "Uh-huh, that's one option. Or you're late."

My gasp is silly loud. "Are you suggesting I'm pregnant?"

Raven holds up a hand. "Is it really that far off base?"

"You've listed a bunch of symptoms, Addy," Delilah unhelpfully points out.

I strike through the air. "Not possible, I'm on the shot."

"Birth control isn't a guarantee. When's your next injection?" Raven asks.

I glare at the ceiling and count backwards. As the dates calculate, I let my jaw go slack. "No fucking way," I mutter. We haven't used a condom once, but I was protected. Until I wasn't. In our haste to tear each other's clothes off, the topic never came up.

My friends both blurt, "What?"

I blink away the blur from my vision. "I let it lapse. How the hell could I be so stupid?" This is the type of careless shit you hear about on bad reality television. Now it's my life? Fuck.

Raven rubs my shoulder. "You've been really preoccupied, Addy. Don't be so hard on yourself. This stuff happens."

"No, it doesn't. I don't need you letting me off easy," I mumble.

Delilah rolls her eyes. "Okay, wenchie. You should have paid better attention and gotten your ass to the doctor."

"Thanks," I grumble.

Raven stands and starts packing up. "It's not for sure. Let's get some tests."

I nod quickly. "Yeah, okay. Good idea. Does it really happen that fast? I feel like this is coming out of nowhere."

Delilah peers over at me. "Is it, though? It only takes once to get pregnant. You guys have probably been going at it nonstop."

I give her a light shove. "I know how reproduction works."

"Just checking," she replies.

I puff up my cheeks and blow all the air out slowly. "I don't need to freak out yet."

Raven rubs my back. "Exactly. And no matter what, you'll be fine."

"I'm not so sure about that," I mumble.

We all bundle up in a hurry although I'm moving on autopilot. My brain is fuzzy, and I have no clue what to think. Dusty spins circles around my legs, reminding me to attach his leash. My friends wedge me between them and we shuffle out of the ice house into the freezing winter.

I toss myself into the backseat with a groan. What am I going to do? Blowing on the window, I draw a little heart with a smaller one inside. I wipe away a few escaping tears, a knot forming in my throat. Crud, I'm already an emotional mess.

I suddenly realize Shane deserves a heads-up of some kind. Not wanting to worry him, I keep it vague.

Me: Something came up and we needed to leave. I'll call you in a bit.

I toss my phone away with a groan. What's Shane going to say?

Fuck, I'm an idiot.

We're all painfully silent on the drive to Kwikee Mart. I rub my forehead. A seed of something sprouts in my belly. The more I think about having a baby, the more attached I become. Wow, everything is happening at light speed, here. Is this how pregnant chicks are? Delilah parks along the curb, and we all shuffle inside the store. My face is on fire as we look over the selections. I pick up a couple of boxes and read the directions.

"How am I supposed to choose?" I whine.

"Easy, we get one of each," Raven says.

"I don't have that much pee." I let out a dry laugh.

Delilah gestures to the coolers. "Go get a Big Gulp or three."

"Too much sugar is bad for—" I cut myself off with a choked breath.

My friends smile. "Aww, the instincts are already kicking in," Raven coos.

I flatten my lips. "We done here?" They nod, and we move toward the register. I freeze, and they collide into me.

"Dude, what gives?" Delilah complains.

"If I buy these, everyone in Garden Grove will know in a hot second," I murmur.

Raven takes a few off my hands. "We'll share the load."

Delilah follows suit and grabs two. "Yup, we're a united front. Marlene will assume we're all preggers."

My eyes get all misty again. "What would I do without you guys?"

"Totally knocked up," Delilah stage-whispers to Raven.

I sniff loudly. "I'm trying to be sentimental."

We all pay separately and haul ass back to my apartment. I pee on at least six sticks with my friends hovering right outside the door. During the two-minute window, I chew most of my nails to nubs. When the timer dings, we all leap for the counter holding the results.

There, staring back at me, are a perfect row of plus signs. Damn, that's impressively clear evidence.

"Well," Delilah starts. "Looks like you're pregnant." She wraps me in a tight hug. "Don't freak out, okay?" She pulls away, and Raven takes her place.

"Whatever you need, we're here for you. How do you feel?" She squeezes my upper arms, jostling me out of my stupor.

I shake my head, trying to clear the fog. "Uh, I'm a little… shocked. I don't really know what to think."

Delilah takes a picture of the sticks. I raise a brow, and she shrugs. "For the future scrapbook. You'll want to remember this moment."

"I can't even think straight right now," I mutter.

"Well, you tell us what to do. Should we give you some space?" Delilah asks.

I swallow. "Yeah, maybe. I need to talk with Shane."

"Of course," Raven soothes and ushers Delilah into the hall. "We'll be waiting for news."

I hug them both once more. "Thanks again, besties. I'd be lost without you."

"We got you, honey." Delilah blows me a kiss.

"Good luck with the mister," Raven says.

I offer a weak wave. "Fingers crossed."

As they're leaving, I hear Delilah's squeal. "We're going to be aunties!"

I smile so wide my cheeks hurt. What a bunch of nuts we make. I stare down at my flat stomach in wonder. A little nugget is in there. I lay my palm on my lower belly and exhale until it sticks out. Crazy.

With a curse, I race to find my phone. There's a slew of messages waiting from Shane, sharing the same theme. He wants to know what the heck is going on and where I am. He's in for quite the awakening.

How do I explain this to him? As the more sexually experienced one—although not by much—it's my responsibility to remember safe sex. Mrs. Drodon's lectures from health class in high school come screeching back. If she could see me today, holding a bouquet of positive pregnancy tests.

I'll keep it simple, for now. My hands shake as I type out a quick message.

Me: Hey, you. Come home, okay? We need to talk.

The subject remains hidden, but anticipation bubbles inside of me. I'm going to be a mommy, which is something I've always dreamed of. Sure, this came a lot sooner than expected. We didn't get a chance to plan or talk about the future first. But we'll just do things a bit backwards. The weight of these last few hours crashes onto me, and I collapse on the couch.

I miss my mom more in this moment than in all of the last year. She'd know just what to say, offering stellar advice to calm me down. Heck, my parents had me when they were twenty-two. They were married and settled in their lives together, but that's not what's important. Or am I trying to fool myself?

I groan and dial her number, needing to feel a fraction of comfort. I'm not going to spill the beans. Shane deserves to hear the news before anyone else. Delilah and Raven were around by default.

The line rings twice, and I almost hang up out of sheer principle, reality sinking in.

"Addison!" Hearing her chirpy voice opens the floodgates, and I hiccup a sob. "Honey? What's wrong?"

I wipe the forming tears away with my sleeve. "Hi, Mama. Sorry to cry in your ear."

She shushes me. "Addy, you don't need to apologize. I'm still your mother, a thousand miles away or not. Now tell me what's the matter."

I gnaw on my bottom lip, searching for a viable reason to be hysterical. "I'm just emotional with the holidays coming up. Dagos has been crazy swamped, and I'm running ragged. Guess I'm just tired."

"I'm sorry we're not visiting Garden Grove for Christmas. Are you going to be okay without us?"

I shrug even though she can't see me. "Yeah, of course. I have my friends and Shane to keep me company."

"How're things going with your boyfriend, Addy? You barely tell me anything."

I almost choke on my tongue. "Uh, he's good. Really great, actually. He should be here any minute." Fun fact—my parents don't know he lives with me. Guess I'll be dropping a few truth bombs soon.

My mom hums. "Oh, that's nice. I hope you two have something fun planned. Sounds like you need it."

"Um, yup. I'm sure we'll think of something."

"You should come to Arizona. The sun is always shining, and it's so darn warm. I've never been so tanned."

I snort and roll my puffy eyes. "Mom, you're cursed with fairer skin than me. Anyway, thanks for the offer, but I'm not sure we can get away." Especially with our cabin trip already planned. I rub my belly and consider how different that vacay will be now.

"You work too hard, sweetie. Come down and relax with us." She sounds so happy and carefree. I'm dumping on her retirement parade.

I clear my throat and throw on some big-girl panties. "I'll try, okay? Tell Dad I miss him. The Holi-Daze aren't the same without you guys."

Her pout is almost visible through the phone. "We're sad to skip out, but next year will be different." Boy, will it ever. She has no idea how much. A twine of guilt squeezes around me and yanks tight. I've never kept secrets from her. Now there's two fairly significant ones stacking up.

I fan my watery eyes. "I should go. Love you, Mama. Give my best to Dad."

"Addison, are you all right?" Her tone is dripping with uncertainty.

"Yes," I say and force my voice to remain stable. "I'm good, don't worry."

"Okay, dear. Please call if you need us."

"I will, thanks."

"Bye, sweetie. Love you." She hangs up, and I sag into the cushions. My body is heavy, and I feel stuck in place. That conversation granted a speck of peace, but I'm still lost. Now what? I check my messages, but Shane hasn't responded. I don't allow the sliver of worry to gain strength. After setting the phone down, I kick up my feet. I'm about to tip his world sideways. My stomach flutters when I consider his reaction. He'll be happy, right? Only one way to find out.

All there's left to do is wait.

CHAPTER 23

SHANE
Daddy

Going from calm to ballistic in an instant is quite staggering. Addison's last text came in as Trey was dropping me off, and this brick in my gut has doubled in size. The possibilities have been looping on warp speed, not all of them good. What's most important in this moment is finding my girl.

When I crash through the door, Addison is pacing and wringing her hands. I stumble in my haste, and she twists toward me with wide eyes. Evidence of upset is written in the tracks trailing down her cheeks. Then she smiles.

I slam to a halt while my pulse beats ferociously. "Adds, what the fuck? I'm freaking out."

She launches herself into my arms. I haul her close, burying my nose in comforting red waves and sweet apples. Addison loops her arms around my neck and kisses me with white-hot passion. That's a good sign, right?

"You're gonna be a daddy," she whispers against my lips.

My mind checks out, and all functioning seems to freeze. "W-what?" I manage to stammer.

Addison pulls back slightly and looks up from under wet lashes. "I'm pregnant."

I blink as my brain misfires and trips over those words. Thoughts and reactions tangle in a web too complicated for me to solve. I let my mouth sag open while shock continues to barrel into me. This is shockingly similar to all those months ago when I'd always be at a loss around this woman. What's the proper thing to say?

"Let's get married," is what pops out. Where did that come from? But the more my suggestion sinks in, the better it sounds.

Addison goes very still in my grasp and time seems to get stuck in a tub of molasses. Why isn't she jumping for joy? That's the normal reaction to a proposal, at least to me. She slowly inches away until there's a gap separating us. Her hands go to my shoulders, and she squeezes.

"Um, what?" Addison says with zero inflection.

I smile wide and try again. "We should get married. I need you to be my wife." I grip her hips and try to draw her into me, but she resists.

Her expression is blank, giving nothing away. "Care to rephrase that?"

"Marry me today," I push.

"Shane, no. We're not getting married."

I shake my head. "Wait, what?"

"Why is that your first point of action?" she asks with wide eyes.

I furrow my brow. "Why isn't it yours? You're mine to take care of, Adds. I love you. It's my duty to do anything necessary to keep you safe and happy. Why wouldn't we get married?"

Her freckled nose wrinkles. "We're having a baby, not planning a wedding."

"You can't have a child out of wedlock. Let me make you an honest woman."

She shoves away from me and holds up a finger. A bright flush races up her pale neck. My gut sinks when all traces of joy vanish from her features. "Oh, no, you didn't. Are you effing serious with that barbaric crap?"

"Am I being unreasonable?"

"Ready to take that foot outta your mouth?"

"Not sure what you mean," I utter softly.

"No? You're sticking to those archaic ways?"

I dip my chin and blow out a huge breath. Maybe I'm not handling this well. I should have kept my big-ass mouth shut. I stare at Addison, her body so tense it's shaking. My hands curl with the need to hold her close, but I doubt that'd be well received in this moment. "You're already a respectable lady," I mumble. "I want us to be together for this, Adds. That's what I meant."

She crosses her arms. "Being married is the only way for that to happen?"

"Well, I guess not..." Every single lesson hammered into me from Pastor Raines bellows otherwise, but that's clearly not the case for her. My attempt at backpedaling falls flat, and she glares at me.

"This baby will be surrounded by love whether we're a couple or not."

My chest gets tight thinking of us apart. I need to fix this and fast. "Of course, Adds. There's no disputing that. I was raised very differently, though."

"I thought you'd moved on from all that?"

"The sermons are screaming at me." I tap my temple.

"You can't stand the idea of a bastard child?"

I flinch at her tone, the words stinging deeply. "Damn, Adds. That's pretty fucking harsh."

"And telling me I need a husband to have a baby isn't? I'm not marrying you, Rooks. I appreciate you stepping up, but this is over the line."

I swallow the pile of ash in my mouth. "I thought you were ready? Isn't that what you meant at the garage?"

"I just meant for more in general. Not necessarily getting engaged, especially not this way."

"What's that supposed to mean?"

"I don't want a proposal out of obligation."

"Good thing that's not what's happening, then," I say.

Addison holds out her palms. "Are you sure? Because I feel otherwise."

"I just want to make you happy, Adds."

"Well, this is definitely not the correct route. I envisioned a very different conversation." Her posture droops with a heavy exhale. "Maybe we should drop it. I'll go take a nap. When I wake up, this Twilight Zone will be gone."

I'm shaking my head before she finishes the sentence. "No way. We've barely scratched the surface, and I want to hear everything." I move toward her, and she immediately steps back. "Why won't you let me hold you?"

"Have you been listening? I'm very confused and want some space."

It's like a bucket of cold water dumped over me. "From me? Why? I'm just trying to help."

"Yes, the poor helpless woman. Way to go."

"Am I being punished for offering to marry you?" I can't seem to stop spewing trash and piling onto the already heaping load. I can almost hear Addison's teeth grinding.

"We're done discussing this." The snarl in her tone makes me cringe.

"Okay, okay. Let's take it easy. I'm not trying to be an asshole."

"Could have fooled me."

"I'm allowed to be off-kilter, Adds. This is a big deal."

"Wow, really? Thanks for noticing."

I scrub over my face and bite back a shout. A coil tightens in my stomach, and I'm barely keeping shit under control. "You're acting really strange. Am I being scolded?" Tossing blame at her is apparently the name of this game. Fucking brilliant.

Addison huffs loudly. "I'm pregnant. For the next nine months, expect me to act like a hormonal mess."

I clench my eyes shut and change tactics. "When did you find out?"

She motions toward the hall. "Thirty minutes ago. Go check the tests for proof."

I gawk at her. "I believe you, Adds. There's no question about it, just piecing stuff together. I'm belatedly realizing we never used condoms. Are you on birth control? Did it fail?"

Her eyes narrow, and I've once again said the wrong thing. "So, this is all my fault?" She clamps her mouth shut and looks away. "It kinda is, but that's not the point. I'm really hurt, Shane. I don't know how to feel. This is a huge upheaval for me, and I was banking on more support from you, not just a proposal."

I lick my lips, picturing us getting on the same path. What a beautiful concept. "I'm trying to do the right thing."

"For who?"

"Us. Why are you being so stubborn? I understand you're an independent woman, but let me be here for you."

Addison laughs, but there's no humor behind it. "That's mighty noble and all, but what the eff era/century are you living in? Being excited and happy about this would be super." Addison's palms rest on her flat stomach, and reality crashes down. My child is growing inside of her!

I blink quickly, trying to clear the moisture. "Why are we fighting?"

"Good question."

"I thought you'd wanna get married. Guess I was wrong," I mumble.

"That's not the priority."

"Since when?" I shoot back.

She shrugs. "I dunno. I'm only twenty-three. There's plenty of time for me to think about the future."

"What about wanting the kind of relationship your parents have?"

Addison glances down, her foot kicking at the rug. "Yeah, someday."

Her meaning hits me like a semi at full speed, and I almost buckle under the pressure. My hackles rise with her dismissal. I should have fucking expected this. Years of lectures and lashings plow to the surface. I'll never deserve her.

Stunning clarity slaps me in the face. "Okay, I get it."

"Finally," she sighs.

"It makes perfect sense. You don't want to spend forever with me." My thoughts are clanging like chaotic pots and pans.

Her face pinches. "Huh?"

"You want the family and happily ever after, but with someone else. It's all right, Adds. I understand. I've been trying to prove myself, but I was always at a disadvantage."

"That couldn't be further from the truth. Where is that assumption coming from?"

I can't hear her over the roaring in my ears. "I thought you loved me."

"I do, so very much. Don't twist my words." She's slowly shaking her head, trying to deny it. But the answer is reflecting in her shimmering green pools.

"You're doing fine on your own. So, you'd prefer to be a single mother?"

"What the actual fuck, Shane. Are you giving me an ultimatum? Marry you or that's the end for us?"

I balk at that. "Not in the slightest. I'm trying to figure out where I fit into your story. You're capable of doing everything alone. I'm used to falling short. Fine, I'll return to the sidelines."

"Okay, this conversation needs to end. We're gonna end up saying a lot of shit we don't mean."

"Too late."

She frowns. "Yeah, you're right."

I can't see past her not choosing me. Fuck, I've been blind. I rock back on my heels and keep digging the hole. "I always knew you deserved better, but you fooled me into thinking otherwise."

Addison sucks in sharply. "I love you, Shane. That's undeniable. I'm thinking too many things right now. One point stands out from the rest, though. We're not getting hitched because I'm knocked up."

I want to tell her about the ring already picked out. I almost blurt that we could have been engaged a month ago if it were up to me. Instead, I bow my head and surrender. "You don't want me."

She yanks at her hair. "Rooks, you're unbelievable, and I'm beyond frustrated. Let's pick this up later when we're thinking clearer."

"I'm seeing pretty damn well. Not sure a few hours will change that."

"How am I the bad guy here?"

"Trust me, you're not. I should have never believed you could really love me."

"I'm not arguing with you. We're uselessly spinning in circles," Addison mutters and stalks toward the foyer.

Panic swells in my gut. "Where are you going?"

"Out."

"Where?"

"Haven't decided."

"When will you be back?"

Her lips tighten into a scowl. "Who knows. I'm a fiercely independent woman all on my own, too damn stubborn to ask for help. I'm also a witch who tricked you into thinking my feelings were real." She tosses my words back at me. They sound so much worse the second time.

I leap into action and reach for her hand, but she shakes me off. "Just leave me be, Shane. I'm gonna mull over my new responsibilities and start planning for changes. Maybe you should do the same." I watch her open the door and leave, effectively slamming a gate between us.

A bolt of lightning strikes my chest, and I double over. What the fuck have I done?

CHAPTER 24

ADDISON
Loon

How did everything get so screwed up? My chest pinches painfully, and I inhale a shuddering breath. Finding out about the baby is reason to be overjoyed and ecstatic. This should be one of the best days of my life, now that the initial shock has worn off. Instead, I'm crying and alone and freezing my ass off. Shane's words slam into me all over again, and I stomp the snow off my boots. I'm not stubborn, but being independent and getting married for the right reasons are important to me.

I furiously wipe at the tears pouring from my eyes. I take a deep breath and knock again.

Delilah swings the door open with wide eyes. "Jeez, I said hold on a second. Where's the fire?"

"Is Zeke here?" I blurt.

"Uh, no. Why?"

"Good." I shove past her. "I'm on a man-hating mission."

She looks at her imaginary watch. "Wow, that flip didn't take long. You were beaming an hour ago. What happened?"

I start searching her cabinets. "I need some wine first." I stop my frantic pillaging and smack my forehead. "Dammit, no alcohol. That's gonna be an adjustment. How else do I cope?"

"First off, that makes you sound like an alcoholic."

I roll my swollen eyes, and she laughs. Delilah opens the freezer and pulls out a carton of ice cream. "Second and more importantly, with extra doses of sugar."

I snatch the container from her and find a spoon. Then, I dig in. I moan when the cool sweetness sticks to my tongue. "Oh, yeah. That's good stuff."

She rests on her hip. "Told you. Works wonders."

"I'm gonna get so fat," I mumble around a big bite.

"And adorably round."

I scowl at her. "Thanks a lot."

Delilah winks. "You're the one who accidentally forgot to get the shot." Her air quotes have me frowning harder.

"You think I meant to get pregnant?" I almost spit out a chunk of cookie.

She pats my shoulder and leads me to the couch. "Of course not, sweet-cheeks. I just enjoy getting you fired up."

I pinch the bridge of my nose. "I've already hit my tolerance level for the day. I appreciate the effort, though."

"Shane didn't take the news well?"

"No!" I chuck my spoon onto the table and it clangs loudly. The noise echoes my thundering pulse. "He asked me to marry him."

Delilah blinks at me, her mouth popping open. She starts to speak, but nothing comes out. Her lips purse, and she squints at me. "I don't get it."

"Right? My baby daddy is being a loon," I complain.

"Um, okay. Never thought I'd hear you complain about a guy asking to marry you."

"This is different. He made it feel like an obligation."

She scratches her chin. "Does that have to do with his religious upbringing?"

I feel my face heat. "Maybe, but he wasn't listening. We barely talked about the baby. He was so focused on getting married and me supposedly not loving him, which is total bull."

Delilah holds up a hand. "Okay, whoa. Rewind a bit. How did the marriage topic come up?"

"That's the first thing Shane said after I told him I'm pregnant. He wants to make an honest woman out of me," I grind out.

She hisses. "Yikes. That's not cool."

"I know! And he wouldn't drop it. I was getting so upset." I sniff as a lump forms in my throat. "Then he accused me of not loving him. It was a disaster spiral with no end in sight."

"How'd you leave things?"

"I stormed out," I mutter. "Pretty much told him to get his head screwed on straight. Who immediately jumps to proposing like that?"

Delilah twirls a piece of her blonde hair. "Plenty of guys, actually. I think it's a common reaction."

I slap my knee. "What? No way. That's so lame."

"Why? I think it's romantic. They wanna support their woman and step up. Not sure there's a bigger display of sticking around than popping the question."

I groan loudly. "Then the foundation of your marriage is based on an accidental whoopsie. After the dust clears, will he still feel the same way? Will he regret asking? I don't want a pity proposal. And now I'll never know if he's genuine in wanting to marry me. We'll always be connected by this kiddo."

She rubs my arm. "Addy, you're being a little dramatic. Try to think of it from Shane's perspective."

I gape at her. "What?"

"Maybe he deserves a do-over. I'm sure he realizes by now you aren't ready for that type of commitment from him."

"That's the farthest thing from the truth. Whose side are you on?" My pitch is bordering on a screech.

"Okay, calm down," she soothes. "Getting pissed is bad for the baby."

"Since when are you an expert?" I narrow my eyes into slits, but take a deep breath and slowly blow it out.

"Stop being a diva," Delilah replies. "Additional stress is known to be unhealthy for pregnant women. Ask anyone."

"Whatever," I mumble. "I should probably keep my distance from Shane if that's the case. He makes my blood boil."

"It's gonna be a long-ass nine months," she murmurs.

I leap to my feet. "All right, that's it. I don't know when you all decided to be mean and unsupportive. I'm not a fan."

Delilah tugs on my hand. "Sit down." I do with a huff, and she laughs. "I'm sorry. I just don't want you to be hasty. This is a really big deal, and being part of a smoothly functioning duo makes it much easier. I was just trying to problem-solve for you."

I flop back into the cushions. "Well, be on my team. I need you in my corner. I really don't wanna be solo for this." I hiccup a sob and cover my mouth. I lower my head to my thighs and let the tears flow. I never cry this much.

"Addy," she whispers and rubs my neck. "You're never alone. No matter what, I'll always be here. Rave, too."

"But apparently I'm stubborn and too independent and meant to be single," I blubber.

"That's not true, girlfriend. You've always been about finding Prince Charming and riding off into the sunset."

I scoff. "Tell that to Shane."

Delilah tsks. "That man needs a stern talking to."

I point at her. "That's better. Say more of that."

"Does he realize how all this came across? You know guys could always use more guidance in the feelings department. Unless we're talking about Zee. He's perfect." Her voice trails off on a whimsical sigh.

I rub my temples, a headache forming. "Uh-huh, that's great for you. My man is trying to steamroll me. And yeah, how he was raised might have a lot to do with it. Or the fact I'm his first girlfriend."

"Oooh, girl. You tamed that wild stallion."

I cough into my fist. "Something like that."

Delilah taps her chin. "Shane will be kissing your butt for weeks. He's crazy about you, boo. Everyone sees that. Sure, he handled this situation poorly, but I'm betting he will fix it."

I avert my gaze, staring at a speck in the carpet. "But the damage is done. He ruined the pregnancy reveal. He said some really shitty things. I'm not sure how we move on from here."

Delilah scoots closer and gives me a hug. "Are you gonna kick him outta the love nest?"

The thought of breaking up with him is a dagger to my heart. I blink away a fresh round of emotion and swallow roughly. "No, I can't do that."

She nods. "Okay, good. That's an important piece of the puzzle. Not all is lost. Yes, he did a lot the wrong way. But I'm assuming his intentions are good. You know Shane. Would he be a jerk on purpose?"

"No," I utter quietly.

"See? Remember that. You two have a little peanut coming, and that's what matters most. So, figure out the logistics and decide what happens next. No drama-llamas." Delilah pokes my cheek.

"Hey," I rub the spot. "This isn't my fault. Well, the faulty birth control is. But I was so excited to tell him and figured we'd be celebrating right now. He had to go and mess up my plans."

Delilah sighs slowly. "This has been quite the day. We should do something fun."

"Ugh, I'm not in the mood. Can we just binge on *Friends*?"

"Nope. You need to get up and do something. Motivate yourself," she suggests.

I snuggle into a squishy pillow. "Exercise is the last thing on my mind right now. Staying in this spot is totally working for me."

Delilah snaps her fingers. "Ooooh, let's get pedicures."

I squint at her. "Did you get into a bottle of wine? It's the middle of winter."

"So? It'll make you feel better. Those massage chairs are so relaxing. And Ruby will spoil your feet."

I cringe. "My legs aren't shaved."

Delilah giggles. "Girl, that's the least of your worries."

I smile. "Preach. Gah, what am I going to do?"

She zips her lips. "Toes first. Problems later."

"You make it sound so simple."

She offers a hand and yanks me off the extremely comfortable couch. "I'm not saying this will be easy, but it's gonna work out. One baby step at a time. Aww, see what I did there?"

I laugh at her bright expression. "You're a goof. Thanks for listening, D."

Delilah slings an arm around my shoulders. "You can always count on me, day or night."

"I'll remember that when we need a sitter."

She bounces in place. "I cannot wait. This kid is gonna be so spoiled. I'll set up a little play area at Jitters. Your little one can hang out and soak up all the attention."

I release a weighty sigh. "This is the reaction I was hoping to get from Shane."

She frowns. "You don't think he's excited?"

"I dunno. He was too fixated on getting married."

"Give him a few hours to catch up. I'm picturing him out buying a little onesie as we speak."

I smile sadly, wishing I could see it. "Fingers crossed."

CHAPTER 25

SHANE
Closure

I park my ass on the bench inside the lobby and let out another long string of expletives. After driving around for an hour, I found myself pulling into Jacked Up. I guess this place is my second home so the destination wasn't surprising. The shop is closed and dark, which means I'm alone with my thoughts. This is exactly what I need.

My face falls into my hands, and I bellow loudly. The pained sound rips from my chest and bounces around the small room. Fuck, I'm ashamed of myself. I can't believe all that stupid shit came out of my mouth. Addison is the most honest and honorable woman. How could I disgrace her with such slander?

The longer I'm replaying our conversation, the worse it seems. I have no excuse or reason other than being too damn excited about her news. Having a baby with the woman I love is the greatest gift. I should have wrapped Addison in my arms and taken her to bed. Instead, I'm wallowing and whimpering in the garage with nowhere to go. I got too confident and cocky, and now she wants nothing to do with me. I deserve her wrath. I can only pray to the heavens above that she'll forgive me.

An idea niggles at my foggy brain, and I grab my cell. I'm hazy and drained, but dialing the number is easy. This isn't the first time I've tried to contact my family since leaving. So far, no one has picked up, but today that doesn't stop me. I so badly want to share this extraordinary news with them.

"Hello?" My mother's clipped tone makes me shiver. I'm already regretting my decision. But I push ahead and follow through.

"Mother, it's Shane," I greet.

If she's surprised, I can't tell. Her stone mask was always hard to read. "What do you want?" Her voice is a fierce whip, but I feel no sting.

I clear my throat. "This won't take long, and I apologize for disrupting your day."

"Spit it out, child," she chides.

"I'm going to be a father."

The line is quiet for a moment, and I'm certain she hung up. Then she asks, "You chose a different bride? When were you married?"

I want to laugh at the irony but know better. Maybe explaining this conversation to Addison later will help my case. "My girlfriend is pregnant."

"Your girlfriend?" Her voice is flat with no hint of inflection. I can almost feel her disappointment bleeding through the speaker.

"Yes," I confirm. "She's having my baby."

"I see," my mother starts, and I hold my breath for her lashing. "That's quite an abolishment, even for you. Having a child out of wedlock? What on God's creation were you thinking? I'm so disturbed by this, Shane. You're my son, but I do not know who you've become." She exhales harshly, and I'm sure she's making the sign of the cross. "Molly would have made a good wife. Pastor Raines wanted that arrangement. You two matched well and would have provided strong offspring for the family. Now you're tainted, even more than before. This is permanent, Shane. Do you realize that?"

Acid churns in my gut at her accusations. "Of course, Mother. I'm aware of my actions."

"I hope your harlot was worth spending eternity in purgatory."

I grind my molars. "She is the greatest thing that's ever happened to me."

She scoffs. "You are more lost than I thought. Simply out of reach. We will pray for you, Shane. You need to atone. You will need all the Lord's forgiveness after such a sinful blasphemy."

"How can you say that?" I whisper.

"Excuse me?"

My defenses rear up, and I release all doubt. "This baby is a blessing. Addison is my perfect angel. We're very happy together."

"You're an outsider, Shane. You no longer belong to the good Pastor Raines or with us. The moment you stepped foot off the compound, your destiny fell from His good grace. You made that choice."

"I did." There's a smile in my voice, and she hears it.

"That wasn't meant as a compliment, son. You should be forever remorseful," she commands.

"I have zero regrets, mother."

"So, you call to rub this dishonor in my face? What shame! I hope you find the Light again, before it's too late."

Her response further proves I've been right all along. I was never meant to stay locked away with them. There were bigger dreams and goals with my name on them. Most importantly, I found my girl, and we created our miracle.

"She's everything I need. I love her," I state with my entire heart.

"Oh my word, Shane. I can't listen to more of this. You're on a path we cannot allow or follow. Do not contact us again."

And with a click, the connection to my family is severed forever. Maybe I should feel broken inside, but the opposite is true. I've never been more whole, the final weight lifting off my conscience. I got the necessary closure to be completely free.

The smile on my face is misplaced, but I can't stop it. Shit, maybe I'm really losing my marbles. The bell above the door jingles, and Jack steps inside. He shakes off the snow from his jacket and takes a seat beside me. We sit silently for a moment and my grin spreads. Warmth suddenly blankets me, and I know he was meant to find me here. Talking to Jack is what I was searching for earlier.

Jack's shoulder bumps mine. "Whatcha doing here, rookie? Thought I told you to take the day off. That includes the evening hours as well."

I scratch at the scruff lining my jaw. "Needed somewhere to think."

"Shouldn't you be at home with your girl?"

"Nah, not right now."

He frowns. "Uh-oh. Trouble in paradise."

My joy dims, and I slouch to hide the shame. "I fucked up."

"Wanna talk about it?"

"Addison is pregnant," I say, and the smile returns for a moment.

Jack hoots and pumps a fist in the air. "Hell, I was preparing for the worst. That's great, kid. Congratulations."

I nod slowly. "Thanks, boss."

He studies me quietly. "I'm sensing a but coming along. Is she upset?"

"Not about the baby. I reacted poorly, and said some stupid shit," I admit.

"Ah, well, you're not the first guy to freak out when getting the news. I'm assuming this wasn't planned?"

"Yeah, it's an unexpected surprise. A happy one."

Jack chuckles. "So, what? You walked out to get some air and think about the next eighteen years?"

I scrub over my eyes and exhale roughly. "I asked her to marry me. That's the first thing I thought to say. It came across wrong, like we had to out of obligation. Then I proceeded to make a bigger ass of myself and gave her more reasons to break things off. I figured she was saying no to being with me in general and I couldn't see past that. I got on a selfish tangent and spewed a bunch of pitiful garbage. Safe to say, I really screwed things up. And here I am." I gesture around the room with a limp hand.

He makes a noise of agreement and leans back. "That's quite the story. I'm sorry it didn't work out quite right, but this is just a bump in the road. Does she know you'd already been thinking about a ring?"

"No," I mutter.

"Got flustered and fumbled?"

"You could say that."

"Well, shit. Don't sweat it, rookie. She'll come around."

"Yeah? I told her I'd make an honest woman outta her. She wasn't too pleased about that."

He sucks in air through his teeth. "Ouch, I imagine not. Modern times and women, rookie. Gotta watch your tongue, right? But your heart was in the right place."

"I'm crazy about her, you know? I just wanna make her happy. I wanna raise our baby together. I really wanna make her my wife. I'm not sure she feels the same, at least not anymore."

"Nah, don't get too down. These misunderstandings happen. Buy her some flowers and apologize. She'll be right as rain tomorrow," Jack assures.

I tug on my ear. "We'll see."

Jack stands up and motions me to follow. "The sooner you start, the faster you can make up."

I cross my arms. "Mind if I crash at your place?"

His brow furrows. "Can't go home? Did she kick you out?"

"Nah, it's not that. I wanna give Addison some space like she asked for. I've already done a great job shoving her away. I'd hate to make it permanent by not following her wishes. A night away from me is probably what she needs." A knife twists in my gut just thinking of sleeping without her, but I made this fucking bed.

Jack rocks on his heels. "Whatever you think is best, rookie."

I offer a humorless chuckle. "Trust me, that's what got me into this clusterfuck. From now on, I'm gonna do a lot more listening and paying attention to her cues."

"Good luck," Jack grunts. "Women are tough nuts to crack. Just when you've got a handle on them? Poof, they change their minds and demand something else."

"I'll do whatever it takes."

He smirks. "Then you'll do just fine."

This small town has become my home. But it wouldn't be possible without her. Addison is the center of it all, and I need to prove that more than ever.

CHAPTER 26

ADDISON
Rents

I wake with a jolt and sit upright, taking in my room. Why am I sleeping in here?

The events from yesterday rain down on me like a storm, and I almost start crying. In a flurry, I dislodge Dusty from my lap and tumble off the mattress. I send him an apologetic look over my shoulder and go in search of Shane. I slam to a halt outside his open door, featuring a neatly made bed and no recent trace of him. He didn't come home last night.

A sob works its way up my throat as panic floods me. I didn't expect him to stay gone. The tendrils of frustration are still weighing down my limbs, but I planned to talk with him today. We need to get on the same page, and fast.

In the next beat, a knock calls out. I race to the front door, expecting Shane to be on the other side. When I swing it open, my jaw drops.

"Mom? Dad?" I feel my eyes bug out. "What're you doing here?"

"Hi, sweetie," my mother says and gives me a hug.

"Morning, Addy," my father greets and kisses my cheek.

I motion them inside and continue gawking. I rest a palm on my forehead and try to calm the pounding in my chest. They take off their coats and shoes while I try to wrap my mind around this unexpected visit. It takes me several seconds before I snap out of the stupor.

"What's going on?" I manage to ask.

My mom pats my head like I'm a toddler. "You sounded so sad on the phone, dear. We needed to be with you. I could feel it. A mother's intuition never fails."

"Wow, that's so nice. I'm really happy to see you." I beam at them, allowing the problems with Shane to roll away for a bit. The weight on my shoulders already seems lighter with them around.

My dad looks around my apartment. "Like what you've done with the place, Addy. Your decorating is very impressive. I like the holiday cheer, and it smells like cookies."

I follow his line of sight and take in the new pieces. I grin when catching Shane's influence sprinkled in here and there. "Thanks. I've had a little help lately. Shane likes to tag along."

"Bargain shopping?" my mother guesses.

"Yup, my partner-in-crime has a great eye. He's especially good at finding those trendy trunks," I say and gesture toward the two nearby.

My mom purses her lips. "Are you all right, honey? You look exhausted."

I sag under her watchful eye and let the truth show. Even my scalp aches, if that's a thing. "I, uh, didn't sleep well last night. I kept tossing and turning."

"Do you work today?" she asks.

"Yeah, just a short lunch shift."

She smiles. "That's good. Then you can rest. Holi-Daze festivities start soon, right?"

I glance at my feet, apologizing to them ahead of time. "Yup, on Wednesday. Let the crazy fun begin."

My dad strokes his still-dark beard. "Guess they found a different Santa."

I giggle. "Don't pretend to be upset. It saves you from dyeing all that hair white."

My mother winks at him. "I like him as a silver fox."

I gag. "Don't start, you two."

She lifts her brows at me. "Speaking of, when do we get to meet Shane?"

A boulder gets caught in my throat. "Uh, I'm not sure."

"Don't be shy, Addy. We want to meet the man who's captured your heart," my mom coos.

"Uh, um," I stammer and scratch the back of my neck. "He's probably working."

My dad squints at the ceiling. "At Jacked Up, right?"

"Yep, the one and only," I mumble. My mother gives me a funny look, and I shrug.

"Maybe we can bring him breakfast?" she suggests.

My father nods. "It would be nice to see Jack."

I wave them off. "He's probably really busy. We can catch up with him later."

"That's too bad, but all right. Is your roommate home?" my mother asks and peers down the hallway.

I gulp down a heavy dose of fear. I told my parents I was living with Shane and they heard Shay. Yes, I'm a chicken shit and didn't correct them when they assumed he was a she. Might as well come clean. "He's not," I drag the words out slowly.

"I think I misunderstood you. Did you say he?" my mom asks.

"Yes." I work up all the fake confidence my wounded pride can muster.

My mother's brow wrinkles. "You're living with a man?"

I'm bobbing my head too quickly, giving away my guilt. "Yup, sure am. No doubt about it."

"I don't understand," my dad mutters.

"Why don't we sit down." I motion to the couch. They follow me into the living room and we all settle in. My parents stare at me expectantly, and I fidget with a fraying seam. My mother stills my hands.

"Sweetie, what is it? You can tell us."

"Promise not to be mad?"

She squints at me. "You can't ask that. Ever since that party you held—"

"Yeah, yeah," I cut her off. "We don't need a history lesson. Okay, so Shane moved in with me in August. He was strictly my roommate for a while. The original plan was to keep it that way. Obviously, that didn't happen."

"Well, that's interesting," my mother murmurs.

I hold up a finger. "Oh, there's more."

My father rubs his forehead. "Maybe I should go to Dagos for a beer. Not sure I want to hear what you two have been busy doing."

I laugh at his pinched expression. "Very funny. I'm an adult and make my own choices."

He scowls. "I don't like what you're implying."

I pat his shoulder. "It's not that bad." It totally is.

"Addison?" My mother signals for me to speed things up.

"Fine, okay." I suck in sharply. "You're going to be grandparents," I blurt in one long stream.

They blink at me, wearing matching expressions of shock. I give them a few moments to let the news sink in, not wanting to cause any panic attacks. After Shane's reaction, I can't be too sure.

My dad keeps gaping, but my mom's stunned face unthaws. "I was not expecting… that."

I spread my fingers out and offer jazz-hands. "Surprise!"

"Have you been to the doctor?" she asks.

I bite my lip. "Um, no. I just found out yesterday."

"Oh, my! You're early on. We arrived at the perfect time." She elbows my dad, and her mouth spreads into a massive grin. "This is wonderful, sweetie."

Now it's my turn to go slack-jawed. "It is?"

The skin around her eyes crinkle. "Of course. I mean, it's always easier when babies are planned. That's not the case here, though. You just have to take the twists as they arrive."

I rub my stomach. "How do you know this was an accident?"

Her smile droops slightly. "Well, I was assuming."

I laugh. "Only kidding."

She pinches my arm playfully. "Such a stinker."

My father scrubs over his face. "A baby, huh? Are you getting married?"

"Seriously?" I cover my face and groan. "For Pete's sake, why is getting married so darn important?"

My mother hushes him. "Your father is more old-fashioned. We know that logic has become more outdated recently. Unless, you want Shane to propose? Goodness, I shouldn't continue assuming."

My belly dips as things get more complicated. "Well, he kinda already did."

"Good!" my dad barks. My mom grips his hand and gives him a playful tug.

"So, you're engaged? Wow, we've missed an awful lot. Good thing we made this trip or who knows when you'd tell us," my mother half-jokes. She picks up my left hand and finds no trace of a ring.

I tap my lips. "Um, yeah. It's kind of a long story. We're still ironing out the details of our, um, arrangement."

She clicks her tongue. "What does that mean?"

I swat the air. "Not important. Let's talk about you guys. How was the flight?"

"Sweetie, you're acting very strange. Are you sick?" My mother checks my forehead for a fever.

I let her fuss over me. "You heard the knocked-up part, right? I feel like that's an automatic excuse to be out of sorts."

She bumps me. "You're pregnant, dear. Let Shane dote on you day and night."

My dad harrumphs. "Oh, great. Your mother will have that poor boy running all around town for you."

I force my features to remain neutral. Being on unstable ground with Shane couldn't have come at a worse point. This conversation would have been so much easier if I knew we were going to be okay.

"I'm not so sure about all that." I try to inject humor in my tone, but it sounds dull.

"I'll do anything to help. I'm going to be a grannie!" My mom is in her mid-forties, but looks far younger. Not sure I know many women her age excited about being called a grandma. I smile at her exuberance, letting it pump me up a little.

I do a little shimmy, and it makes me need to pee. "Next year is going to bring a lot of fantastic changes." My movements still as I think more about that. "And you'll be in Arizona."

My parents share a glance, and my mom frowns. "That does present some challenges. We're here now, though. Let's focus on that." Despite her best efforts, sorrow seeps into the room.

I try to hide the moisture collecting in my eyes. "But you'll be leaving again. How long are you in Garden Grove?"

"We're staying through Christmas. We got a room at Grove Inn

Bed and Breakfast," my mother says.

I brighten slightly at that. "Oh, that's good. We can attend some festivities while you're in town."

Her hazel eyes sparkle. "That's the plan."

I glance down at my nonexistent bump. "Although wine-tasting and snow-tubing will be out for me."

Even my dad laughs at that. "Good thing there are plenty of other options."

"Oh!" My mother sits up straighter. "Marlene and Betty can save you a spot at the bingo table. There's also a knitting seminar."

I wrinkle my nose. "I'd rather eat my way through Raven's cupcakes and check out the ice sculptures."

"Sounds fantastic. I'll meet you there," my mom replies.

"And we can host here on the eve. I'm already kinda set up." I nod toward the tree. "Shane will be glad to celebrate with you." I lean on my mom glancing between them. "Have I told you this visit is the sweetest surprise? I'm so glad you're here."

She points to my stomach. "You have a better surprise all bundled up in there."

Flutters erupt as if the tiny peanut can hear her. "You know what I mean, *Mama*."

She brushes hair off my face. "Yes, sweetie. We couldn't stay away."

"Could have fooled me," I grumble.

My mom laughs. "Don't be a grumpy Gus."

I give her a side-eye. "I just miss my family. I'll do my best to appreciate the time we have together while you're here, though."

My mom claps. "That's the spirit. Plus, there's a baby on the way. We have so much to be thankful for. We're blessed with amazing gifts."

As if on cue, Dusty trots toward us from wherever he was hiding. He scratches my leg, and I scoop him up. My mother covers her mouth.

"Oh, he's precious! So much cuter in person." She strokes his curly fur. "That fiancé of yours is a real winner."

Am I a horrible person for not correcting her? The truth will come out eventually. Plus, it's becoming more and more clear that I probably overreacted to Shane's proposal. It's not like I don't want to marry him. I'm not opposed to the idea under the right circumstances. He still has some explaining to do, though. My chest threatens to cave in when I recall the sadness reflecting in his honey eyes while we fought. Maybe I was too hard on him like Delilah said. I gnaw on my bottom lip and consider sending him a quick message. I mostly want to make sure he's okay and stayed the night somewhere safe.

Actually, my skin is starting to crawl with the urge to reach out to him. Damn, I really do love that man something fierce.

I shove the stirrings of guilt to the side for now. I'll solve things with Shane soon enough. For now, I'm going to focus on some happy. I nuzzle Dusty's soft fur, give him a few more pets, and pass him over to my mom. She cradles him like a baby, and he licks her chin.

"I'm practicing for daycare duty. How do I look?" She titters when Dusty wriggles to get closer. "Oh, I'm so excited."

I let out a long sigh. "Me too."

Her red hair swishes when she looks at me. "Are you sure? This is a big change for you."

The smile lifting my lips is genuine, and I relax into the couch. "I am. It'll be even better once a few things get cleared up." My mom waits for me to say more but doesn't press when I stay silent.

She continues lavishing Dusty with affection and asks, "How about breakfast? I haven't had the Greasy Spoon in far too long."

We all get up when my stomach rumbles at the prospect. "That sounds perfect."

CHAPTER 27

SHANE
Loved

It was nearly impossible to wait for Addison's shift to end. Like a stalker, I sat in my truck outside of Dagos and watched her work for hours. That's the behavior of a desperate man in need of his girl. Although others might consider my leering straight up psycho. Either way, I couldn't stay away for another moment.

My view is obstructed by the array of neon signs littering the glass. I've never paid much attention to the glowing advertisements until now. Maybe I should tell Grayson to remove some. There's got to be a safety code I can quote to defend my case. But being on this side of the glass isn't a habit I plan to make.

I can see enough to appease this insatiable hunger churning inside of me. Barely. Addison's red hair is knotted in a messy bun, shining like ruby waves from the overhead light. My hands curl around the steering wheel, imagining the soft silk sliding between my fingers. If all goes well, I'll be burying into those strands soon.

The clock ticks on, and Addison circles back to a familiar older couple. I recognize them from the pictures on our mantle. I haven't had the pleasure of meeting her parents yet. The opportunity is almost enough to blow my cover and walk inside the bar, but I resist. I wasn't sure how my presence would be received.

My breath fogs up the window when I blow out a heavy exhale. Talking with Jack last night was vital and boosted my ego back to a normal level. I'm confident in my ability to win Addison back, now… if she gives me the chance.

She smiles at a customer, and my gut tightens, wishing that joyful expression was aimed at me. Will her green eyes twinkle in that special way when I show up on the doorstep?

I continue waiting as Addison finishes up and says goodbye to her parents. She strolls out of Dagos, and I notice the sudden lack of bounce in her step. Awareness pummels into me, and more than ever, I need to repair the damage I've caused. My truck follows her car down Main Street toward our apartment. My heart rate reaches dangerous peaks as we get to the parking lot.

Walking slowly behind her, I'm mentally preparing my apology speech. The words swirl faster and faster with each measured crunch of my boots through the snow. Addison climbs the steps at a snail's pace, and I feel almost positive she's dragging this out on purpose.

My theory is proven when she glances down, her face barely visible through the layers of her scarf. She tugs the wool away, and a half smile tips her lips. My girl turns and unlocks the door, walking inside our place. That's all I need to take off racing up the stairs after her.

I pause on the threshold, unsure about crossing the line without a proper invitation. She catches my indecision and motions me forward. My feet move on their own, following her command without hesitation. I loom silently by the front closet and wait for her to continue leading this show.

Addison leans against the dining table, facing me dead-on with no sign of shying away. She crosses her arms. "How long were you parked outside Dagos?"

I startle, and a heat creeps up my neck. "Uh, just for a bit."

"You sure it wasn't my entire shift?"

I scratch the burn at my nape. "Might've been."

Her shoulders rise with a deep inhale. "Why didn't you come in and eat?"

"Wasn't sure I was welcome."

"Rooks, you stop by almost daily. You're my best customer."

When Addison uses my nickname, a warm sensation passes through me. It's been twenty-four hours too long since I've touched her.

"Today was different," I mumble.

"How?" She settles back against the ledge.

I take the opening she gives me, shrugging sheepishly. "I'm not in your good graces and didn't wanna cause a scene. After the way I treated you yesterday, I'd expect you to kick my ass to the curb."

"I would have served you like usual. I'm not that unreasonable," she huffs.

"I'd deserve a beer poured in my lap."

Addison's freckled nostrils flare. "You think I'm that bitter or callous?"

I broaden my stance, making no room for argument. "I'd never use those terms to describe you. I'll only call you beautiful and gorgeous. Maybe wife someday, if you're willing. But I'll gladly accept you being my girlfriend for the rest of our lives. We never have to get married if you don't want to."

"We've already discussed this," she reminds me.

I bob my head, drooping slightly. "I should have broached the subject differently and paid attention to your needs. But I was freaking out, Adds. You're carrying my baby. Don't I get one free pass at least?" I take a few steps toward her, needing to erase the distance. My muscles tense in preparation for her to dodge my advance. Instead, Addison hops off the table and shuffles forward, bringing us closer together.

"Would a hug be too presumptuous?" I murmur.

She clasps my outstretched hand but doesn't move further. "Flinging myself into your arms would be so easy, but I need to be certain. Taken off guard or not, you can't just take words back. I want to make sure you're in this relationship for the right reasons."

"You know me, Adds." I pound on my chest. "I'll always want to do right by you. I'm gonna fuck up and say stupid stuff, but that will never change how I feel. I love you so damn much, nothing else exists. Where you end is where I begin, connected in an infinite loop. Please give me another chance, Adds. You can trust me." My skin prickles as she silently studies me. I gulp down some humble-pie, readying myself to beg at her feet.

Addison's smile is weak, but it's there. "I can. That's true. This was a totally unexpected situation for us, and you know what? It's a really huge freaking deal. We've gotta buck up and be ready for our baby. I have to be confident that you'll be there for us. I need a reliable partner by my side to share the load." Her fingers squeeze mine. "I want to be more than a woman serving your procreation needs. I want us to be equals."

My gut seizes, and I almost hunch over. "I'm so damn sorry if that's how my proposal came across. There's no room for excuses. You're everything to me, Adds. I'm going to prove it. Marrying you has been on my mind far longer than our baby has been in your belly. I wouldn't have asked if I didn't want to spend forever with you. I'll take you in any capacity or title, under whatever terms. No matter what, I'm not surrendering you or my child. You're both mine, dammit."

She shivers, and more than ever, I want to haul her into me. Addison licks her lips, the bright red a beacon in my darkness.

"I'm a fan of you being a growly alpha, but read the scene before barking demands. There's a time for you to be a dominant asshole. When I'm making a baby announcement isn't one of them."

I tug on her arm, and she folds against my chest.

"How about now?" I rumble in her ear.

Addison's small form shakes as she laughs. "I hope you're making a joke."

I tip her chin up and kiss her softly. "Yes, Adds. I know when you like me gritty and rough."

She blinks quickly. "I need to apologize too."

I furrow my brow. "For what?"

She cuddles into me, her breath hot on my throat. "I'm at fault too. I jumped to conclusions and assumed the worst. I should have taken a timeout and explained myself a little better. We both can learn from this."

"Yeah?"

"Uh-huh." Her fingers claw into my shirt, making a statement. "I realized you're trying to be helpful by doing it all, and it came across as overbearing. I get that you didn't mean it that way. I acted like a brat, and I admit it."

I press her harder into me, wanting to eliminate the last remnant of space between us. "I understand why you were upset. I'd never place blame on you."

Her exhale puffs out in bursts. "But I do, and it's deserved. I've had too much time to obsess about it. Is it silly that I missed you like crazy and it's only been a day?"

"I'm so fucking sorry, Adds. You're the only one who gets me. Being away from you was torture. I can't fucking sleep without you."

She lifts a shoulder and the collar of her shirt shifts, exposing a sliver of tempting skin. "And you didn't come home last night. I woke up in my bed super-confused."

My mouth rests on her temple. "I spiraled and lost my wits thinking you didn't want me. I was giving you space."

"I'll always want you beside me, Rooks."

"Thank the Lord for that. I won't make that mistake again."

Addison stills, seeming to hesitate. "Are you, uh, upset about the baby?"

I pull away and stare into her wide green pools. "How could you even consider that?"

"You never said anything about it..."

I clench my hands into fists at her hips and hiss out an exhale. How foolish can I be? Shame threatens to split me in half as I silently plead for her forgiveness. "Adds, I am so sorry. I can't stop thinking about being a father. This child is a miracle I'm not worthy of, and I will never take it for granted." I swallow roughly. "I called my mother."

Addison's lips part in surprise. "When?"

"After I left yesterday."

"What happened?"

I comb through my hair, trying to ward off the toxins that conversation brings forth. "I told her about you and the baby. It was a blood bath. Long story short, I'm guaranteed a life of struggle and suffering."

She gasps. "That's terrible. Regardless of her beliefs, she's still your mother."

I sigh, knowing full well those ties to my family are over. "I might have taken creative liberties with the phrasing, but that's the gist."

Addison cups my jaw. "We're making our own family. You could never be anything except good. Your heart is too pure for anything else."

I brush my nose along hers. "And all yours."

"Love conquers sin, and we have plenty to go around."

"Do you really believe that?" I murmur.

She nods quickly. "Yes, we can beat anything."

I crash to my knees and hug her to me. My forehead rests against her flat torso, and I smile. I kiss the center of her belly where our baby grows. "I'm going to make you proud. Don't lose faith in me."

"You'll be a great dad." Addison scratches along my scalp, and I groan.

"Will you help me? When I goof shit up?"

She giggles. "This is all new to me, Rooks. We'll figure it out together."

"I love the sound of that." I prop my chin on her stomach.

Addison freezes in my grip. "Oh my gosh, ow, ow."

I jerk backwards. "Did I hurt you?"

"No, it's just," she sucks in a sharp breath, "really bad cramps."

"Has that been happening?"

Her eyes get misty. "No."

"The baby?" My voice wobbles.

Addison's face crumples in pain. "I'm not sure. Something doesn't feel right."

I move my ass, dashing to the closet and grabbing our coats. I get her shoes on, gritting out, "I'm taking you to the emergency room."

CHAPTER 28

ADDISON
Seedf

Two hours later, my feet are secure in a pair of stirrups. I'm wearing a hospital gown with my butt hanging out. There's a large baton-type instrument in my vagina that should be extremely uncomfortable, the walls are too white, and the room smells sterile. None of that fully registers. My full attention is locked on the little black and white screen.

The doctor adjusts the wand and taps a few keys. All I see is a blobby blur through my cloudy vision. She's a patient woman and has been handling our panic without ruffling any feathers. Her serene tone and mellow demeanor put me at ease even under this potentially traumatic circumstance. Shane is by my side, our hands clasped in a vice-grip. His chaotic honey pools are pleading with her to hurry up.

I'm sure mine reflect the same. He's been murmuring encouraging words and sweet-nothings to keep me calm, but I'm ready for the news. Fingers effing crossed it's on the good side.

The doctor points to the middle a circle. "And there's your baby."

"Where?" My voice is near hysterics at this point.

She pats my shin in a signal for me to calm down. "Take a deep breath for me, Addison." I follow her orders on autopilot, and she smiles. We all glance back to the monitor.

"Right here," she says and draws her finger around a barely-there speck.

I squint and lean closer. "That tiny dot?"

The doctor drags the machine over so we can have a better view. "Yes, that's your poppy seed."

My watery gaze swings to Shane. "Do you see it?"

He wipes under his eyes. "Yeah, Adds. I do."

"But I don't hear anything," I whisper urgently. "Shouldn't there be a heartbeat?"

The doctor's expression is kind. "This little one is only four weeks old. Things are just getting started. The heart doesn't begin functioning until closer to eight weeks. There's nothing to be concerned about. From what I can tell, you have a perfectly developing embryo."

Shane squeezes my hand, placing a kiss on the inside of my wrist. "And what about the pain she was experiencing?"

She doesn't miss a beat. "Cramping is a normal symptom in early stages of pregnancy as the uterus stretches to make room. It's a scary feeling since women associate that type of pain with their period.

But don't fret, Addison. Everything is looking right on track." She scribbles on a pad and passes me the paper. "Here's the name of a recommended prenatal vitamin you can get over the counter at any local pharmacy. I'll also print out some helpful literature and websites you can browse. If you experience any discomfort, stick with Tylenol. You can always call with more serious questions and concerns. On your way out, don't forget to schedule your next appointment. I'll be seeing you monthly until the third trimester."

My mind is spinning so I just nod slowly and whisper, "Thank you."

The doctor gives me another reassuring smile. "Do you need anything else right now?"

Shane gestures to the screen. "Can we, uh, have a picture of our poppy seed?"

As if he didn't already own my heart. This man, my word.

"You're so thoughtful," I whisper.

"For the memory scrapbook," he murmurs. If I wasn't already knocked up, Shane's smirk would do the trick. Good grief, those dimples are an aphrodisiac.

The doctor prints out a few copies, and I clutch them in a trembling grip. The tears are pouring down my cheeks in earnest, and I don't bother trying to stop them. I look up at Shane and find him crying too. So masculine and stoic, he's wearing his emotion like a badge of honor. I tug on his arm, and he dips down toward me.

"I love you," I murmur.

He kisses my forehead. "Love you, Mama Bear."

"Oh gosh," I sob out.

I'm zoned in on his handsome face while the doctor finishes up the exam and removes the instrument. His light brown eyes are brimming with so much feeling, there's no escape. Not that I'd be anywhere else but suspended in this moment with him. I hiccup a shuddering gasp, and Shane full-on winks at me. The swagger-swoon is on full display, and I'm having a tough time remaining still. He's so effing fine, and all mine.

A screech of metal knocks me out of his orbit, and I blink quickly.

"I'll give you two some privacy," the doctor says and stands from her stool.

"Oh, wait!" I stop her. She turns to us, and I feel a severe blush coming on. I fidget with the fabric against my thighs, trying to get the words out. "Um, is it okay to have, uh, sexual intercourse as usual while pregnant?"

Her smile spreads wide, and my nerves vanish. "I get this a lot, and yes, being intimate with your partner is not only fine. It's healthy and certainly encouraged."

Pretty sure a groan rumbles in Shane's chest. *Down, boy.* I giggle and shift on the tissue paper beneath me. "Okay, thanks," I squeak out.

The doctor nods and leaves the room. Shane is busy staring at me in all my mostly-naked glory.

"See something you like, Rooks?" I ask.

"Is it weird that I'm wicked turned on? Knowing you're pregnant with my baby is doing something to me. I have this primal urge to take you, right here and now." He shakes his head. "That makes me sound like a Neanderthal."

I yank on his shirt until our lips press together. "This is one of those instances I don't mind you being all possessive and barbaric. Let your caveman show, Rooks." I hum when he adjusts the bulge in his pants.

"Let's go home, Adds. We have more making up to do."

"Oh, yeah? What'd you have in mind?"

His nose dusts up my jaw, and he murmurs, "I'm gonna feast on you for hours. I wanna know what all your freckles taste like."

My toes curl, and the temperature spikes to sweltering. "Uh, yep. That sounds good."

"But first, we're gonna sleep because you need rest."

My raging libido shakes an angry fist at him. "You're such a tease. I was already left high and dry last night."

Shane helps me off the bed, and I reach for my clothes. He beats me to it and grabs the stacked pile. I lift a brow but don't argue, allowing him to take care of me. The tie at my nape loosens, and the material slides away, pooling at my feet. My body heats under his watchful gaze. I'm turning his favorite shade of red.

He remains on task, but his eyes are burning pools of honey. I step into my panties and he slides them up around my hips. The lace bra is next, covering my pebbled nipples. Shane brushes soft kisses across my shoulders as he secures the clasp, and I sag into his hold. The scruff on his cheeks is a harsh rasp against my sensitive skin, and I shiver against him. Before I can offer to strip, he tells me to lift my arms and tugs my sweater on. My leggings are tight and present more of a challenge, but he handles the stretchy fabric easily enough. When he draws the waistband up my thighs, I wonder if he can tell how wet this is making me.

Damn, he's good. I've never been so effing aroused while putting clothes on in my life. Shane gives me a playful spank, and I offer a scowl in return.

"Problem, Adds?"

"I'm gonna have to change my underpants after that display."

"Me too," he laughs.

"We make quite the pair."

He points at me. "I see what you did there."

Shane opens the door, and we walk into the hall toward the scheduling desk. He drapes an arm around me, and I curl into his side.

"Where'd you stay yesterday?" I ask.

"Jack found me at the garage. I crashed on his couch."

I bury my nose in his shirt and inhale his woodsy goodness. "You should have come back to the love nest. I wouldn't have kicked you out."

Shane's grip tightens. "I'll know for next time."

I pinch him, and he yelps.

"Don't plan for things like that," I say.

He kisses my temple. "Just teasing, baby. If we do fight, it will be very amicable."

"Better," I mutter.

We reach the front desk, and get an appointment set for January. Thinking about a month from now is slightly bittersweet. I press a palm to my nonexistent bump and focus on the good. Shane catches my wilting grin and rubs my arm.

"What's wrong, Adds?"

"My parents are in town."

"That's a bad thing?"

"It's only temporary. I got kinda sad thinking about it. They'll miss all the baby fun being away."

His brow furrows. "I'm not used to that type of parental relationship. We'll have to video chat and send plenty of updates." He ushers me outside, and we rush to his truck.

Once we're settled in the cab, I sigh heavily. "It's just different not having them around."

He laces our fingers together over the center console. "We'll spend every day with them while they're in Garden Grove if you'd like. Our work schedules permitting."

"They're so excited about our poppy seed," I say, and my joy inflates.

"I can't wait to meet them. Should we make plans for dinner?"

I nibble on my lip. "Let's take a nap and see where the evening goes. We can hang out with them eventually."

Shane turns onto Main Street, which bustles with traffic. "Welcome to Holi-Daze season."

"Things don't kick off until tomorrow."

"Tell that to all these folks." He chuckles and pulls into our parking lot. "Luckily we don't have to fight for a curb spot."

I lean back in my seat and let the events from today roll off my shoulders. "I'm lucky you were with me earlier. Thanks for stepping up and taking charge."

Shane kisses my knuckles. "That's my job, beautiful. I'll always keep you safe. I'm so fucking glad the baby is okay. It's been less than two days, but I'm already really attached."

I blow out the air trapped in my cheeks. "Me too."

"We're gonna be parents. It's officially confirmed."

I laugh and recall the tests littering my bathroom. I suppose this procedure was final proof. Plus, this little visit has put my initial worry to rest. "Yeah, kinda crazy. And here I just wanted a roommate."

He flashes me those dashing dimples. "Too bad, Adds. You're getting so much more."

CHAPTER 29

SHANE

Jolly

My gloved hand clutches Addison's mitten-clad one as we stroll down Main Street. Twinkling lights are strung up on every lamppost, wreaths hang from shop doors, and the sweet smell of pine warms the wintry breeze. Garden Grove doesn't mess around when it comes to their festivals. This Holi-Daze is vastly different from the last, all due to the girl beside me. I can't keep the grin off my face, but who can blame me?

"What should we do first?" I ask. Addison's cheek is red from the cold, and I place a kiss at its center.

She flutters her lashes at me. "Well, my parents are at Jitters. Wanna start there?"

"Were they disappointed we didn't meet them last night?" My plan was to do whatever Addison wanted. She chose to spend the evening in bed having make-up sex. I definitely wasn't denying her that.

She kicks at a chunk of ice on the sidewalk. "They understand, trust me. I told them we needed to be alone after the stressful afternoon."

"We sure did, gorgeous," I growl in her ear, and she giggles.

Addison bops my nose. "Behave and maybe I'll reward you later."

I haul her into my arms, spinning us around, and she squeals in delight.

"I'll do my best," I say.

"Oh, Betty, look," I hear from behind me. I turn slightly to look over my shoulder and see Marlene standing nearby with her friend.

"It's the adorable lovebirds," Betty says. "Hey, you two."

Addison tries to hide against my chest. "I have a bad feeling about this," she mumbles.

I hug her close and turn until we're facing them. "Morning, ladies. Always a pleasure."

They're wearing matching knit hats, and I wonder if a stand is selling them nearby. Both of them wave and take a few steps toward us.

"Isn't this weather glorious?" Marlene coos.

Mother Nature decided to give us a pass by providing pleasant temps for the highly anticipated kickoff. At least by December-in-Minnesota standards. I'll take forty degrees and sunny this time of year any day. I appreciate my body not feeling like an ice cube.

"Sure is," I agree and tip my chin to the sky. "It'll make being outdoors more bearable."

Betty's eyes sparkle. "Yes, we wouldn't want anyone getting sick.

Especially those in delicate conditions."

Addison tenses next to me. I do my best to hide the cringe, wary of how this will play out. I want to snuff out their interest so we can move on. I'm also aware that Addison can handle this confrontation whether I want to protect her or not.

My girl straightens and rolls her shoulders. "I'll make sure to pass along the wise words."

Marlene smiles, and the expression is kind. "You'll be great parents. We're all very happy for you."

Addison's jaw drops, and I manage to keep my features neutral. "Um, do you mean someday?" I deflect, not willing to spill the baby secret quite yet.

Betty titters. "Barbara saw Delilah, Raven, and Addison buy a bundle of pregnancy tests at the Kwikee Mart. Rumor has it the other two girls were enjoying some adult beverages at Boomers yesterday. Process of elimination."

Consider me impressed. These women are better than Sherlock Holmes. I scrub over my mouth, unsure how to respond. Addison takes the reins and saves me from deciding.

"You two work real fast," she says.

"Thanks for noticing." Marlene gives us an exaggerated wink. That gets a laugh out of me.

Addison makes a noise in her throat. "Well, it's still very early on, and we weren't planning on spreading the news so soon. Can we count on any form of discretion?" She tacks on a sugary sweet grin for impact.

The ladies make a show of buttoning their lips, and we laugh. Yeah, right. At least their effort is good for comedic effect.

"We appreciate that," I say.

They nod and quietly announce, "Congratulations."

Addison presses her palms together. "Thank you both. We really need to be going. Shane is meeting my mom and dad for the first time."

Marlene leans forward and gives her shoulder a squeeze. "Tell them we say hello. Make sure to stop by the bingo hall for a game or two."

"We'll see," Addison replies.

I give them a wave. "Enjoy the celebration."

Addison loops her arm through mine, and we continue on our way. "I was waiting for the other shoe to drop. I think they genuinely meant it."

"Underneath it all, I'm sure they mean well. It doesn't always come across that way, though."

Addison huffs. "You can say that again. I knew we'd be the talk around town quick enough."

"Is that so bad?"

"Nope, I actually don't mind one bit."

I kiss her and pull open Jitters' door, the telltale ding alerting everyone to our presence. Addison's parents are seated on a blue couch by the front window. I guide her over to them, sticking my hand out in greeting.

"Mister and Missus Walker—"

"You can call us Peggy and Joe, dear." Addison's mom knocks my palm away and gives me a hug. "I'm glad to finally meet you."

"The feeling is very mutual," I greet. When she pulls away, Joe steps in and offers a shake.

"Heya, Shane. How're you doing?" he asks.

I catch Addison's twinkling gaze and smile.

"I'm living the good life."

He chuckles. "That you are. Recently found out you two are rooming in that apartment together?"

My stomach drops, but I shove off the guilt. I'm not ashamed of anything when it comes to Addison, especially the love we share. "Yes, sir, that's right. Best way to protect her is staying close."

He studies me silently, looking for bullshit in my brown eyes. I'm more than happy to let him try, certain he won't find any.

Peggy elbows her husband. "You stop giving him a tough time," she scolds.

"It's my fatherly role," he says proudly.

"It's quite all right, Ma'am. I don't mind proving myself." I've been doing it for years. What's a conversation with her dad going to hurt?

"Atta boy," Joe replies. "You're great stock. I like you."

I try to hide my grin. "Thank you, sir."

"Okay, okay," Addison chides. "Enough with the grilling. I need coffee."

I let her lead me to the counter where Delilah is waiting.

"Hey, lovebirds," the bubbly blonde greets. "Welcome to Jitters."

Addison rolls her eyes. "You're a dork."

"If I break character now, all the newbies will think they've stumbled into some other cute cafe along Main Street," Delilah explains.

"Uh-huh, right," Addison drawls. "I'll have a large hazelnut, and Shane wants that motor oil mix you've got."

I grunt out a quiet laugh. "The dark roast will do, D. Thanks." I slide her some cash across the counter, and she shoves it right back.

"Your money's no good here," she chirps. "But smiles are always appreciated." Delilah turns away to make our drinks.

Addison bumps her hip into me. "Hey, you."

I lean down and kiss her softly. "Hi, Adds."

"Never have I ever had a date to Holi-Daze."

"Me either," I murmur.

"Will you be mine?"

"Thought I already was?"

Her freckled face glows under the muted lighting. "Just double-checking."

I dip to her ear. "I'll always be your anything."

Addison yanks on my coat collar and presses our lips together. "Good," she whispers.

"Here you go." Delilah passes over two takeaway cups.

Addison inspects the one in front of her. "Why's there a huge D on the lid?"

"For decaf," Delilah explains. Addison tries to return it, and her friend backs out of reach. "You're preggers, girlfriend. You can't have too much caffeine. Think about the baby."

Addison's wild green gaze flies to mine, maybe for backup. "I can't have regular coffee?"

LASS

"Only in moderation. This"—Delilah taps Addison's cup—"is a big portion. Just watching out for you, boo."

I scratch my temple. "Uh, sounds legit. We could call the doctor?" I suggest.

Addison huffs. "I know what they'll say. D is right. For whatever reason, she has a crazy amount of pregnancy knowledge."

Delilah makes a noise of agreement. "That's right, sweet-cheeks. It never hurts to be informed."

"Speaking of," Addison starts. "Way to blow our united front by going out for drinks with Rave. Marlene and Betty are all over this." She points to her stomach.

Delilah tosses her head back and cackles. "Oh my gosh, those two are something else."

I tug on Addison's belt loop. "Everyone's gonna find out eventually."

"Yep, and that time is now." Delilah is still giggling.

Addison points at her. "You think it's funny now. Just wait until you're expecting."

Her friend scoffs. "I'll just bring Marlene with me into the bathroom. Cut out the middleman."

"Whatever," Addison grumbles. "There's no privacy around here."

"As if you'd have it any other way," Delilah says.

Addison looks up at me and smiles. "Guess not."

Delilah shoos us off. "Go on and have some fun. Those sleds aren't gonna slide down the hill themselves."

I lift my cup at her. "Thanks, D."

"Yeah, I appreciate the zero caffeine," Addison mutters, yet she's grinning at her friend.

Delilah blows her a kiss. "Love ya, bestie."

We step away from the counter as more customers filter in. My palm finds its place at the small of Addison's back, and she leans into me. We meet her parents by the entrance before heading outside. The cooler air is a relief, and I squint against the late morning sun.

We make our way toward the park where stands and booths dot the snowy landscape. Groups of people are huddling in each direction, clogging the path.

"Looks like it'll be another successful event," Peggy says and twists to avoid those passing by.

"Mom, look," Addison gasps. "Nancy has sweater mittens for sale."

The two women squeal with glee, appearing more like sisters than mother and daughter.

Joe glances around the lot. "Those two will be occupied shopping for hours."

I swallow roughly as opportunity falls into my lap. I motion over to the chainsaw sculptures and meat raffle. "Should we leave them to it?"

"All right," he says and follows my lead.

My pulse is a jackhammer on the highest setting. I do my best not to stumble while words mash together and clang inside me. I shove my fists deep into my jacket pockets.

Joe raises a dark brow. "Got something on your mind, son?"

The term rattles something loose in my chest, and I falter. "Ah, sir?"

He shakes his head. "Didn't we already handle this? Call me Joe."

I dig my boot into some melting ice. "Okay, Joe. I was hoping to ask you something?"

He blinks at me, the bushy mustache making it hard to tell how he's feeling. "You're building the suspense. What's up, Shane?"

"I'd like to marry your daughter. Maybe not today or tomorrow, but in the future when she's ready. I was hoping to get your permission," I blurt.

Joe chuckles. "Oh, son. If my wife heard this, she'd never let the patriarchy comments go. I like your style, though. Will you treat her well? Put her above all else? Tell her she's right when we know that's not true? Be a great father to your kid?"

I nod along with each question, silently agreeing. "There's no doubt about it. It'll be my life's mission to make Addison happy."

Even through the beard, I catch his grin. He offers me an outstretched hand, and we shake. "It'd be an honor to accept you into our family. I've never seen my little girl in love before, and let me tell you, it's an amazing sight. You're already doing a great job."

Fuck, my eyes are burning. I dip my chin and manage to murmur, "Thank you."

"Dad, are you terrorizing my baby daddy?" Addison giggles behind me. I twist slightly and smirk at her. She takes in my expression and freezes as if an unspoken understanding passes between us.

"Oh," she mumbles.

"Hey, Adds." I make sure my dimples are on display, just for her.

She bites her ruby-red lower lip. "Hi, Rooks."

I draw her into my side where she belongs. Forever.

CHAPTER 30

ADDISON
Cheers

Delilah and Raven lift their mugs to clink against mine. We sip piping hot cider and settle deeper into the couch. The fireplace is crackling in front of us, spitting out smoky heat and filling the cabin with a rich aroma. This is the way to vacation.

I kick my feet up on the table. "Great choice, ladies. I love this location."

"Right? It's even better than the pictures," Raven says.

Delilah takes another drink. "Not sure I'll want to leave on Sunday."

"Happy New Years, besties. I have a feeling this one will be the best yet," I say.

Delilah pats my stomach. "How's Poppy Seed?"

"Now a sweet pea. Growing big and strong, I hope." I pop another dill pickle chip into my mouth. "Baby sure loves these."

Raven laughs. "Already using the baby as a scapegoat."

"It's only natural!" I retort.

"When's your due date again?" Delilah asks.

"August twelfth."

"That's really far away," she mutters.

I bump her with my shoulder. "Are you in a hurry?"

Delilah steals Dusty off my lap and cuddles him to her cheek. "Um, duh. This one is cute and all, but he's messy and drools."

I laugh. "You just described a child."

"Meh, but babies are different," she murmurs.

"Someone's having the fever," Raven stage-whispers to me.

Delilah huffs. "They're only cute when I don't have to take care of them constantly. I'm not ready for kids."

I rub my belly. "I wasn't either. Now I can't imagine it a different way."

Raven hums. "Motherhood is looking good on you. I'm sure Shane is noticing."

I glance at my chest. "There are perks to all this."

Delilah's fingers comb through my hair. "I have luscious locks envy. Seriously, it's so silky and smooth. I could just stroke it all day."

"That's what she said," I tease.

"Good one," Delilah shoots back.

"You're feeling well?" Raven asks.

"Other than the heartburn and bouts of nausea. My pregnancy hormones are no joke. I'm drawn to Shane in a totally addictive way. I can't keep my grabby palms off his sexy ass." They're practically falling off the couch in full-on cackle mode. I shake my head and grab another handful of chips.

"Oh my gosh, I bet he's loving life," Raven wheezes.

"I can't stop picturing Addy's pincher fingers on Shane's rear. Do you chase him around the apartment? Oh, ow, my lungs are burning," Delilah adds.

"Hardy, har. He has zero complaints, thank you very much." My face warms recalling how thoroughly he loved me last night. I have whisker burns on the inside of my thighs and all around my boobs. That man leaves no space untouched. I shift, and a small smile tips my lips, feeling the lingering evidence. It's a good thing we have our own corridor in this place.

"Do you think Shane is going to propose tonight? I was assuming he'd pop the question on Christmas," Raven says.

I almost spit out my cider. "Nope, not happening. I scarred him for life."

Delilah arches a brow. "Are you okay with that?"

I bob my head. "Yeah, we're rock-solid and in a groove. I wouldn't change anything. We'll get married one day, maybe."

"To each their own," Delilah muses.

I poke her arm. "Mind your own bobber."

"That frame Shane made is almost better than a ring," Raven says.

"Ohhhh, yeah," Delilah agrees. "He's really sweet, Addy."

"I'm pretty spoiled. Shane is very creative with gifts." I feel my smile stretch wider while thinking about the sonogram he framed. He wrote *Miracles come in all shapes and sizes* above the image. I openly sobbed for twenty minutes after opening it. The heart-shaped key I gave him seemed weak in comparison, but Shane acted like it was a priceless treasure. I love that man.

Raven sets her mug on the table. "Speaking of, what are the guys doing out there? Aren't their balls getting icicles at this point?"

I snort into my cup. "That'd be a sight."

Delilah gestures toward the bay window. "They're splitting wood and drinking beer. You know, man stuff."

I squirm just thinking about Shane out there, axe in hand, hauling a pile of wood to the shed. Being all masculine and delicious and irresistible.

Good grief, woman, I berate myself. *Keep it together for a few minutes.*

"Addy, what are you thinking about?" Raven swats me.

My lust-bubble bursts and I leap back to the present. "Huh?"

"Are you thinking about sex?" Delilah accuses.

I tap my toes on the table's edge. "Um, no. Just, uh, lost in a daze."

"A Shane haze?" Delilah wags her brows.

I suck air through my teeth, disliking my transparency. "They'll be busy for a bit out there. Should we watch a movie?"

Delilah grabs the remote and starts scrolling. "How about *Parks and Rec*?"

"Perfect," Raven and I answer together.

"So." Delilah breaks the silence. "Did you parents make it home okay?"

I pout. "Yes, they're safely back in Arizona."

"Aww, I'm sorry. I bet they're already missing you," Raven says.

"My mom promises they'll visit again soon. She's got FOMO." I rest my head against the couch, reclining further.

"I give it a few months," Delilah bets.

"Maybe sooner," comes from Raven.

I feel my eyelids begin to droop. "If they're here in August, I'll be happy."

"Someone's crashing," Delilah murmurs.

I yawn loudly. "I'm gonna hit the hay."

"Already?" Raven studies the clock. "It's only ten-thirty."

"Only? I'm beat. I stayed up well past midnight yesterday to ring in the new year. This baby needs bedtime," I tell them with another yawn.

"Okay, mama. Sweet dreams," Raven says.

Delilah smiles widely. "I'll have a pot of decaf ready for you in the morning."

"Brat," I mutter playfully. I give them both a hug, scoop up Dusty, and trudge off down the hall.

The room is cold and dark when I enter. I shiver from the uninviting chill and almost text Shane to come cuddle me. I scoff at myself, refusing to voice that codependency. At least not yet. I'm so darn tired that passing out while still standing is a possibility.

After stripping off my jeans and sweater, I slide under the cool covers. Just as sleep is taking me under, I hear the door creak open. Fabric rustles, and the mattress dips. Shane crawls onto the bed and fits himself behind me like a big spoon. He smells of campfire and woods and mine. The heady scent assaults my nostrils, and I inhale greedily. His bare skin is scorching along my heated body.

Shane groans while settling into the mattress. "Missed you, Adds."

I stretch my neck to kiss his shoulder. "I missed you, Rooks."

His hand drifts across me, from ass to upper thigh and hip, before settling on my stomach. His palm and fingers splay, practically covering my entire midsection. The move is becoming familiar, and I find it sexy beyond belief. He's going to be the best daddy to our little one.

I snuggle further into him, letting peace and serenity blanket us. He tightens his hold, and the love between us expands, reaching out and around until we're engulfed. This is my favorite part, just being with him.

Without saying another word, Shane stakes his claim on my heart. His drawn-out sigh and pounding pulse are all I need to hear. My man is content and exactly where he wants to be.

So am I.

EPILOGUE

SHANE
Promise

Addison lies on the bed, propped up on her elbows. Her seductive body is gloriously nude and mine for the taking. I let my eyes slowly scour every sinful inch of her. Pregnancy has added more curves and softness in all the right places. As if I needed more reason to be insatiable for my woman.

A rumble stirs in my chest when Addison arches and pushes her enlarged tits higher in the air. She spreads her legs wider, the invitation unnecessary but appreciated. My mouth waters at her little show, and I'm fucking famished. I palm my cock, giving the shaft a few cursory strokes.

"You gonna keep staring or actually do something with that?" Her taunt is a velvety purr wrapping around my length. Damn, I'll come just listening to her.

I pounce, crawling toward her on the mattress. She shuffles backward and settles against the headboard.

"You're being a naughty lass," I murmur against her silky-smooth thigh.

Addison's nails scratch along my scalp. I let my lids hood and blow softly against her slit. She shivers, her freckled skin pebbling. I'm sure her nipples are diamond-hard. I want those stiff peaks between my teeth.

"I want you inside me, Rooks. Don't make me wait," Addison mewls. She tugs on my hair for good measure.

"Let me enjoy you, Adds." I drag my tongue up and across to her hip. "Be patient."

Her limbs tremble. "I've waited long enough."

I blindly drift my fingers along her sides, reaching her breasts, and engulf them completely. My mouth finds those three freckles on her lower abdomen, their shapes altering as her skin stretches. The precious life forming within is getting bigger with every passing day.

The lust cools in my blood, replaced by a fierce need of another variety. I trace up the slope of her swollen belly and lay my cheek at its center. I shut my eyes, wishing for a flutter or kick or any sign of movement. Addison cups my jaw, and I glance at her glowing features.

"It's too early," she reminds me.

I stay in position, not ready to surrender my post. "You get to feel it."

Her torso vibrates with laughter. "On the inside. I'm barely five months."

I pout. "When's it my turn?"

Addison brushes over my furrowed brow. "Soon, baby. Hopefully in the next few weeks."

"Do you think we're having a boy or girl?"

She taps her chin, contemplating the question I ask almost daily. "A boy."

"Oh, yeah?" I inject my voice with surprise, but her answer is always the same.

"Yep. A little guy who'll be just like his daddy."

I nuzzle against her satin skin, my stubble a sandpaper rasp. "We're having a girl, and she's gonna be just like you. Perfect, beautiful, and the light of my world."

Addison hums. "We'll find out soon enough."

"You're okay not knowing until she's born?"

She shakes her head. "My stubborn man, so certain he's right. And yes, I'm sure. I love surprises."

I press my lips on her tummy. "Me too."

"Glad that's settled until tomorrow," she jokes.

With a sigh, I sit up and settle my hands on her stomach. I rub my palms around the barely-there bump and stare in awe. "You're giving me the greatest gift. I'll never be able to express what this miracle means to me. What can I ever do to even the playing field? I'll be forever in your debt, Adds." I kiss her navel, imaging our growing child, and feel the undeniable connection vibrate within me. Together, our halves are forming a whole.

Addison's hands cover mine. When I look up, she's near tears. "You've already given me everything."

Except one thing.

The idea sprouts and takes shape before I can stop it. With the stealthy moves of a ninja--at least in my mind--I reach into the nightstand drawer. I set the small velvet box on the top of her belly and snap open the lid. Her gasp lets me know I've hit the intended target. One glimpse at her beaming face and the assumption is proven.

"Marry me, Addison Jaymes. This time for real, because we want to. For no other reason but our love. Marry me because I can't live without you. Nothing could keep me away from you, and I want it in writing. Marry me and agree to be my family, with our little blessing in tow. Marry me because I'm fucking crazy about you, Adds." I take a shuddering breath, gathering more steam if needed.

She blinks away the moisture on her lashes, fingers lifting to her open mouth. "Is this really happening?"

I smile at her. "Make me the happiest and luckiest man to walk this earth. Will you be a Rookston with me?"

Her fingers tap-dance on my forearms. "On one condition."

I almost choke on the fear of rejection. "You setting more rules, Adds?"

"Just a stipulation."

I pluck the diamond and ruby ring from the case. "Name it."

"We get married this summer." Addison's green eyes shimmer.

My gut tightens. "Before the baby is born?"

"Uh-huh."

I quirk a brow and smirk at my soon-to-be fiancé. "You're suddenly in a hurry?"

What's with the complaining? I scold myself. *Just shut up and get this done.*

Addison wraps her arms around my shoulders. "Ever since you first proposed, I've felt horribly guilty for saying no. I was emotional and rash and not thinking clearly. To be honest, I've almost popped the question to you a dozen times since then."

I part my lips, air wheezing out. This is very unexpected, but extremely pleasant. "Really?"

She nods. "I've been kicking myself since Christmas. Put me outta my misery."

"No more waiting?" Lord knows I already have plenty of experience on the matter.

"I want to be your wife."

"Fuck, Adds." I slide the metal band onto her third finger and she gawks at the collection of clear and red gems.

"The center stone is huge," she murmurs and twists her wrist. The diamond sparkles brilliantly, and pride fills my veins.

I dust a kiss over her knuckles. "Only the best for Future Missus Rookston. That bonus from Jack sure came in handy."

"I wasn't anticipating our afternoon delight turning into an engagement."

"It just felt like I needed to ask in that very moment."

"I'm glad you did." Addison bounces lightly on the mattress, her expression a brilliant ray of sunshine. "We're doing this?"

I nuzzle into her neck. "I agree to your terms. We'll get hitched tomorrow, fly to Vegas or whatever you want.

A giggle comes from deep within her throat. "You're a nut."

"I'll be anything for you."

Her nails stroke down my back. "Just promise to be mine."

I adjust my position between her legs, ready to seal the deal. "That's easy, Adds. I've been yours from the start."

EXTRA EPILOGUE

SHANE
Ruby

A soft coo calls to me as I enter the hospital suite. The lights are off, but the morning sun casts a bright glow across the small space. Elation paints the plain white walls, making them bold and colorful and full of energy. Above the sterile odor of cleaning supplies, I catch hints of lavender from the bouquet by the window. This room is overflowing with affection and genuine joy. I'm drawn to the far corner like a magnet, but my swift steps are quiet. The pounding in my ears tapers off when I stop beside them.

My wife and baby are cuddled up on the standard-issue bed. Emotion blurs my vision as the enormity of this moment cloaks me. I clear my throat softly, not wanting to disrupt their serene moment.

Addison lifts her gaze to me and smiles. The deep purple smudges under her eyes scream of exhaustion, but she's still beaming. There's no manual for parenting. The progression is a stumbling crash course. But I'm quite certain of one thing—we'll never rest easy again.

One look at the tiny angel swaddled on Addison's chest and another concrete fact lands in my lap: sleep is highly overrated. She's worth any amount of soundless nights.

Ruby starts to fuss, and Addison gently rocks her. We named her after our favorite color, or maybe it's just mine. Either way, Addison gave me the honor of choosing. My wife snuggles our newborn closer, and my heart kicks up. She's such a natural at this. I can only hope to hone a sliver of her skill.

I drag over a chair and take a load off. I set Addison's coffee, on the table and she reaches for it eagerly.

"Hazelnut?" she asks and takes a swig.

I nod. "Decaf." My answer makes her scowl, but the expression is playful.

Addison has another small sip. "How long until I'm allowed to have a normal amount of caffeine again?"

"The books suggest in small moderation until you're done breastfeeding."

A low groan escapes her lips. "But I'm so tired."

I hold out my hands. "Want me to take her? You can nap."

With some minor shuffling, she passes Ruby over. I return to my seat and begin swaying slowly.

"This is some seriously hot mommy porn," Addison murmurs.

I lift my gaze at her seductive purr. If looks could strip off clothing, I'd be buck naked. She makes her perusal more blatant, and I have to avert my eyes. Getting turned on while holding my child sounds all kinds of screwed up.

I chuckle to cover the desire clogging my throat. "Six weeks, Adds. Doctor's orders."

That earns me another grumble. "There's plenty else we can do."

"Go to sleep, beautiful. Stop tempting me."

Addison relents with a huff and relaxes against her mountain of pillows. "She's a lucky little lady," my wife drawls groggily.

Her lashes flutter shut, and I release a grateful exhale. Ruby's mop of dark hair sticks out from the blanket cocoon. I'd been rooting for red to match her mother's, but there's not an ounce of disappointment. Maybe this means she'll take after me in some small ways. I can only hope she takes the best from us both. I kiss her tiny forehead, inhaling the sweet scent of our miracle.

Ruby's little fingers curl around my much larger pinkie. Something starts tingling in the very center of me, like a sparkler in my chest. Heat spreads and flows through my veins. The sensation grows into a very recognizable feeling. I'm whole, finally complete.

For the second time in my life, I've fallen instantly. There's no describing the fierce instincts and protective urges that occur upon first sight. I cannot guarantee she'll never experience fear or loss or sorrow. I can only hope love perseveres and conquers, just like Addison told me.

Damn, I am truly blessed.

While in the presence of this precious baby girl and my gorgeous wife, I take a moment to ponder. Can a man's life be too fulfilled? I glance between them, both snoozing silently, and take back my questioning. The answer will always be a resounding no. They make me a better man, my sweet angels. These two have redeemed me.

Not sure what I did to deserve all this. My heart beats wildly, the pulse strong and sure. By some stroke of luck or chance or fate, I get to spend the rest of my days basking in this glory. They're my entire universe, and I'll never get enough.

Addison stirs and blinks open bleary eyes. I stand and move toward my drowsy wife. I press my lips to her temple, and a heady dose of cinnamon apple greets me.

"Thank you, Adds."

Her lips tip up in a lazy smile. "For what?"

"Letting me move in. Giving me a chance. Loving me. Agreeing to spend your life with me. Most importantly, allowing me to share this gift with you." I lay Ruby on my shoulder so she's included in our moment.

Addison tilts her face, and our mouths meet in a brief kiss. "I can say the exact same to you, Rooks. I'll be forever grateful you interrupted my conversation with Myla that day."

Our privacy is interrupted when a nurse comes in, bustling about for a few moments. She tests Addison's blood pressure and other vitals. The monitor she's clutching beeps steadily, signaling everything is stable.

The older woman pauses near the bathroom. "Would you like to give little Ruby a bath this afternoon?"

"Yes!" The single word comes from Addison and me in a unified blurt.

"Well, then," the nurse says with humor lacing her tone. "I'll make another round in a few hours for tubby time." After a quick wave, she walks out.

It sounds like such a simple thing, but I know better. All these small, seemingly insignificant events will not be taken for granted. I will treasure each breath from her lungs. I shut my eyes and thank the heavens and stars above.

It was all worth it.

All the lonely years and forced isolation and conflicting emotions were mere steps on the path to Addison. My choices to leave those troubles behind led me here.

"Knock, knock," calls from the door. Peggy and Joe poke their heads in, wearing matching grins. "Can we come in yet?"

It seems their patience has dried up. I was beginning to wonder who'd show up first.

Ruby was born last night, and we held off on having visitors until today. Being able to bond with her alone was important to us. Spending these sacred hours together has been pure bliss, but it's time to spread the love. I can't complain about people wanting to meet our bundle of joy. I'm surprised Addison's folks didn't put up more of a fight to stop by earlier.

It probably helps that they've moved back to Garden Grove permanently and have every intention of providing full-time daycare.

They might have to fight Addison's friends for that position. I glance at the clock and smile. Raven and Delilah should be storming the grounds soon. We've become a big patchwork family. I wouldn't have it any other way.

Peggy and Joe rush forward, zooming in on their granddaughter in my arms.

"Oh, my," Peggy murmurs and softly strokes Ruby's head. "She's absolutely perfect."

Her fingers are twitching, and I'm certain she's about to steal my baby away. She's trying to remain polite, but I'm afraid to test her limits.

"Would you like to hold her?"

The moment my words are out, Peggy scoops up Ruby and cradles her tight. With our daughter securely occupied, I sit on the bed next to my wife. Addison rests her cheek against my shoulder, and I kiss her forehead.

"You did real good, Adds."

"We, Rooks. This is a team effort." She links our fingers together and squeezes.

I relax deeper into the stiff mattress. "You give me far too much credit, sweetheart."

"And you don't give yourself nearly enough."

I smile against her velvet skin. "Call it even?"

"Forever?" Addison whispers.

"And always."

The End

BONUS CONTENT #1

ADDISON
Savior

I slump against the counter after battling my way through the rowdy crowd. The server station feels like home base and I've just slid in safe, for a quick minute at least. I glare at the rude bunch who'd recently stumbled into Dagos. As fate would have it, they found their way to my section of the bar. I very rarely complain about customers, especially when they're running up a big tab, but tonight has been wild enough. These visitors are far more handsy than usual. The holiday cheer has them loose and taking liberties. I've smacked more than a few unwanted hands away from my ass this evening.

What happened to manners? Or common decency? How about a man treating a lady with respect?

My lonely heart pangs and I rub at the hollow ache. With all these extra people around for Holi-Daze, snagging a date with a semi-decent guy shouldn't be challenging. No, scratch that. I'd settle for a polite conversation at this point. What's wrong with men these days? They get a few drinks in their system and think it's totally appropriate to play grab-ass with the server. What world are they living in? Definitely not mine.

"What's that look for?" Myla asks.

My frown deepens. "Man problems."

My co-worker winces. "Was it Trey? I saw him storm out earlier."

I wave that off. "Uh, no. I'm used to him being a dick." I nod toward a table of boisterous customers, currently engaging in what looks like a belching contest. "Would it hurt them to be gentlemen? I mean, really? It's Christmas."

Myla laughs. "Right? But that's typical behavior these days. Swoon-worthy dudes are harder and harder to find."

I mock-sob and hang my head. "You're so lucky to have Grayson." I blindly gesture toward the bartender hustling to fill drink orders. "He's one of the good guys."

She tracks my flailing movement, looking at her boyfriend. Her gaze gets all dreamy and my chest tightens. I want that look. Myla bites her lip and gives my arm a reassuring squeeze.

"I had to pick through a lot of weeds before finding him. Your one is out there, Addy. Just wait and see," she tells me with more confidence than I'm feeling.

All I can offer is a shrug while Grayson brings over a slew of drinks. I grab mine, trying to hold back a defeated sigh.

"Wish me luck," I tell them and lift the hefty load to my shoulder.

"Always," Myla offers with a thumbs-up.

I dip and dodge through the masses while trying to keep my balance. My full tray tips when people refuse to move and knock into me. A few girls get spilled on and scowl, but they still don't get out of the way.

Don't mind me, I'm just working. The faster you move, the quicker I can deliver.

But I smile politely and carry on. The tips from this week alone will pay my January rent. Maybe even February. I reach my waiting table and drop off their beverages. After scribbling down their food order, I turn away to begin the process all over again.

I take a deep breath and cringe. Rather than getting a refreshing lungful, sticky-stale air burns my nostrils. Gross. There's far too many folks stacked in here and not enough ventilation. If it wasn't so cold outside, I'd open a few windows. Maybe I'll do it anyway.

I check the time on my phone, mumbling a pep-talk to survive the remaining two hours of this shift. When I glance up, there's a man blocking my path. I attempt to swerve around him, but he follows.

Alrighty, then.

I huff loudly. "May I help you, sir?"

His arms cross over a massive beer belly. "Aren't you a sight."

He lewdly licks his lips and I wrinkle my nose. I peek down at my red sweater, checking for a stain or whatever he's leering at. This move is mostly for show, letting him know I see straight through his crap. He doesn't take the hint.

I snap in front of his face. "Eyes up here, pal." I'm sick of these horny assholes. If one more guy ogles me, I'm gonna lose my mind.

He points to my red hair. "Does the carpet match the drapes?" The moron chuckles while receiving encouraging cheers from his buddies.

I roll my eyes. "Wow, how original."

Before he can spew more creativity, someone looms closely behind him.

"These guys bothering you, Addison?"

Shane.

Without looking, I know it's him. I don't know much about the guy, other than he works at Jacked Up and mostly keeps to himself. He's so damn quiet, only talking when something really needs to be said. Like right now, apparently.

I peer around one of the douche bags, catching his glower. I give him a finger-wave and say, "Hey, you."

The loser in front of me cranes his neck to see who I'm talking to. I notice the moment he takes stock of Shane, his body locking up and practically trembling. This imposing mountain of muscle stands there, waiting and watching. Actions are screaming louder than words. Shane's are very clearly announcing that this man better back the fuck off. The stranger's gaze bounces back to me and he sneers.

"Not worth the trouble," he mutters.

"Ouch, my ego." I barely refrain from another eyeroll. "Now, if you'll excuse me." I shoo him like the pest he's being.

He shuffles away, tail appropriately tucked between his legs. His posse follows and I track their sloppy movements. One less group of dicks to worry about.

I smile at Shane, stepping closer so he can hear me. "Thanks for that. I appreciate you stepping in. You're my savior of the night." I'd swear his cheeks turn a little pink, but it's probably the overhead lights.

"It was nothing more than what anyone else would do. Just offering a helping hand." He shrugs those impossibly wide shoulders.

"You'd be surprised," I grumble.

Shane's brow lowers. "You deal with that type of shit a lot?" His voice is more of a growl, but I'm not scared in the slightest. His narrow stare pierces into the door those guys just scurried through.

I touch his flexed forearm, the need for his attention prodding at me. "It's all right. I'm used to it. They're all harmless, really."

Shane's honey eyes focus on mine and my breath falters. He looks down at my grip, his features immediately softening. I shiver despite the room's suffocating heat. A bead of sweat rolls down my spine while I continue gawking. How haven't I noticed his hotness until this moment? I bite my lip, trapping the lie. Shane has always been sexy in my eyes, but he's so… impossible.

I blink quickly, clearing my jumbled mind. I should get back to work before I do something embarrassing, like hump his very muscular thigh.

I clear my throat and glance at his empty hands. "Can I get you anything to drink or eat? Where are you sitting?"

"At that far high-top," he says and points toward the corner. His gritty tone strikes me deep and I can't stop my eyes from lifting to his.

"Did you order anything yet?" My voice is far too breathy. Shane probably can't hear me.

He shakes his head. "I've been waiting."

I tilt my chin. "For?"

Shane rocks on his heels, taking his time to respond. After rubbing the back of his neck and avoiding eye contact, he says, "A certain lass."

I feel my face blaze at that, remembering similar words from a different day. Where is this swagger of his coming from? I get tingly all over and my knees definitely wobble. What the eff is going on? I place a palm on my balmy forehead and exhale slowly. I open my mouth, but nothing comes out. How do I respond to that?

I'm just feeling indebted to him—or more inclined to jump his bones—because he stepped in to save me from those drooling idiots. That's all. I mean, we've barely spoken more than three words to each other since he moved here two years ago. There's nothing going on here other than some gratitude, which I already extended. Case closed.

Yet I'm still standing here.

And so is he.

BONUS CONTENT #2

ADDISON
Halloween

I plop my drink on the table and glance at the door. Again. Where the heck is Shane? I've been waiting on him for what feels like decades. It wouldn't be so bad if Dagos wasn't packed to the gills. I can hardly take a step without bumping into someone. But I'm beginning to think those not-so-smooth moves are intentional.

I've never regretted dressing up for Halloween, until tonight. If one more guy asks me to heal their ache, I'm going to vomit. News flash, jerk wads: I'm not going to perform mouth-to-mouth and offer sponge baths. Maybe I should have been a cat or witch or something even more cliché.

All that nonsense floats away when the man I actually want groping me walks into the bar.

Holy shit.

My breath rushes out in a forceful exhale. Shane has no right to look so good.

I immediately want to smack myself on the forehead. It was my foolish idea for him to wear a uniform. I only have myself to blame. Somebody better check my pulse—there's a good chance I'm going to faint.

Shane whips off his aviators and scans the crowded room. He looks so effing badass. How am I expected to resist climbing him like a stripper pole?

My pleather bodysuit is suddenly restricting and I'm becoming uncomfortable. The temperature in here is stifling, even with the chilly fall breeze wafting through the open windows. I should have worn less clothes.

A fast glance down at my scanty costume causes another huff to escape me. I can't afford to lose any material.

Shane saunters toward me in all his police officer glory. This man was made to wear a badge and holster. If I didn't know better, I'd believe he was the real deal. The blue fabric hugs his upper body in a way my body is extremely jealous of. His sculpted pecs and biceps bulge, threatening to pop the buttons and seams. Would that be the worst thing?

I fan my face and determine it would. I'd likely burst into flames at this rate. My nurse getup was meant to be alluring, but Shane is tipping the scale big time. I tug at the hem of my dress and contemplate hiding out in the bathroom. Maybe he'll follow. I roll my eyes to the sticky floor, realizing the lack of oxygen is getting to me. Before I can contemplate ditching this scene, Shane's boots come into view.

I slowly lift my gaze, getting a full view of him wrapped in this sexy cop package. My perusal ends on his handsome face and I sigh at all the masculine beauty. I want to lick those dimples clean. His honey eyes are smiling and I'm almost certain he can hear my dirty thoughts.

"Hey, Adds." His voice is a sandpaper rasp over my heated skin. I sway in my heels and he reaches out to steady me. "You okay?"

I'm nodding like a bobble head. "Uh-huh, yup. Right as rain. Just hot. So very hot."

He quirks a brow and studies me closer. "You do look a little flushed. Need some ice?" Shane places two cool fingers to my scorching cheeks and I almost moan.

Take it easy, I scold my starving lady bit. He's not our next meal.

But he could be.

"Can I get you something to drink?" he offers.

I point to my glass. "I'm covered. Grayson probably has a Coors already set out for you."

Shane doesn't answer and one look at his expression tells me why. His stare is glued to my chest. I bend forward slightly to offer a better view. My movement snaps him out of his stupor.

Shane rubs the back of his neck. "I, uh, like your outfit."

I cross my arms, offering my cleavage on a silver platter. "Thanks. I figured everyone loves a naughty nurse."

He covers his gaping mouth with a palm. "I sure do."

I lift my chin at him. "You make a hot cop."

"Yeah?"

I rake my gaze over his flexing muscles. "Definitely."

Shane shifts his stance. "Whatcha gonna do about it?"

I wink at him. "Buy you a beer."

BONUS CONTENT #3

SHANE
Busted

I settle behind the wheel and fasten my seatbelt. When I glance over at Addison, she's munching on her bottom lip and staring out the window. I reach for her fidgeting hand and lace our fingers together.

"We don't have to leave her," I murmur against her knuckles.

Addison faces me and smiles. "My parents shoved us out the door. There's no way we're snatching Ruby away. Plus, this will be good for us. We're long overdue for a date night."

"You sure?"

She nods. "Let's go before I change my mind."

I put my truck in reverse and back out of the driveway. "Dagos?" I suggest with a laugh.

Addison pokes my arms. "We're not spending our first evening alone at that bar. Try again, stud."

I glance at her and lick my lips. The low-cut neckline of her shirt gives me a great view of her rack. Addison's tits are more than a handful thanks to breastfeeding. I have big plans of becoming very familiar with their new shape. I shift slightly when my jeans grow tight. Fuck, how am I supposed to wait through dinner.

Addison catches me leering and leans closer. "See something you like?"

"Tease," I grind out.

She does a little shimmy. "Oh, I'm sorry. Are you suffering, baby?" Her fingers begin walking up my thigh and I almost leap out of my seat.

"Whatcha doing, Adds?"

"Just a little preview," she purrs. Her touch wanders up and it takes all my control to keep the truck moving in a straight line. She grips me through my jeans and I groan.

"Fuck, Adds. You're playing with a loaded gun," I warn.

Addison hums. "Never have I ever given road head." She makes quick work of opening my pants. I hiss when her smooth palm makes contact with my straining cock.

"And you're about to change that?" I manage to choke out.

Her fingers tighten around me and she gives me a few smooth tugs. "Would you like that?"

I slam on the brakes too hard at a red light. Is she serious with that question? I blink and try to find the words. "Uh, yeah. But I'm driving."

"No one will see. It's dark out."

"I'm not so worried about that. I doubt my skill of being able to multi-task." Addison begins jerking me harder and my brain gets fuzzy. "Damn, you know how I like it."

She rests an elbow on the center console and kisses my cheek. "Let's find somewhere to park, Rooks. I wanna make you feel good."

My eyes nearly cross. "Shit, Adds. Keep talking like that and I'll have a mess in my briefs."

She increases her pace, stroking my length at just the right speed to get me off. "This will just take the edge off."

I still her wrist. "When I come, it'll be deep inside you. I've already waited this long." In that moment, I make an executive decision that a pitstop is mandatory. I take the next left onto Maple and turn into the bank's deserted lot. No one will bother us here on a Saturday night.

I hitch a thumb toward the backseat. "Ladies first."

Addison doesn't hesitate and I'm hot on her heels. She's almost vibrating in place while I settle in the middle of the bench seat. I tug my jeans lower, pat my lap, and Addison eagerly straddles me. I roam my palms up her smooth legs, need coiling tight. Six weeks without being buried deep inside my wife is far too fucking long. Patience is no longer one of my virtues. We're about to make up for this forced dry spell.

"This is gonna be quick and dirty," I say and tug her thong to the side. "Good call on the skirt." I drag my fingers along her wet slit and she moans.

"Yes," Addison mewls. "Just get inside me. Right now."

She'll never need to tell me twice.

I plunge into Addison's slippery heat and she welcomes me with a moan. Her legs stretch wider, making more room, and shoving me deeper. She's primed and ready for me, like always. The push and pull are a smooth rhythm, our hips rocking together in rotating cycle. Our movements are fluid, joining as one, as if we've done this a thousand times. Maybe we have by now.

It's been too long since I've had her last. I watch my dick enter her as she rides me, sliding into home after too many nights away. The sight is enough to make me blow immediately. I grab her ass and slow our pace, the shallow strokes staving off my release. She squirms in my hold.

"Harder, Rooks. I want all of you," Addison demands.

Filthy pleas keep spilling from her red lips and I'm commanded to oblige. I rut into her, deeper and faster. I buck my hips and punch up in rapid bursts. She tosses her head back with a squeal.

I pluck her nipples, well aware how overly-sensitive they are. "You like that?"

"Oh, oh," Addison chants and arches into my touch. The stiff peaks poke through her shirt, begging and seeking.

"More?" I ask.

She nods, wriggling in my arms. "Yes, always more."

I move my fingers between us and circle her clit, applying pressure that'll get her off. Her core clamps around me and I see stars. Telltale tingles gather at the base of my spine.

"Fuck, Adds. I'm gonna come," I warn.

"Yes, yes." Spasms jerk her limbs. "I-I'm right... t-there."

That's all it takes to tip me over the edge. I thrust into her once more and let go. Black spots dot my vision with the force of my release. Pleasure floods my veins in a rush and I suck in sharply.

"Holy fuck," I bellow with a final surge. I slump against the leather seat, utterly sated and satisfied. Addison hums and snuggles against my chest, mirroring my contentment.

A loud rap on the window makes us both startle. Addison smashes her body to mine as if that will hide the evidence.

"Shit," she spits. "It's Carl."

I follow her gaze and find Garden Grove's nosey sheriff peeping in. I offer him a wave and he shakes a finger at us. "Think he'll let us off with a warning?"

Addison buries her face in my neck and giggles. "We already got off."

"Worth it, Adds?"

She pulls back and smiles wide. "Abso-freaking-lutely."

ACKNOWLEDGMENTS

Hey there! Thanks for reading LASS. When I first started planning my small town of Garden Grove, I had a feeling Addison and Shane would be something really special. Writing their story was nonstop fun and I had the greatest time. Don't tell the others, but I have a new favorite. I really hope you fell for them like I did.

As always, I first need to thank my amazing husband. He continues to be the most patient man I know, especially when I'm nearing a deadline. If it wasn't for him, I couldn't do this author gig. I'll never be able to express how much he means to me. Above all else, he's an amazing father to our wild toddler. Many of the ridiculous Shane-ism were straight out of his mouth. I hope you love those as much as me!

I must give a huge shout out to all the readers, reviewers, and bloggers. You're what keep authors going. I'm so very grateful for each one of you for taking time out of your busy schedules for us. I hope you know how much I appreciate everything. Thank you so very much for loving books and this amazing community.

I have an epic team in my corner and I'll never be able to thank them enough. Talia, Candi, Sunniva, Ace, Melissa, Tijuana, Danielle, Sarah, and Lauren—I wouldn't be able to publish without you!

A huge thank you to all my wonderful author friends who keep me going with all the love and encouragement. Kate, Michelle, Nicole, Leigh, Annie, Tia, Suzie, Victoria, Ella, Logan, Lauren, Maria, KK, Parker, Cassie, and many more—thank you for just being there when I need a pal.

A super special virtual hug to Jacqueline, Megan, Cindy, Shauna, Autumn, Keri, Crystal, and Vanessa. You're all lovely and generous and fantastic peeps!

I've got to thank my dynasty—Peggy, Lisa, and Jessica—for all the inspiration and stories that helped me build the Garden Grove crew.

I owe so much to Candi Kane PR and all the ladies of Give Me Books. I have the greatest marketing and promotional services around. I couldn't manage without your help and dedication. Thank you, thank you, thank you!

Thanks to Reggie, the very talented photographer who shot the image of BT and Jess. Thank you for giving me a beautiful cover photo for this story.

For my Hotties, the bestest reader group an author can ask for. I'm so thankful to each one of you for taking this journey with me. I appreciate you more than words can describe. Thank you for being dedicated to me and our bookish community. I love our special place on social media!

Harloe's Review Crew, thank you so very much for wanting to read and review my words. Somedays, I still pinch myself. I appreciate you going above and beyond to support and promote me during releases. I'm eternally thankful to all of you!

A huge thank you to Nadege from InkStain Design Studio for making the interior of LASS look its absolute best.

And last but certainly not least, a huge shout out to YOU for reading LASS. The fact you chose to read my book when there's so many amazing titles available makes me giddy. You all play a role in my author life and I'm grateful. Just continue loving books and reading for me, okay? You've made me a very, very happy author!

ABOUT THE AUTHOR

Harloe Rae is an Amazon Top 100 bestselling author. Her passion for writing and reading has taken on a whole new meaning. Each day is an unforgettable adventure.

Harloe is a Minnesota gal with a serious addiction to romance. She's always chasing an epic happily ever after. When she's not buried in the writing cave, Harloe can be found hanging with her hubby and son. If the weather permits, she loves being lakeside or out in the country with her horses.

Harloe is the author of Redefining Us, Forget You Not, Watch Me Follow, GENT, MISS, and LASS. These titles are available on Amazon.

Find all the latest on her site: www.harloe-rae.blog
Subscribe to her newsletter at: http://bit.ly/HarloesList
Harloe's Hotties Reader Group: www.facebook.com/harloehotties

Follow her on:
BookBub: http://bit.ly/HarloeBB
Amazon: http://bit.ly/HarloeOnAmazon
Goodreads: http://bit.ly/HarloeOnGR
Facebook: www.facebook.com/authorharloerae
Instagram: @harloerae
Book & Main: www.bookandmainbites.com/harloerae

Want to learn more about Trey and Raven?
What about Delilah and Zeke?
Well, keep reading for sneak peeks of...

GENT & MISS

GENT Sneak Peek

CHAPTER 1

TREY

Ma'am

"Did you hear what I said?"

At her question, my gaze shifts to connect with the woman's stare. She's an unfamiliar face, probably lured into town by the specialty shops off Main Street. Sitting closer than socially acceptable, she's almost stuck on me. The bar is crowded tonight, though. I let the proximity slide, but her attempt at conversation is pushing it too far.

I came to Dagos for a few beers after work, not to engage in chit-chat. Usually I won't hesitate sampling fresh meat, gladly gobble up what's being offered, but not today. Try as she might, this chick is striking out with me. I have zero intentions of giving her the quick fuck she's been practically begging for since sitting down.

I clear my throat. "Ma'am, I'm not interested."

"Excuse me?" she says as her eyes widen. "Ma'am? That's what you call a grandmother. Do I look old to you?"

The dial on her annoying meter cranks up a few notches. I'm not stupid enough to fall into her trap, but still bite my tongue to keep the insults from barreling out.

I quickly scan her pinched face, covered with powdery shit likely meant to hide her age. I was trying to be polite by using a respectful term, but she's clearly not the type. I rub my forehead while blowing out a breath, frustration already building like a storm cloud.

"I mean no offense," I grind out between clenched teeth, "but I'm spending the evening solo. Cheers." I raise my bottle in a lame-ass salute.

The yappy broad huffs and rolls her eyes. It seems she might spit more crap my way, but then her attention darts to a man across the room. She eagerly slips off the stool, nearly spilling her drink with the jerky movements. She glances back at me, shooting daggers from her eyes.

"Asshole," she shoots over her shoulder before sauntering off.

Good fucking riddance.

I lift the nearly empty beer to my lips, but a burst of laughter interrupts me.

"Wow. You sure know how to pick 'em. How are you still single with suave moves like that?"

"Not you too," I mutter without turning around, recognizing the raspy voice immediately. "Was the entire female race set on driving me fucking crazy?" My chin tilts skyward as I silently ask for patience... or a fucking break. Neither will come for me.

"Would it kill you to be nice?" Addison rests her arms against the bar next to me.

I puff air through my clenched teeth. "Most likely. And I was nice. I called her ma'am."

"You know girls hate that," she shoots back. "It's a dig more than anything and makes us feel old. Might as well call her a raging bitch or wrinkled hag."

"Those names seem more appropriate. Thanks," I chuckle but there's no humor behind it.

"Don't start, Trey. You know I'm right."

"I'm not saying shit. Just thinking I might use those instead."

"You're impossible."

"That's the point."

"What-ev-er," Addison singsongs while glancing around. "Where's Jack?"

"Still at the shop."

"Burning the midnight oil?"

"In more ways than one. Had a rough day."

She tilts her head and gives me a once-over. "You too?"

"Don't I always?"

"Meh, I suppose. You're always a grump so it's tough to tell the difference."

"And here I thought we were exchanging pleasantries."

"You and pleasant will never go together." Addison hitches a thumb over her shoulder. "Running off that lovely lady is a prime example."

I grunt and shake my head. "She deserved it for being so desperate."

She snorts and elbows me. "Why are you such a dick? All that handsome is going to such shameful waste. You need to find someone to treat right."

Peering at Addison, all toned limbs and tan skin, I consider a quick fuck after all. I grip the cool bottle, picturing her soft flesh giving in to me.

"Why haven't we ever—"

"No way. I know that look," she says. "I see you give women those bedroom eyes every Friday night only to watch them turn cold the following morning. I haven't fallen for them yet and I don't plan to start."

Just like that, our breezy banter slams to a halt. Tension strains my shoulders after being cut off. *Again.* What is it with chicks bulldozing me tonight?

Having Addison call me out does nothing to help my mood, but it's no surprise she sees straight through me. Although I've known her since kindergarten, it still pisses me off. Moments like this make living in a small-town suffocating. There's nothing and no one new around here. I know useless shit about everyone from Garden Grove, whether I want to or not.

I roll my neck and restore my typical look of indifference. "I never get any complaints. Your loss, Addy."

Addison shakes her head. "So fucking cocky. I ain't giving you any ass, but how 'bout another?" She asks and gestures to my beer.

I grumble, "That'd be great," without looking back at her.

Addison just stands there so I give in and glance over. Her arms are crossed as she raises a slim brow my way, seemingly waiting for…

"Please," I grit. The irritation from earlier whooshes in my ears and I'm ready to get gone.

Right after this drink.

She snickers and says, "That's better. We'll make a gentleman of you soon."

"Don't hold your breath, *ma'am*."

Addison gasps and flames rise in her hazel eyes.

Before she digs into me, I add, "Chill out. I'm just fucking with you. But seriously, get back to work. I'm thirsty."

"You really are an asshole," she says while patting my cheek with more force than necessary. I'm sure she'd love to slap the shit out of me but won't risk getting in trouble for it. She shakes her head and turns away, strutting off to serve other waiting customers.

My eyes lock on her swaying hips, losing myself in the rhythm of her movement for a moment. No harm in looking, right?

Sweet-smelling perfume wafts in as the abandoned stool next to me shifts slightly.

"Is this seat taken?"

The notes are soft but rise above the booming noise in the space. The feminine lilt of her voice snakes around before I feel a twisting in my gut. I quickly shove that fluffy shit away. My jaw ticks while I ignore her heavenly scent closing in around me.

"Don't even bother," I growl loud enough for her to hear.

"Excuse me?"

Disbelief colors her voice and I can't help swiveling toward her.

Holy shit.

Bottomless blue eyes greet me, sparkling with fierce emotion. The glittering sapphires are hypnotizing, the type of pull any man would fall victim to.

Except me.

MISS Sneak Peek

PROLOGUE

ZEKE
Gone

I storm out of my father's house for the final time, ignoring the burn blazing up my side. I'm more than ready to get gone and wrench open the truck door. As I toss my duffle across the seat, soft steps sound behind me. I know it's her without turning around. My heart beats wildly, even faster than when he was threatening my life a few moments ago.

Will she understand? Here's hoping.

I turn slowly and my breath falters at the sight of her gorgeous face painted with worry. My beautiful girl looks scared and I'd do anything to wipe the concern away. But I can't stay.

My feet shuffle toward her and piercing pain radiates from my ribcage. I do my best not to wince. He got me good tonight, but never again.

"Where are you going?" she whispers.

"Away. At least for a while."

A quiet sob hiccups from her throat. "W-why? I don't want you to leave."

I cup her jaw and tilt her face up. My eyes devour her porcelain perfect features. "The last thing I wanna do is be without you, Trip. But staying in that house, with him, is ruining me. I don't wanna go but if I stay, there won't be much of me left. He won't stop until he's destroyed me."

"Take me with you," she pleads. "I can't make it without you, Zee."

My shoulders sag under the pressure of her green stare. I hate disappointing her. "You gotta finish school, Trip. And you're so strong. I'm holding you back, feeding off your goodness. You'll do better without me, at least how I am now."

Her bright gaze is fierce and pins me in place. "You take that back. If I'm strong, it's only because of you. Having you here with me is the greatest gift."

I stroke her velvet skin, letting her kindness sink into my soul. I let the memories of simpler times rush in, easing the agony slightly. Our younger selves were full of so much happiness.

"Remember the day we met?" I ask into the darkness.

She nuzzles deeper into my touch. "How could I forget? I still sleep in that ridiculous shirt."

"And you stumbled in the grass rushing over to me. My little Trip." She laughs, and a hint of a smile tilts her lips. "That's right. Think of the good."

"I know what you're doing," she murmurs.

"Is it working?"

Moisture coats her lashes as she blinks rapidly. "No".

"Should I try harder?"

"Does that involve you sticking around?"

I don't respond. Words can't express the war waging in my heart.

Trip sighs. "Okay. I'll be strong. For you."

"For you too. Don't let them win. Keep your head up," I demand. A loud bang shatters the calm around us. I glance at house before focusing on her. "He'll be looking for me soon. I gotta go now."

My fingers twist a few locks of her blonde hair, committing the silky texture to memory. Her bottomless green eyes are shining with emotion, and nothing I say will stop her tears.

"No. Please, stay," she cries and clutches onto me tight. I suck in sharply when her fingers dig into the fresh bruises on my torso.

"Trip, baby. I can't. He's gonna kill me if I don't get to him first." I brush away the tracks streaming down her cheeks. Her tears slam into me harder than his fists ever have. With regret pooling in my gut, I lay out the truth. "I can't survive there another minute. But know if I could, I'd do it only because of you."

She stays silent because she knows it's true. Living next door, she hears the constant fighting. When Trip clings to me harder, my teeth grind to force the ache away.

"Where will you go?"

"I have distant family spread all around. No one stays in contact with my dad, but they'll take me in."

"Are you going far?" Her lip wobbles, and my thumb presses against it.

I shrug, helplessness soaking into my bones. "I'm not sure. We'll see when I get there."

"Will you call me? Tell me where you are?"

"Of course. You're all I'll think about. You know that, right? I've always loved you."

She sniffles and wraps tighter around me. "I love you so much, Zee. It hurts knowing you won't be here tomorrow."

"But it's only temporary. We'll be together again soon."

"O-okay," Delilah stammers.

I clear the tightness from my throat and whisper, "Knock, knock."

Her head moves against mine. "I'm not in the mood, Zee."

I'm desperate to dry her tears. "Please humor me?"

Her body quakes with a shuddering exhale. "Who's there?"

"Butch and Jimmy."

"Butch and Jimmy who?"

I nuzzle into her neck. "Butch your arms around me and Jimmy a kiss."

Delilah laughs, but it's forced. She snuggles closer and I grip her harder. Silence envelopes us, but my mind is screaming, and time has run out. I can't leave her with nothing but a faded shirt and cheesy jokes. I fiddle with the chain looped around my neck. As always, my mother's ring hangs from the center. I pull it off and place it over her head.

Delilah gasps and clutches the silver links. "No. I can't accept this. It's all you have left of her."

She's right, of course. That necklace is the only possession I've ever cared about. I tug on the metal strand and tell her, "It's to keep you safe. Like it has for me all these years. I don't need it now that I'm leaving. Wear this and know I'm always with you."

She's crying openly, the tears pouring freely without pause. "I'll never take it off."

"That's right. Hold on to it for me."

Trip nods. "And I'll wait here until you come back."

A knot pulls tight in my stomach at her words. Why does this seem like a gamble? I don't want her betting on false hope, grasping at a future that might not come, but damn, a life without her isn't one at all. So, I let us both believe.

"I'll come for you soon. Don't worry, baby girl. I'm gonna get a job and save up every penny. I'll get us a cute little place we can share. And when it's ready and you've graduated, I'll come for you."

"I believe in you. I know you'll make this happen for us."

I'm counting on her having enough faith to keep our love burning bright.

Printed in Poland
by Amazon Fulfillment
Poland Sp. z o.o., Wrocław